Mekong Memories

Books in the Tom Stone series by Michael Patterson

Playing at Murder
Deadly Retribution
Ring of Truth
Death or Honour
Fatal Love
Mekong Memories

Mekong Memories

Michael Patterson

The Choir Press

Copyright © 2024 Michael Patterson

All rights reserved. No part of this publication may be reproduced or transmitted in any form or by any means, electronic or mechanical including photocopying, recording or any information storage or retrieval system, without prior permission in writing from the publisher.

The right of Michael Patterson to be identified as the author of this work has been asserted by him in accordance with the Copyright, Designs and Patents Act 1988

First published in the United Kingdom in 2024 by
The Choir Press

ISBN 978-0-78963-477-8

To my old friend, Glyn, for your continued support and encouragement.

Chapter 1

'You're going where, sir?' asked Milner, in a voice which clearly betrayed his amazement. As he ended his question, he suddenly realised he was addressing DCI Stone as though he were still his boss, despite the fact Tom had retired from the force a couple of months earlier.

If Tom had noticed this, he wasn't about to mention it. 'I've told you already,' he answered, with a touch of annoyance in his tone. 'Why? Don't you believe me?'

'It's not that,' replied Milner. 'It's just, well, you've always said how much you dislike going on foreign holidays and, let's face it, *Vietnam* not only sounds very exotic but is also not exactly nearby.'

They were both seated in the kitchen of the house, in Bagshot, which Tom shared with his partner Mary.

'Well, that was all in the past. Everyone has the right to change their mind,' Tom said, before adding, almost as an afterthought, 'even me.'

Milner wasn't about to let it go. 'It wasn't too long ago you told me just how bored you were the last time you went away on holiday.'

'I wasn't retired then. If you remember, I was busy trying to make sure our part of London was a safer place to live. Bad people don't stop doing their stuff just because we go on holiday. You might want to remember that, Milner, the next time you are thinking about booking some time away.'

His comment was quite apt as Milner was, in fact, looking to go on holiday. Milner decided, however, that he'd pushed his luck far enough already.

Although Milner had worked with DCI Stone for a few years now, he was still never quite sure if his former DCI was being serious or simply taking the opportunity to have a bit of fun at his expense. He thought it was probably the latter but wasn't about to test his theory.

David Milner had originally been transferred to the team at a time when DCI Stone's career was at its lowest point. This was reinforced by the simple fact that the *team* consisted of just the two of them. Despite over thirty years' experience within the force, Tom was apparently considered by many of his colleagues to be well past his professional shelf life, and simply killing time before he could take retirement. What was even harder to take was how he could sense that his colleagues – many of whom he had worked with over the course of his time in the force – had started to pity him. Other younger, more ambitious officers had even quite openly gone out of their way to avoid him, not wanting to be associated with someone whose star was now rapidly descending. There had other been low points over the years, but nothing on this scale, and none with such negative effects on his sense of self-worth.

Milner, meanwhile, at the time was just a very callow and raw detective constable who, it was felt, was unlikely to do much damage whilst working with Tom. This was especially so as Tom was now being given some of the more routine, mundane inquiries which his colleagues probably deemed to be beneath them.

In a further slight, Tom had been assigned to help out on an investigation which was being run by a different London police force. They were short of manpower and needed people, mainly to carry out the more administrative tasks and thereby free up other officers for duties at the sharp end of the investigation. Tom had agreed to do this, mainly as it meant he didn't have to face his colleagues every day and, anyway, it would help pass the time until his retirement. It certainly wasn't the way he had thought he would end his career, but now, however reluctantly, he had to accept that his standing had fallen so low he no longer held any real influence.

But all of this, due to a combination of good fortune and his traditional policing skills, was soon to change, setting both Tom and Milner on an unexpectedly upward career path.

That first case, far from being the routine, run-of-the-mill one which everyone had anticipated, had quickly developed into one of the most nationally high-profile cases of recent times. Tom, unexpectedly at this stage of his career, had found himself at the centre of it and so right in the national spotlight.

Afterwards he had returned to his own force, with his reputation and, more importantly, his self-esteem hugely restored. There were, of course, some colleagues who openly resented his newfound fame and were convinced it wouldn't last long. But they were proved to be wrong, as Tom soon found himself leading other complex but ultimately successful murder investigations, assisted by Milner. The result was that the two of them actually further increased their professional and public profiles. From being *persona non grata* amongst his colleagues and superiors, Tom had suddenly become one of the most respected officers in the force.

Another consequence of all of this was that he and Milner had developed a surprisingly strong and personal relationship of their own. It was a relationship which, despite Tom's natural inclination to be wary of openly displaying emotions, especially around subordinates, had gradually extended beyond normal work-related matters.

Tom was of the generation where work and private life should never be mixed. It was a rule he had tried to apply throughout his career, whether downwards with subordinates or upwards with superiors. There were, of course, many within the force who were very good at ingratiating themselves with their superior officers. Tom wasn't one of those, not least because 'networking' didn't come naturally to him. Saying what people wanted to hear, in his experience, eventually ended badly.

Nonetheless, he had become very fond of Milner. Sometimes, and with a growing sense of unease, he found himself starting to see him almost as a substitute son.

When he had first met Milner, Tom had been estranged from his own birth son, Paul, for over thirty years, not helped by the fact Paul had lived in Australia for most of that time.

After Tom and his wife Anne's divorce, Anne had emigrated, taking their son with her, and, later, had remarried. Tom had only recently found out that Anne had died of cancer a few years earlier. All these things had increased his sense of guilt, especially not having kept in contact with Paul.

Then events had taken another dramatic turn, not least due to Mary's own covert efforts to effect a reconciliation. Paul, together with his family, had planned to visit the UK, and this had been the opportunity for them to meet. Initially, it had been a stressful time for Tom, with his anxiety increasing further the closer it got to Paul's visit. In the event, it had turned into one of the most emotionally charged, but most rewarding, periods of Tom's life, as they had all spent extended periods of quality time together.

This had more than compensated for his recent retirement, as it had given him another, different, purpose in life. Tom's retirement would now allow him to focus on his 'new' family without the pressures of wondering what was happening back at work.

After a brief silence, Milner asked, not unreasonably, 'So, what attracted you to Vietnam?'

'Well, it's a part of the world which has always interested me,' Tom answered. 'You might have read about the war there, in the 1960s and early 1970s. It will be interesting to see for myself what changes there have been since then. And it's a lot closer to Australia, so we'll also be taking the opportunity to visit Paul and his family in Melbourne.'

'That makes sense, then,' replied Milner. He hesitated before adding, with genuine feeling in his voice, 'You must be really looking forward to that.'

'I am, although I can't say that I'm looking forward to all the travelling. That's the problem with going abroad on holiday. You have to leave this country.'

Chapter 2

'Anyway,' Tom said, 'that's enough of my holiday plans. What are you currently involved in? Anything interesting?'

Milner, anticipating that this was the real reason why he had been invited to Tom's house, had prepared for this question. DCI Stone was not the type of person who could retire one day and then have forgotten all about it the following day. Milner suspected it might take some time, if ever, before that day finally arrived.

'Doesn't seem the same without you there to give me the benefit of your advice.' A hint of a smile appeared on Milner's face. 'I even miss your little sayings.'

'Well, I'm sure that you will soon forget all about me, and, anyway, that's probably a good thing.'

'I'm not sure about that, sir. It's still all a bit strange.' Milner hesitated briefly before continuing, this time with undisguised emotion in his voice. 'To be honest with you, at the moment, I feel out of place. I don't seem to have the same enthusiasm I used to have when we worked together. Plus, I'm not sure everyone was happy to see me join the team.'

Tom looked directly at him. 'Firstly, it's usually best to be honest, especially with me. And secondly, that's perfectly normal. You haven't been there that long. A few weeks, isn't it? Remember how you felt when we first started working together. I'm sure you had a few doubts then.' He continued. 'Now it's my turn to be honest. I definitely had big doubts about whether or not you would be up to the job. But,' he immediately added, 'I couldn't have been more wrong. You've been a credit to the force and to me. It just goes to show how you shouldn't jump to conclusions. Just try to remember that.'

'Do you mean that, sir?' answered Milner, a slight tremor in his voice.

There was the briefest of pauses before Tom replied. 'I

think we've worked together long enough now for you to know I wouldn't say something like that if I didn't believe it.'

Milner knew that overt sentimentality, and this touchy-feely type of conversation, did not come naturally to Tom. It was certainly not something for which he was known amongst his colleagues, and so Milner found himself suddenly quite moved by his words.

As Milner remained silent, Tom continued. 'You've gone through so much over the past couple of years – particularly with what happened to Gary – that I would have been surprised if you didn't have any doubts.'

This was a reference to the last case they had worked on. Milner had been promoted to acting detective sergeant and then, not long afterwards, to full DS, with DC Gary Bennett reporting directly to him. His rapid promotion had been largely influenced by Tom's personal lobbying on his behalf. But during that last case DC Bennett had gone rogue, having taken it upon himself to pursue a suspect without keeping Milner fully informed. One evening, whilst following the suspect alone, DC Bennett had been stabbed to death during a confrontation. Ironically, it had occurred when he had gone to the assistance of the suspect, who was being viciously attacked by two men. It had been a massive loss to both Tom and Milner, but especially to Tom, who had worked with DC Bennett on and off for many years.

The ensuing internal inquiry into DC Bennett's death had found that Milner was seriously at fault for not being aware of what DC Bennett was doing and, more importantly, not providing the appropriate level of close supervision expected of him. He was subsequently given the option of either immediately resigning, from the force or being demoted to detective constable and reassigned to another unit.

Milner was still only in his mid-twenties, and the resulting demotion simply confirmed – at least as far as some of his colleagues were concerned – that he had been promoted too far and too fast. It had taken all of Tom's powers of persuasion to convince Milner that his future was still with the force and that he would eventually find his way back onto his previous upward career path trajectory. Milner had, with some reluctance and even less expectation, agreed.

The other major consequence of the inquiry related to Tom's own career. As it had been Tom who had strongly recommended Milner's promotion to full detective sergeant, the same review also found there was some culpability on his part. At the time of DC Bennett's death, Tom had taken a few days' holiday in order to spend time with Paul and his family whilst they were in the UK. Although this was not a major official factor in the review, Tom was under no illusions about how it had probably been held against him. The upshot of this was that Tom had been offered just one option: early retirement, albeit with full pension benefits. Once again, it wasn't the way he had intended to end his police career, but the recent reconciliation with his son had certainly softened the blow.

All of this was now weighing on their minds as they remained seated in Tom and Mary's kitchen.

'Remember what I said to you at the time,' Tom said. 'I really believe, one day, you could be commissioner of the Met. But, as you are finding out, it's never a smooth ride to the top. There are always ups and downs. Believe me, I should know. You are still very young, with lots still to learn, but I know you have it inside you to get there. You've been in the force long enough now to know how teams can be very wary of newcomers, especially when they are replacing somebody else. It threatens the dynamic of the group. Sometimes it's due to resentment that the newcomer has got the job ahead of someone else. Sometimes it's just envy, and sometimes it's because of some loyalty to the previous person. I wouldn't worry about it too much. You just need to be yourself and do the job to the best of your abilities. People will ultimately respect you for that.' He paused. 'Now, I'm interested to know what you are currently working on.'

Milner, still quite emotional as a result of Tom's openness, took his time before answering. 'As I said earlier, it's all a little strange. You might have heard how a DC John Shipley was recently found dead, having apparently committed suicide. It looked like he'd taken a deliberate overdose. Well, I'm his replacement. He was part of a specialist team set up earlier in the year, directly by the commissioner, code name Operation Deliverance. It was formed to investigate an organised gang network, which is thought to be responsible for supplying the bulk of illegal drugs throughout West London. There's also evidence to suggest they are involved in other major forms of criminality. Organised burglaries, money laundering, human trafficking. That type of thing. What's even more concerning, however, is it looks like they might also be responsible for the spate of recent murders we've seen in our area.'

'Yes, I did read about DC Shipley. Very sad. Do you have any idea what drove him to it?' asked Tom.

'Not really. You know what it's like. There are all sorts of rumours and speculation circulating. The most frequent one is that he was taking money from the organised drugs syndicate and was on the verge of being discovered. But, as I said, it's all just speculation. Anyway, there's a major inquiry ongoing and, until that is completed, it's a bit of a no-go area. What is apparent, however, is how it seems to have set back the progress of the operation. It's like the officers working on the case are always looking over their shoulders, as though they don't trust anyone any more. You can almost feel the tension amongst them.'

Tom didn't immediately respond, still thinking about what Milner had just told him. Eventually, though, he said, 'So, what is your role? Have you taken on all his caseload?'

'I don't think so. Although I have been asked to review all his files and notes and follow up any specific leads he was working on. From what I can see, though, the named individuals in his files are all low-grade dealers. Street corners. Clubs. That sort of thing.' He paused briefly. 'There are a couple of other names I came across, though, apparently deliberately hidden in the sleeve of one of his files, which I intend to follow up on. I'm assuming there must be a reason why he tried to hide them.'

'And here's me thinking we had got on top of this type of crime,' replied Tom, almost wistfully.

'From what I've already seen, these OCNs are bigger than ever. There are lots of gangs in West London, obviously, but most of them are small, local ones, based around a tower block or even an individual street. These are on a different scale entirely. Far more organised, with a clear command structure, and, worryingly, much more ruthless and brutal in the way in which they enforce things.' Milner folded his arms. 'There's been an upsurge in violence, both within individual groups and amongst the larger competing groups. Just in the past couple of weeks there's been at least three murders which we're pretty sure are related to this gang. This specialist team was set up specifically to take this particular gang down. Another team has also been formed to do the same thing as us, but with another major gang which is operating mainly in North London.'

'Is there coordination between your two groups?' asked Tom. 'An overall command structure, a system to share information? CCTV, for example?'

'I'm not sure if you've come across him previously, but Commander Fernley is overall lead officer. I'm too far down the food chain to be privy to any strategic issues, though.' He hesitated briefly. 'What I have picked up, however, is that apparently there's real rivalry between the two groups.'

'That's not surprising,' replied Tom. 'Would you say that it's a positive, competitive rivalry?'

'Not at our level, no. Just the opposite, in fact,' Milner replied. 'It's not been helped, of course, by what happened to DC Shipley and the rumours of how he was involved with the OCN in our area.'

'That doesn't bode well,' mused Tom. 'In my experience, unhealthy rivalry usually leads to sloppy policing, corners being cut and, inevitably, mistakes being made.' After a momentary pause he continued. 'So, does DCI Shaw head up your group?'

'He does,' answered Milner. 'I haven't seen a lot of him so far, although he did make a deliberate point of welcoming me in front of my new colleagues when I started. I really appreciated that.'

DCI Richard Shaw had previously worked with Tom. Although their relationship was now based upon a mutual professional respect, that had not always been the case. Tom was the very antithesis of DCI Shaw. Tom was old-school, taking his time to gather the facts and consider all the options available before settling on a course of action. It was an approach based upon his experience accumulated over many years.

DCI Shaw had seemed to Tom to be the perfect example of a young officer in a hurry, more willing to take risks and far more fixated on achieving his own personal, well-calibrated ambitions. Tom had taken an instant dislike to him, whilst DCI Shaw had made it equally apparent that he considered Tom to be a dinosaur, the epitome of what was holding back the force as it attempted to implement modern policing techniques.

To the surprise of both of them, however, this mutual antipathy had noticeably changed over the past year or so. Circumstances meant they'd had to work together, and it was during this period that they had both developed a respect, albeit somewhat grudging at first, for each other. Whilst it was unlikely they would choose to spend any leisure time together, they now nonetheless felt comfortable enough with each other to both offer and seek advice.

It was against this background that Tom had spoken with DCI Shaw, asking if he would be willing to add Milner to his team. The fact DCI Shaw had readily agreed had simply reinforced this new detente.

What Tom had not been aware of, at the time, was how DCI Shaw must have known he had been asked by the commissioner to set up this specialist unit. Notwithstanding just how important this was to DCI Shaw's career prospects, he had still agreed to Tom's request. Tom's admiration for DCI Shaw was increasing substantially.

'Do you think the unit is making any progress in eliminating the OCN?' Tom asked.

'To be honest, I don't really know. There are quite a lot of suspects, and some arrests that have been identified as being part of the gang, but nothing so far that has materially moved things forward. As I said, they seem to be extremely well organised, along a type of pyramid structure. I'm still finding my feet, though, so I don't yet have access to everything that's going on. The meetings I've been part of so far have just involved our small group.'

'So, who is your immediate boss?' asked Tom.

'I've been assigned to DS Gordon's team. It's still early, of course, but he seems to know his stuff. There's myself and a couple of other DCs in his team. As you can imagine, it's been a bit tense since DC Shipley's death. I suppose it was always going to be difficult for whoever replaced him. There's another DS, DS Foster, who heads up the other team.'

'That seems a bit unusual,' said Tom. 'Wouldn't having two DSs on the same investigation lead to a bit of confusion as to who was in overall charge?'

'It might do, I suppose, but so far, from what I've seen, there doesn't seem to be any problems. Anyway, they both report to DI Richards. It's quite a big team working directly on the case, plus, of course, the usual backroom people, specialist forensics, technical support and legal people who we can call upon.'

Tom nodded. 'That is quite a big resource.'

'It's become a major priority to take down this OCN, especially since the upsurge in gang killings. I also understand that the North London team are similarly resourced.'

Tom was silent for a moment before speaking again. 'It sounds like it could become a bit dangerous. Make sure you look after yourself.'

It wasn't clear if Tom still had the circumstances of DC Bennett's death in mind as he said that.

Chapter 3

Just then they heard the noise of the front door being opened, and not long afterwards Mary walked into the kitchen. 'David, I thought it was your car parked outside. Lovely to see you again.'

Mary had known Milner for a while now and had, like Tom, become very fond of him. This feeling had become much stronger during the period when Tom had been recuperating after being shot by a vengeful criminal. Milner had spent a considerable amount of his own time providing both Tom and Mary with practical support, which had undoubtedly helped Tom's recovery.

It was during his recovery that Tom had moved into Mary's house in Bagshot. The idea was that this would be a temporary move, allowing Mary to take better care of him during his rehabilitation. Whilst his leg injuries were not life-threatening, they had necessitated regular physiotherapy, combined with extended periods for rest and recovery. Although they had only been together for a couple of years, Mary knew, due to Tom's natural impatience, that it was highly unlikely he would give his injuries the necessary time to fully heal. This temporary arrangement had quickly turned into a more permanent one, confirmed when Tom had subsequently taken the big decision to put his own house in Staines on the market.

Since his divorce from Anne, Tom had had one or two brief relationships, but none of them had developed into anything remotely permanent. He'd soon realised that the intense nature of his career, combined with his occasional tendency to selfishness, was not a good environment for any meaningful or permanent relationship.

Looking back, he was now able to see how the pursuit of his career had always taken priority and had therefore become the main source of tension between himself and Anne. Even the birth of Paul, early into their marriage, hadn't changed his priorities, and so it was no real surprise when their marriage failed. In recent years, he had found himself looking back on those times with a sense of increasing personal shame, and this feeling of remorse had only become stronger during the time he'd recently spent with Paul and his family. He couldn't help thinking just how much he had missed by not making the effort to re-establish contact with Paul. It was something he now realised he would likely regret for the rest of his life. But he couldn't change the past; all he could now do was ensure the future was different. Not for the first time, he was grateful for Mary's involvement in arranging his reconciliation with Paul.

It was during a particularly dark phase of his life that Tom and Mary had first met. During that period, Tom was not only assessing his professional career but also re-evaluating what he wanted to do with the rest of his personal life. If he didn't do something about his situation, he knew he would soon move into the next, and perhaps final, part of his life as a lonely and increasingly bitter old man. Although at the time he was still only in his early fifties, he felt both mentally and physically exhausted, but he knew it was probably his last chance to find happiness and some meaning in his life. As his circle of friends had always been very limited, the chances of him meeting someone with whom there was a mutual attraction were virtually nonexistent.

So he did something which was completely out of character. He subscribed to a dating agency: You're Never Too Old for Love. Even now he couldn't quite believe he had actually gone ahead and done it. His decision to join was on the basis it might prove to be quicker than if he tried to develop a relationship in the traditional way. In truth, probably due to his innate cynicism, he hadn't held any great hopes.

His first experience had not gone well, reinforcing his low level of expectation, and he had almost cancelled his subscription straight away. But, fortunately, he hadn't, and it was on his second date that he and Mary had first met. Mary had been a widow for a few years and, after her husband's death, had opened a small florist shop in Bagshot. This had provided her with the distraction she needed, as well as a small but regular income.

In terms of personality, they were very different people. Whilst Tom was very calculated in his actions, rarely showing his true emotions and not prone to making sentimental or spontaneous decisions, Mary was far more extroverted in nature and not afraid to show her emotions. In fact, she was an active member of the local Camberley Amateur Dramatics Society, which, like her flower business, had provided her with great comfort and a sense of purpose in recent years.

Mary was also far more trusting of people, always likely to see their good points first, whereas Tom's initial instinct was to be wary, especially of more naturally outgoing people. Sometimes he tried to rationalise this by suggesting it was the nature of his job, over time, which had caused this cynicism. The reality, however, was that his job had simply exaggerated a personality trait that already existed.

Despite all these differences, it had come as a great surprise, not least to Tom, that they had enjoyed their time together and then had, quite quickly, become increasingly attracted to each other. More and more, Tom had found himself thinking of Mary and looking forward to the time when they would be together again.

There had, of course, been times of stress and strain in their developing relationship. It was inevitable with two people who had diametric personalities. Those stresses had first surfaced during a period when Mary had found herself being personally targeted, in an attempt to intimidate Tom, by gang members he had previously arrested. Unsurprisingly, Mary's own family had voiced their concerns regarding the dangers of being in a relationship with a serving police officer, particularly one who came into contact with such dangerous criminals. It was not long after this that Tom had sustained his injuries and moved in with Mary.

Mary gave Tom a significant look. 'You haven't been talking shop, have you?'

Before Tom could reply, Milner answered. 'Not really. We

were discussing your holiday. DCI Stone was just telling me how much he was looking forward to it.'

A faint smile appeared on Mary's face. 'I'm not sure "looking forward to it" is exactly what he would have said, but, now we've booked it, there's no going back.' Without giving Tom the opportunity to contradict her, she went on. 'Anyway, how are you and Jenny getting on together? I hope you're making time to see one another regularly.'

Jenny had, at one point, been Tom's PA. It was during the period when Tom had been asked to become acting station superintendent, until a permanent replacement could be appointed. He had reluctantly agreed to it, but his time there had simply confirmed what he'd always suspected: he was not naturally cut out for a deskbound role. Whilst he was aware that such a position required good management and leadership skills, he had underestimated just how many diplomatic and 'politicking' skills were also needed, something which he instinctively lacked. Jenny had not long been there, and so they had, in a way, helped each other find their way in their new roles. Inevitably, Milner had first met her when he attended meetings in Tom's office. Somewhat surprisingly, he and Jenny had started to develop their own personal relationship. For a while they had managed to keep this secret, but, as so often happens in such a close environment, the more they tried to keep it a secret, the more their behaviour subtly changed. It had become obvious to everyone, but especially Tom, that their relationship was more than just platonic or professional.

'Thank you, she's fine,' answered Milner. 'In fact, we are hoping to go away on our own holiday shortly.'

'I'm really pleased to hear that,' replied Mary, with genuine feeling. 'Where are you planning to go?'

'Portugal. Well, the Algarve, actually. You both went there a couple of years ago, didn't you? I remember DCI Stone telling me how much he enjoyed it.'

This wasn't exactly true, as Milner knew only too well. Tom had told him how, by the second week, he had become bored with simply doing nothing and couldn't wait to return to work. By now, though, Milner was not averse to having some fun at his former boss's expense.

'I'm not sure that's entirely true either. But we did have an enjoyable time,' she said, looking expectantly at Tom. 'Didn't we, Tom?'

'It was very enjoyable,' answered Tom, without any great feeling.

Mary stared at him, her eyes slightly narrowed, and then she turned back to Milner. 'Well, I'm sure you'll both have a wonderful time. Can I get you another drink? Apart from wanting to say hello to you, I came in to make myself one. I think I need one before I tackle the packing; I really don't know what to take.'

Milner shook his head. 'No, thank you, Mary. I've still got some left. Have you ever been to that part of the world before?'

'No. Never. I think that's why I'm looking forward to it, especially the river cruise along the Mekong River. It sounds so adventurous; just saying those words sounds exotic. Then, of course, we are flying on to Australia to visit Tom's son, Paul, and his family. I can't wait to see them again.' Her excitement was clear in her voice.

'I'm sure you'll both have a wonderful time. How long will you be away for?' asked Milner.

'We leave on Friday. The Vietnam trip is about ten days, and then we'll spend another two weeks with them in Australia,' she replied.

Milner, now turning to face Tom, said, 'Is that the longest time you've ever been away, sir?'

'It is,' answered Tom, in a matter-of-fact tone that gave no sign of whether that meant he was looking forward to it or not.

'Anyway, lovely to see you again, and don't forget to say hello to Jenny from us,' said Mary, picking up her mug of coffee. 'I'm sure we'll have plenty to tell you about when we get back.' She left the kitchen.

When Tom next spoke, it was clear that any more talk about holidays was over. 'You were telling me how you had a few leads to follow up on. What are you planning?'

Even though Tom was no longer in the force, Milner still

felt a sense of loyalty to him and so had no problem in sharing work-related issues. 'The names which were hidden in DC Shipley's file, you mean? They could just be other low-level street dealers, of course, but why would he try to hide their names like that? I'd guess that either they're important or he wanted to protect their identities. Anyway, at this stage it's early days and I'm still trying to make sense of his files.'

'Could they be informers?' asked Tom.

'I did think that, but why would he have mentioned their correct names? It just seems a bit risky.'

'Maybe they were their code names,' mused Tom. 'My suggestion would be to go back over all of DC Shipley's files, both written and electronic, to see if they throw up anything else. Look out for any connections and coincidences, because, as you know—'

Before Tom could finish his sentence, Milner interrupted. 'Because you don't believe in coincidences.'

'So you have learnt something from me? That's good to see,' said Tom, a thin smile suddenly on his face.

'How could I not, considering everything we've been through together over the past couple of years?'

'Anyway, it sounds like there's plenty for you to get your teeth into.' Tom hesitated before adding, 'If there's anything you'd like to run by me, you know where I am. You've got my email address and mobile number, so you can always contact me when I'm away.' He cleared his throat. 'Of course, I don't want to interfere or step on DCI Shaw's toes. If that happened to me, I suspect I wouldn't be best pleased, but, if I'm only acting as a sounding board, there can't be too many issues with that.' His delivery was not especially convincing.

'Thank you, sir,' replied Milner. 'I'll bear that in mind.' He stood up and offered his hand to Tom. 'It was really good to see you and Mary again. I hope you both have a wonderful holiday, and, of course, that you enjoy your time in Australia with your son and his family. I'm sure it will be a real adventure, and one you'll both never forget.'

Little did he realise just how prescient his prophecy would prove to be.

Chapter 4

A few days later, Tom and Mary were in the arrivals hall at Hanoi airport. To Tom's great surprise, although their journey to get there had been a long and tiring one, it had gone remarkably smoothly. Their flights had taken off and landed on time and, best of all, their luggage was waiting for them when they arrived in Hanoi.

They made their way towards a man who looked to be in his early forties, dressed in a red polo shirt and black trousers. He was holding up a laminated sign on which was printed the name of their travel company: *Mekong Cruises*. An identically dressed but slightly younger-looking man, with a clipboard in his hand, was confirming the names of other passengers against his checklist.

There was already a group of about thirty people milling around the two men. Apart from a younger couple, most seemed to be in their fifties or sixties, with a few older still. Each of their pieces of luggage had a distinctive red tag attached, identifying them as part of the same group. Tom waited his turn before approaching the men and giving his and Mary's names.

'Welcome to Vietnam,' said the man with the sign, in his excellent English. 'My name is Lan, and I am your tour director. I will be with you for the entire trip. We are just waiting for three more couples to come through, and then we will be boarding our coach to take you to your hotel in Hanoi City.'

Mary, meanwhile, was in conversation with a couple they had befriended whilst waiting in the departure lounge at Heathrow. They were a few years older than Tom and Mary: probably in their late sixties or early seventies. Tom joined them.

'I was just saying to Sue how it all seems so real now we are in Vietnam,' said Mary. 'I can't wait to experience Hanoi.'

'I agree,' replied Tony, Sue's husband. He was a tall, well-built man with a distinctive Yorkshire accent. 'I still can't believe we are in a country which has suffered so much from war. It will be interesting to see how much it has recovered since then.'

'I think the Vietnamese refer to it as the American War. At least, that was what I read,' said Tom, who had spent some time on the flight reading a recent history of Vietnam. When the trip had been confirmed he'd contacted a retired former colleague who he knew had a particular interest in recent military history, especially the Vietnam War. His colleague had provided Tom with a number of articles to read relating to that particular period in history.

Just then Lan called for everyone's attention. 'Thank you for being so patient. I know you must all be very tired after your journey. Everyone is here now, so if you could follow my colleague, he'll lead you to your coach. Depending on traffic, we should be at the hotel in about forty-five minutes. Just to let you know, there will be a more formal welcome in the hotel tonight at 7pm. We will then be joined by our other guests who have flown in from the United States.'

When they reached their coach Tom was surprised to see just how luxurious it was. He quickly realised that his assumptions about the country were likely to change dramatically over the next couple of weeks.

This became even more evident when they reached their towering hotel. It dominated the skyline of Hanoi and would have looked impressive in any major western city. Its visual impact was even more spectacular as it had been built on one of the hills that dotted the landscape. The road to the hotel entrance was very wide and wound its way around the hill until it reached the hotel entrance, in front of which was a large fountain, with a circle of lights fixed beneath the water level.

As they got off the coach, they were met by a small army of hotel staff, all immaculately dressed in their white uniforms. The staff were clearly used to this as all the luggage was quickly and efficiently recovered from the coach's storage area, loaded onto high-sided trolleys and wheeled into the hotel.

As they entered the hotel lobby they were met by a group of young ladies, each wearing a long, tightly fitted white dress, in traditional Vietnamese style, and carrying a tray of drinks.

'Ladies and gentlemen,' said Lan, the tone of his voice instantly demanding attention, 'welcome to Hotel Emerald. I hope you will enjoy your welcoming drink whilst your luggage is taken to your rooms. The hotel has already allocated your rooms, and you will get your room numbers and keys from my colleagues at the table over there in the corner.' He pointed at the table in question, where three more Mekong Cruises personnel were seated, each with a number of large, white envelopes laid out in front of them.

'In your Welcome pack you will find your room keys together with the itinerary for the rest of today and tomorrow. The pack also includes a full list of the names of everyone who will be on this Mekong Cruises trip. If I could remind you that the official welcome meeting will take place this evening at 7pm, in the Ambassador Room, which is situated here on the ground floor. During your stay at the hotel, if there is anything you need, one of my colleagues will be available to help at our reception desk.'

He held up his own drink. 'So, ladies and gentlemen, here's to a memorable adventure. I know you will enjoy your stay here in our beautiful country, and that it will provide you with a lifetime of memories.'

Chapter 5

Milner was seated at his desk, rereading one of the files laid open in front of him. Taking DCI Stone's advice, he had spent most of the morning trying to spot any key connections amongst all the names listed in DC Shipley's files. Some names did crop up more than once, and so he made a separate note of those, planning to obtain their addresses and phone details later.

After he had finished reading the file he examined the list of names in front of him, each of which had been recorded at least twice. Alongside each he'd written the number of times they'd been mentioned. In total there were four different names, although, unfortunately, the two names he'd found hidden in the sleeve of one of DC Shipley's files were not on the list. What was immediately obvious, though, was that two of the surnames were identical. As none of the names were immediately known to him, he decided he needed some help.

'Do you have a minute?' he asked, turning to face his colleague DC Darren Grey, who was seated close by.

'Of course,' DC Grey replied.

Milner handed him the list of names. 'Before I start accessing the database, I wondered if you have come across any of these individuals before.'

DC Grey examined the list. 'Well, two of them stand out straight away.' He pointed at one of the names. 'Daniel Melton, for one. He was found dead not too long ago. He'd been murdered. Well, that's what the report said. But it looked like he'd been tortured before being shot. Very nasty. The other one, Clinton Melton, is his younger brother.'

'What do we know about the older brother? Did he have a record?' asked Milner.

'As long as your arm. Started young. Petty crime: joyriding, shoplifting, car crime, burglaries. The usual stuff. Then progressed into dealing, and then God knows what.'

'Where was he found?'

'At the bottom of a stairwell in a block of flats in Shepherd's Bush,' DC Grey said. 'I thought you would have known about it. It should have been uploaded onto the system.'

Milner considered what he'd just been told before answering. 'I should have, but it might have been during the time when my personal details were being added to the system. I remember there were a few tech issues. It might have been that they simply forgot, and it just wasn't updated.'

'Sounds familiar,' replied DC Grey. 'You'd think it was just a question of pressing another button. I swear that sometimes those techies deliberately make it as complicated as possible, just to try and impress us.'

'What about his brother, Clinton?' Milner asked. 'Same thing?'

'More or less. As he's a few years younger, his record isn't yet quite as long as his brother's.' DC Grey looked again at the list. 'There's one other name I'm aware of. Dennis Farmer is also known to us – although, unlike Daniel Melton, he hasn't yet been found dead. The other one – Curtis Seton – doesn't ring any bells, though.' He handed the list back to Milner. 'Anyway, what's so special about these names? There are probably another hundred just like them on file.'

'The names appeared in the files I inherited from DC Shipley. I'm just trying to get a handle on what he was working on,' Milner answered. He had decided, at this stage, not to mention the two additional names he'd come across.

'Good luck with that,' replied DC Grey. 'The inquiry team have been all over his stuff with a fine-toothed comb. They copied everything. All his digital and electronic stuff, paper files. They even took away the screwed-up paper he'd thrown into his waste bin. I'm told they did the same with his personal stuff at home.'

'So they are sure he was involved in something shady. Is that right?' asked Milner.

'Nothing official yet, but apparently the clincher was when they conducted a more thorough search of his home. They found money – quite a lot, I hear – hidden in the washing machine, as well as a sizeable quantity of drugs, mainly coke, in one of his wardrobes. They also found a few wraps amongst his socks. Presumably for his personal use. So, looks like he was dealing and using, as well as being on the take.'

'What makes you think he was on the take?' asked Milner.

DC Grey looked at him in surprise. 'Well, where to start? Cash and drugs in his personal possession would be enough. But I don't think it was a coincidence how, after his death, we started to have some successes with our raids. Admittedly not spectacular, but better than the period immediately before then.'

'Are you saying there weren't any results at all before he died?' asked Milner.

DC Grey shook his head. 'There were, but nothing of any significance. Well, at least as far as I was aware.'

'So, pretty much the same as after DC Shipley died.'

DC Grey didn't reply, and Milner, recognising that his question might have been interpreted as questioning DC Grey's professional assessment, decided to leave it there, especially as they were both of equal rank. The last thing he wanted to do was set DC Grey against him so early in their relationship.

Instead, Milner simply said, 'Thanks. That's really useful background information. Anything that helps me piece together DC Shipley's thinking will be of real help.'

'Happy to help,' DC Grey replied.

Milner took a moment to reflect on what he'd just been told. He'd heard rumours, of course, but nothing as detailed as this. It prompted him to ask an obvious question. 'Can I ask you how you know all this? I thought the inquiry was still ongoing and being carried out by a separate unit.'

A faint smile appeared on DC Grey's face. 'That's all true, but this is the police, remember. There's just as many leaks here as anywhere else.'

He went briefly silent. Milner decided to keep his own silence, and it was DC Grey who first began to speak again.

'I have a mate who works in the unit. We go back quite a way. He knows I worked alongside John, so he wanted to give me the nod.' A look of concern suddenly appeared on his face.

'All of this is still confidential. I probably shouldn't have told you, but, as you are new, and you've taken John's place in the team, I thought that it might help.'

Milner decided to help him with his obvious unease. 'I really appreciate that, and it does help. Rest assured I'll keep all of what you've told me to myself.' He paused. 'What was DC Shipley like? Were there any obvious clues, even in retrospect, to suggest how he might have been involved with the OCN?'

DC Grey took time to formulate his reply. 'He was the type who liked to keep himself to himself. I wouldn't say he was a team player, for example. Some of the other guys in DS Foster's team thought he always seemed reluctant to share information with them. My impression was that, although he wasn't disliked, he wasn't especially popular either. He did sometimes socialise, after work for example, but I always thought he didn't really enjoy it. It was almost as though he felt it was the thing to do, or at least to be seen to do. You know what working in this type of unit is like. People can be quite judgemental and unforgiving if you are even slightly different. That old rule is especially true of police officers: if you're not there, expect to be talked about.'

'I would agree with that,' replied Milner. 'But he must have been good at his job, otherwise he wouldn't have been selected for this unit.'

'I suppose so,' DC Grey simply replied. 'But it's clear now that all the time he was in the pay of the OCN. God knows what information he was able to pass to them. You know what some cops can be like when they're together, especially after a few drinks. Sometimes they can be incredibly indiscreet in the most public of places. Anyway, that's why everyone was so angry. I'm sure there won't be too many tears shed when all of this comes out.'

'Was he married?' Milner asked, determined to get as much background information about his predecessor as possible, without raising DC Grey's suspicions.

'Yes, he was. I think he'd only been married for a couple of years, though.'

'Any children?'

'No. Well, at least I don't think so.'

Milner decided to leave that line of questioning and instead return to something DC Grey had said earlier. 'You mentioned how relatively unsuccessful the team had been just prior to his death. Were there any examples of failed operations which can now be traced directly back to him?'

'Nothing proven, no,' he answered. 'But there was one suspicious occasion where we had followed a car, which we were sure was involved in a spate of recent violent robberies. They'd changed the number plates a few times, but we managed to get a locator on it so that we could track its movements and hopefully catch them in the act. After it had been parked up, we staked it out, expecting them to return, but it never moved again. That was a bit suspicious, and of course the rumour mill started.'

'What sorts of rumours?'

'Well, it was convenient to blame John for everything. Human nature, I suppose.'

Milner, impressed with DC Grey's honesty, asked, 'But what about when all of this first came out, after he was arrested? Was it a big surprise?'

'Massive,' he answered. 'It came as a huge shock to the team. Since then, though, that shock has turned to real anger. Everyone is really concerned that any progress we were making has now been compromised. We're all wondering what else he might have done which has still to come out, too. It's making everyone nervous and has definitely affected the morale of the team.'

'But, looking back, you can't think of anything specific, traced back to him, that might have been a red flag?'

For the first time, DC Grey's expression changed to one of outright suspicion. 'We've all been through this already with the inquiry unit. They were very thorough and, anyway, I've probably said more already than I should have.'

Milner decided not to pursue this particular line of conversation. 'Yes, it must have been very uncomfortable. Anyway, thanks again. As I said, it's been very helpful.'

'I've got a question for you,' DC Grey suddenly said.

'Okay,' replied a surprised Milner.

'Were you selected for this unit or just appointed? It's just that some of the team were a bit surprised when you joined.'

Adopting DCI Stone's advice that honesty was usually the best policy, Milner said, 'Actually, I was recommended to DCI Shaw by my previous DCI.'

'Was that DCI Stone? He's quite famous, isn't he?'

Choosing to ignore his second question, Milner said, 'It was, yes. I was part of a team which, at one point, also included DCI Shaw. That's how the connection was made.' He hesitated slightly before continuing. 'You might have heard how I was a DS in that team but, well...' It was a struggle to think of the right words, so he simply said, 'I screwed up, and my DC was murdered as a result. Something I'll never forget.' His voice was beginning to waver. After a brief pause, he continued. 'Anyway, there was an inquiry, and I was subsequently demoted to DC.'

'We had heard something along those lines. I probably need to tell you that some of the team knew your DC. That's why it was a bit of a frosty welcome when you arrived. I'm sure you could sense that.'

'Yes, I did notice, but it was totally understandable. It would probably have been my reaction as well.'

'That must have been tough for you. Weren't you tempted to just jack it all in?'

'I was, yes. It wasn't the best time of my police career, that's for sure, but eventually I was persuaded by my DCI not to do that. It was a short while afterwards when DCI Shaw offered me a DC position here.'

'And that's another thing you should be aware of, while we're being open with each other,' said DC Grey. 'It's not often that a DC is directly recruited by a DCI, especially into a specialist anti-crime team like this. A few of the team have already mentioned favouritism.'

Milner didn't immediately respond to DC Grey's comment. When he eventually did, it wasn't entirely clear whether he was speaking to DC Grey or himself. 'Well, at least I know what I'm now up against.'

Chapter 6

After the welcome meeting, Tom had collected their travel information envelope and he and Mary had gone up to their room. The room was far more luxurious than they had envisaged, and even Tom was impressed by its size, layout and contents. The most impressive feature, however, was the spectacular view they had from their seventh-floor window. Below them was a bend of the Red River, which seemed the very epitome of a busy working river with all types and sizes of boats, small fishing boats and laden barges making their way up and down the river. It was the type of vista which, without caution, could have an almost hypnotic effect, taking up far more of your time than intended as the scene continued to change.

After they had unpacked and finished exploring their room, they headed down to the reception area to meet up with Sue and Tony. Inevitably, the initial conversation was about their rooms.

'Our room is fantastic,' said Sue. 'I must admit I didn't expect that.'

'I know,' answered Mary, clearly equally excited. 'Ours is the same. Did you see the view over the river?'

Tom, thinking it might be a bit churlish, resisted the temptation to mention the high cost of the trip. Mary had, inevitably, been the one who had researched the holiday and then carried out all of the associated administrative tasks. They had briefly discussed it, and Tom must have expressed some interest, because a couple of days later Mary had presented him with the confirmed booking details.

Earlier the four of them had agreed to take a short, exploratory walk around the surrounding streets, so as to get their bearings as well as to experience some of the local culture. They were not disappointed. Just a short distance from the peace and tranquillity of their hotel surroundings, they suddenly found themselves walking down a street which was bursting with noise and activity. The chaotic sight of seemingly thousands of motorcycles of varying size and roadworthiness, on which the riders all appeared to be using their horns at the same time, was mesmerising. Very few of the riders seemed to be wearing a helmet, and many had more than two people riding pillion.

They decided to stop at a small bar alongside the street so they could take in the full experience. It was certainly the first time they had deliberately sat by the side of a road just so they could watch the traffic pass by. There were a few local people already there, all of whom were seated on undersized blue plastic chairs placed around an upturned blue plastic crate, which served as a table. There were plenty of unused ones, and so they took their lead from the locals and sat down at one of the makeshift tables, each of them now filling out their own chair. A man soon appeared to take their order. After ordering four beers, they once again turned their attention towards the street.

'How does anyone manage to cross the road safely?' asked Mary. 'I certainly won't be trying.'

'Me neither,' replied Sue. 'It's like a river of motorcycles going both ways.'

'They do seem to know what they're doing, though,' said Tom, with a touch of admiration in his voice.

Just then, as if to prove his point, a local man began to cross the road, a phone held up to his ear in one hand and a cigarette in the other. There didn't seem to be any hint of anxiety in his body language, or of concern for his personal safety, as he successfully negotiated his way across both lanes of the road without apparently paying any attention to the traffic.

'It's almost as though it's the responsibility of the motorcyclists to miss the pedestrian, rather than the pedestrian taking any special care. It's unbelievable,' said Tony. He took out his phone and pointed it in the direction of the road. 'I must get a video of this to show the grandkids.'

They stayed there longer than they had originally intended, having had another round of beers, almost spellbound by the mass of mounted humanity just a few yards in front of them. Someone had suggested that they play a game of 'spot the motorcycle with the most people on it'. So far, the record was five people: dad, two small children, and mum carrying a baby.

Just as they were thinking of paying the bill, five people – three men and two women – took their place at a table closely alongside theirs. They all looked as though they might be in their mid-seventies. The men were wearing knee-length shorts, long white sports socks and various branded baseball caps, whilst the women wore loose-fitting dresses and had their heads protected from the sun by broad, floppy hats.

'Are you with Mekong Cruises?' asked the tallest of the men in an unmistakeable American accent, as he took off his cap and wiped his forehead.

'We are. How did you know that?' asked Sue.

'Just an inspired guess, I suppose,' he replied. 'And anyway, we're not that far from our hotel.' He stood up and offered his hand, firstly to Sue and then to the others. 'Hi, I'm John, and this is my wife, Joany.'

One of the other men then also offered his hand. 'I'm Bob and this is Ruth.'

'And I'm Jim,' said the last man, who was slightly frail-looking and the smallest man of the group. 'I'm afraid I'm here by myself. My wife Barbara passed away a couple of years ago.'

'I'm really sorry to hear that,' replied Sue, with genuine sympathy.

'Thank you,' he answered. 'Fortunately, my two kids and my sister, Peggy, have been there for me.'

Sue made their introductions, after which John asked, 'Is it okay if we pull up our chairs and crate and join you?'

Without waiting for a reply, he moved their table to link up with where Tom and the others were seated. The newcomers then picked up their own chairs and placed them alongside the table.

'We're just about to order a beer. Can we get you guys one?' John asked.

'That's very generous of you,' replied Tom. 'We were just about to leave, but I'm sure we can share another one with you.'

This prompted a slightly puzzled look from Mary. Tom was not exactly known for open bonhomie, especially towards people whom he had only just met.

'So where are you guys from?' asked John after he had ordered their drinks.

'We're all from the UK,' answered Tom. 'What about you?'

'We're all from the States,' replied John. 'Joany and myself are from Kansas City, and Bob and Ruth are from Chicago. Jim lives in Florida.'

Tom couldn't help making a mental note that John seemed to be the main spokesperson of the group.

'Is this your first time in Vietnam?' John asked.

'It is,' replied Sue. 'What about you?'

'Well, it is for Joany and Ruth, but Bob, Jim and myself were all here fifty-five years ago.'

'Was that during the war?' asked Tom, quickly doing the maths.

'It was,' replied Bob. 'This trip is a sort of pilgrimage for us. Every year trips come here from the US, partly funded by the US Military Association, for veterans from different companies. This year our company was one of those which was on the list. There are five of us who were all in the same company back in '69 and have made the trip.' He gestured to himself, John and Jim. 'The three of us here have always kept in touch with each other and still meet up every few years for a reunion. Unfortunately, there are less and less every time we meet, so we decided we should take advantage and make a last trip together, while we can. Some of us are not in the best of health now.' He suddenly seemed to remember something else. 'In fact, there are others from the US, also here on the trip, who were also in 'Nam at some stage, although I'm not sure when. Over the past few years, this has become a very popular trip for 'Nam veterans.'

The brief pause which followed suggested a collective hesitation, as though it might be difficult to find the correct follow-up words. It was Mary, though, who broke the ice. 'How many of you are there from the US?'

Joany answered. 'I think there are about sixty in total from the US, although we haven't had the chance yet to get to know everyone. It was only yesterday that we all flew into Hanoi, from various places in the States. Some are veterans, together with their wives and, I think in some cases, children.'

'So,' asked Ruth, speaking for the first time, 'where in the UK do you live? London?'

'We live in Sheffield,' Tony answered quickly, clearly irked at the insinuation that everything revolved around London.

'Sheffield?' repeated Ruth. 'I don't think I've ever heard of that particular city.'

Before Tony could answer, Mary said, 'And Tom and I live about thirty-five miles southwest of London.'

'Near to London, then. Thirty-five miles doesn't seem that far,' suggested John.

'I suppose it's not, but the UK is a very small country compared to yours.' She then added, almost as an afterthought, 'Actually, Tom did spend most of his life working in London, though, before he retired. Didn't you, Tom?'

John turned to face Tom. 'So, Tom, you worked in London. We've been there a couple of times on vacation, haven't we, Joany?' Without giving Joany any time to reply, he immediately carried on. 'So, you're retired, Tom? You don't look old enough to be a retiree. What was it you did?'

'I was a policeman,' replied Tom, slightly annoyed with Mary for opening up this discussion topic.

'In London? How wonderful,' said Ruth. 'Your policemen look so good in those big blue hats.'

Tom, who was becoming slightly embarrassed with the way the conversation was going, resisted providing any more information. 'Returning to Vietnam must generate a lot of mixed feelings for you all,' he said instead.

'It sure does,' answered Bob. 'I was only here for a year, and it was a long time ago, but I can remember it as though it was only yesterday.' There was a slight pause before he continued. 'It affected some guys in different ways. I learned yesterday that some of the other guys on the trip were imprisoned here during the war. They were pilots who were shot down, got captured and then spent the rest of the war in the Hanoi Hilton.'

'The Hanoi Hilton? What's that?' asked Mary.

'It's the name the captured pilots gave to the prison where they were held here in Hanoi,' answered Tom. 'Some of them were there for over six years.'

'You seem to know a lot about the war,' said Bob.

'Not really,' Tom said. 'It's mainly from watching documentaries. A previous colleague of mine is a bit of an expert, though, and in fact he's visited Vietnam regularly over the past ten years or so. I read one of the background reference books he gave me on the flight coming over here.'

'And some of those prisoners of war are on this trip?' asked Mary, directing her question at Bob, a mixture of disbelief and admiration in her voice.

'They are,' he replied. 'As far as I make out, there are about five guys who were prisoners here in Hanoi.'

'I wonder if that's the same prison we are visiting tomorrow?' asked Sue. 'I did wonder what that might be.'

'As a matter of fact, it is,' answered Bob.

'I can't imagine how they will feel going back there again,' Sue said.

'Anyway, that's enough of the war,' said Ruth, before anyone could follow up on Sue's comment. 'Are you guys retired or still working?'

After Mary had given them a brief summary of her florist business, it was Sue who spoke next. 'I've been retired eight years. I was a primary school teacher.' She nodded to her husband. 'Tony retired about the same time from his job as a warehouse manager. Funnily enough, before that he'd spent over twenty-five years in the British army. Didn't you, Tony?'

'I owned my own trucking business,' interjected John, 'but sold it about ten years ago. Best thing I ever did.'

'Yes, as Sue just said, I was also in the army,' said Tony, choosing to ignore John's last comment, with a slight detectable annoyance in his voice. 'I joined as a squaddie when I was seventeen years old. Then did various other things. By the time I retired, I'd worked my way up to become a warrant officer.'

'What's a squaddie?' asked John.

'It's the name given to young privates when they first join,' answered Tony. 'The lowest of the low.'

'Like we were, then,' John said, with a slight laugh. 'Did you spend any time on operations?'

'Well, I did two tours of Northern Ireland in the late eighties and then was involved in the first Gulf War in 1991.'

'I expect you saw a bit of action, then,' said John.

Tom had already known Tony had spent time in the army, but he hadn't been aware of what Tony had just revealed. He wondered how Tony would answer John's question. When he did, having in the short time they had known each other quickly recognised John's natural bluntness, he was surprisingly diplomatic. 'As you say, a bit, but probably not as much as you all did.'

To the relief of Mary, who was concerned that the topic could become uncomfortable for some people, there was no more conversation relating to war and military careers. Instead, they spent the next ten minutes or so sharing more family-related things with each other, such as how many children and grandchildren they each had, after which the Brits decided it was time to head back to the hotel.

'It's been great meeting you,' said Mary, who, being the most naturally outgoing of the British group, seemed to have become their spokesperson. 'I'm sure we'll see you again at tonight's welcome meeting.'

They all once again shook hands with each other, before the British group started to walk back to their hotel.

'Christ,' said Tony. 'There's over another fifty of them.'

Chapter 7

It was just before seven in the evening, and Tom and Mary were seated in the Ambassador Room at their hotel. Next to them were Sue and Tony, who now seemed to have become permanent attachments as their new best holiday friends.

Whilst Tom recognised most of the people who had been on the same UK flight, there were now lots of others in the room who were unfamiliar. He assumed these were the rest of the US contingent. As he looked around the room, he could see that, unlike the Brits who were there, the majority of the others were in their seventies. This tallied with what John and Bob had told them about their tour of duty in Vietnam during the late 1960s. He knew that the age of the average GI in Vietnam was just nineteen.

Exactly at seven o'clock, Lan took hold of a microphone and began to speak. Behind and to the side of him sat two other men, both wearing the same distinctive black trousers and red polo shirt emblazoned with the Mekong Cruises logo. Immediately behind him was a screen in front of which a laptop had already been placed onto a small table.

'Good evening, ladies and gentlemen. First of all, thank you for being here on time.' Just as Lan said this, the door opened, and two couples slowly walked into the room. Lan immediately, and very deliberately, stopped speaking until they, rather sheepishly and conspicuously, found seats at the back of the room.

After they were seated, he continued. 'As I was about to say, my full name is Phan Duc Lan, but please call me Lan. I think it's easier for everyone to say and, of course, it will save a lot of time,' he said, with a slight laugh. 'I have the honour to be your cruise director for this trip. Before I give you more information about what we have planned for you over the next few days, I want to introduce you to two other members of the Mekong

Cruises team, who are here to help you enjoy your visit to our beautiful country. First, Sang,' who Tom recognised as the person ticking off the names when they had passed into the arrivals hall at the airport. Sang briefly stood, held up his right hand in acknowledgement and then sat down. 'Second, Dung,' who also stood and waved an acknowledgement.

Lan resumed speaking. 'We have a brief presentation, which hopefully will not only tell you what is ahead, but also provide you with a bit more background information on the places you will be visiting whilst on your trip. Please keep any questions you might have for after the presentation, and we will do our best to answer them. After that, we will all have dinner in the Banquet Room. For your information, there are ninety guests on this cruise, thirty from the UK and sixty from the US. By the end of the cruise, I'm sure you will all have made new lifelong friendships.'

Lan then spent the next half-hour or so highlighting some facts and figures about Vietnam, its geography, culture and history, including a brief section on the war and its aftermath, after which he briefly summarised the travel itinerary. After he'd finished, and any questions had been answered, the formal part of the meeting ended, and they all made their way to the Banquet Room for dinner.

Tom and Mary found themselves seated at a table with two other couples. Tony and Sue, of course, but also Mike and Shelley, who were about their age and lived in Exeter.

After they had introduced themselves, Mike said, 'I don't think anyone is likely to be late again to any of Lan's meetings. He certainly made it clear that he wasn't happy.'

'I know,' said Shelley. 'There's nothing worse, though, than some people always being late, whilst all of the others have made the effort to be there on time.'

Sue added to the conversation. 'As an ex-teacher, I know how important it is to keep to a timetable. If people can just turn up when they want, then nothing will get done.'

As Tom looked around the room, he said, 'It's interesting that all the Brits are sitting together, as are all the Americans. I wonder if it will be like that by the end of the trip.'

'I'm sure we will all be mixing by then,' replied Mary in her usual optimistic manner.

'Hmm, we'll see,' Tony muttered. It was unclear whether he disagreed with Mary or simply wasn't looking forward to it.

By the time they had finished dinner it was almost 10pm.

'Why don't we have a quick drink at the bar before we turn in?' suggested Tony.

It was Tom, now uncharacteristically starting to get into holiday mood, who quickly responded. 'I was reading in the hotel brochure that there's a Sky Bar. It's open until about one in the morning. Why don't we give it a try?'

Mary, not wanting to dampen his unexpected enthusiasm, said, 'That's a good idea. We are only here for two nights anyway, and there's another dinner arranged for tomorrow night, somewhere in Hanoi City. The Sky Bar is in the open, and the brochure says the views from it are fabulous, especially now, as it's dark.'

With the others in agreement, they all made their way to the lift and then up to the Sky Bar. Although a section was currently undergoing some maintenance work, and therefore not open to guests, the rest of the outside seating area was still large enough that they could easily find somewhere to sit. The area was rectangular in shape, with the bar sited along one of the shorter sides. There were a few small tables and chairs in the centre, but also a number of comfortable-looking leather settees all around the outside. Most of these were already occupied. Tom recognised a few Brits there, but mostly they were taken by people from the American group.

As he continued to look around the space, he suddenly recognised a voice.

'Hey, Tom, Tony, come and join us and have a drink,' John said, in a way which suggested he'd had a few drinks already. 'We'll make some room for you.'

'That's just what I need,' whispered Tony, just loud enough that Tom could hear.

'Let's make room for our Brit friends,' said John. Although the five Americans were already seated, with a bit of rearrangement, space was soon found for the new arrivals. 'Are you two Brits as well?' asked John, directing his question at Mike and Shelley.

'We are,' answered Shelley. 'I'm Shelley, and this is my husband Mike.'

'Nice to meet you both. Do you live in London?' John asked.

Tom smiled to himself, guessing Tony's reaction without the need to look at him.

'We don't, no. We live in Exeter, although I don't suppose you are familiar with it.'

'Can't say as I am,' replied John.

'It's a city in a place called Devon, which is a county in the southwest of England,' Shelley explained. 'We used to live in Totnes, a small town in Devon, but moved to Exeter about ten years ago. My father was born in Totnes and didn't want to move. I think he wanted to be near his own mum, my grandmother. She was a wonderful lady,' she said, wistfully. 'She'd had a very difficult time when Dad was born, and he wanted to be near her in her final years.'

'I've heard of Devon,' Jim said, to their surprise. 'I've never been, but Dad was based there for a few months during World War II, just before D-Day. He always spoke about how much he enjoyed his time there and how friendly the locals were. He often talked about going back there someday, but, unfortunately, he never did.' Before anyone could respond, he added, 'Hi, by the way. My name is Jim.'

'Nice to meet you, Jim,' said Shelley, before being introduced to all the others.

When they were all finally seated, John asked, 'What can I get you all to drink?' whilst simultaneously beckoning to one of the bar staff. 'I can definitely recommend one of their cocktails.'

'Why not?' said Mary. 'We are on holiday, after all. It's not every day you get the chance to drink a cocktail in a bar whilst looking out over Hanoi.' She paused briefly before adding, 'It really is beautiful. It looks so different at night.'

'It is now,' said Bob, suddenly. 'At least compared to when we were last in Vietnam.'

'I expect, like everyone who was here during that time, you

can still remember a lot about those days,' suggested Tom.

Bob didn't immediately respond. Finally, he simply said, 'I suppose so, but there are lots of things I'd rather not remember.'

An uneasy silence followed, before John said, 'Here's the barman. Now, what are you guys going to have? They're on me.'

After they had all placed their drink orders, Sue said, 'Those people seem to be enjoying themselves. Do you know them?' She was watching a group of maybe a dozen people, men and women, who were all seated at the far end of the open area.

'Based on their noise levels, I think they've all already had a bit too much to drink,' Ruth said, disapproval evident in her voice. 'It was the same last night.'

'They're just letting off a bit of steam, Ruth,' said Bob. 'I think at our age everyone should be allowed to do that.'

'I assume they were also here during the war,' suggested Tom.

'They were,' replied John. 'Two of them were in the same company as us, although in a different platoon.'

After they'd had another cocktail, Mary whispered to Tom, 'I think I'm ready for bed now. It's been a really long day and it's all starting to catch up. You don't have to come, though, if you'd rather stay here.'

'Good idea. I think I'll turn in as well,' he answered, 'before John orders any more cocktails.'

The other Brits took their lead from Tom and Mary and also stood to leave.

'Thank you so much for such an enjoyable evening,' said Mary. 'It's been a very long day for us, though, and I'm starting to flag a bit.'

'We should do it again soon,' suggested John.

As they made their way out of the bar, Tony said, 'I don't know why, but I really don't like that John. The others seem okay, but there's something about him that annoys me. Did you notice earlier today how he couldn't wait to tell everyone he'd owned a truck business? Plus, he keeps throwing his money around as though he's trying to impress. Well, it doesn't work on me.'

'I wouldn't worry about it,' Tom answered. 'He is a bit full-on, but it's still early days. You never know; you might be swapping addresses by the end of the trip.'

'Somehow, I don't think so,' Tony replied.

Chapter 8

Following his revealing conversation with DC Grey, Milner had gone back to reviewing the files, after which he tapped Daniel Melton's details into his computer, thinking that might be the best place to start. Sure enough, a long list of increasingly serious offences and convictions appeared on the screen, finally ending with Melton's own recent brutal murder.

In a way, Milner couldn't help but feel some degree of sympathy for him, especially for the way in which he had died. But he knew he had to balance this with the likelihood that, due to Melton's actions, other young people were probably now on the same inevitable path that he had tragically followed.

There was an address in Shepherd's Bush on Melton's file, together with a telephone number. As far as Milner could tell, Melton was DC Shipley's main lead, and so he decided he would arrange to focus on Melton first, starting with a visit to his address.

*

'I've told the police all this already,' explained Mrs Melton. When Milner had phoned earlier, she had made it clear that, as far as she was concerned, there was no point in his proposed visit, as all she wanted now was to carry on with her life as best she could.

They were seated in a small open-plan room which also included a smaller kitchen area. The flat itself was located on one of the side streets within a short walking distance of the main shopping area. Milner also knew the flat must be quite close to where the body of her son had been found. This would have made it even more difficult for Mrs Melton, especially as she would inevitably sometimes have to pass it.

Milner had arranged to be at the flat at 1pm and, knowing what the traffic would be like, had given himself plenty of time to get there. Despite this, it had been almost 1.15pm before he had knocked on Mrs Melton's door, having spent a frustrating amount of time trying, unsuccessfully, to find somewhere to park. In the event he'd had to drive back the way he'd come until he found somewhere, and then walked to her address. As he was the type of person who prided himself on his punctuality, his lateness didn't bode well for his meeting with Mrs Melton.

'I've just been assigned to the investigation and wanted to meet you personally,' Milner said. 'I've read the file, but, in my experience, you can learn so much more by hearing it yourself. As I mentioned earlier, though, if at any time you'd like to stop then I will leave. It's not a problem.'

Milner could see she was, suddenly, quite upset and had started to dab at her eyes with a handkerchief. He patiently waited until he felt she was able to continue.

'I understand Daniel was your eldest son,' Milner said at last. 'What was he like?'

She hesitated momentarily before replying. 'He was such a good boy when he was young. Good at school, good at football, and wanted to take care of me, after his father died.' Once again, she began to quietly cry, but, between sobs, she managed to continue. 'I blame myself. I wasn't able to give him the time and attention he needed at that age. I also had Clinton and Shannon to bring up while I was working. I should have noticed Daniel was getting in with a bad crowd. When I did, it was too late.'

'Please don't blame yourself. It must have been very difficult,' Milner said, with genuine feeling. 'Was there one specific point when you realised what sort of company he was keeping?'

'It was when the police first started to come round, although his school reports had begun to get worse before then. I was called into school to talk to his teachers. It was only then I found out how much he'd been skipping school. After that I just couldn't do anything to get him to stay away from trouble. He'd quite often bring me nice things, but I told him that I didn't want any of them if they'd been stolen. Eventually, he was arrested for stealing cars and sentenced to serve time in a young offenders' prison. He was only there for six months, but, when he came out, he seemed to have become a man. He immediately started again, and, if anything, things got worse. I just didn't know what to do.'

'Was he still living here then?' asked Milner.

'On and off. Quite often, though, he'd just disappear for a few days. At first, I was worried sick, as I never knew where he was or what he was doing. In the end, though, I was relieved when he was away.'

'Why was that?' Milner asked quietly.

'He was having such a bad influence on Clinton. Shannon was too young, but Clinton always looked up to him and just wanted to be like him.' She hesitated briefly. 'But it was too late. Clinton started doing all the things that Daniel used to do, and it wasn't long before he was in trouble with the police as well. I just knew that would happen.'

'Does Clinton still live with you?'

'Not really. Well, he still has his room, but he's hardly here these days. In many ways, I worry more about him than I did with Daniel. He's not as clever as Daniel was and is more easily influenced by other people. I just know he's going to end up like Daniel.'

Her last few words clearly affected her, and she began to cry again, more loudly and interspersed with deep sobs.

'Do you need any water?' asked Milner, quite moved by Mrs Melton's distress.

'No, thanks. I'll be fine soon. Just give me a minute.'

Milner patiently waited, and this was rewarded when she began to speak again.

'After Daniel became a father, he seemed to grow up very quickly. He and Diana were so happy. They managed to get a flat in Acton. Although it was very small, they had tried to make it into a real home. I was so proud of them.'

'When was that?'

'Just before Daryl was born. He's coming up for one now.

How is Diana going to look after him and work? I don't know what they'll do now.' She dabbed her eyes with her handkerchief again.

'Do you get to see them?' asked Milner.

'It's not easy for them to get here, so I try and go there when I can,' she answered. 'Every time I see the baby, he just reminds me of Daniel when he was that age.'

'Hopefully that's some comfort for you,' suggested Milner.

For the first time, a smile appeared on Mrs Melton's face. She suddenly stood and walked over to a nearby set of drawers, opened the top one and brought out a photo. 'It is, yes. At least I've now got Daryl to remind me.'

She passed the photo to Milner. It showed Daniel with his arm around Diana, whilst she held a baby.

'They look so happy,' Milner said, before handing the photo back to Mrs Melton.

'I know. That's what upsets me so much. I honestly thought that Daniel would change after his son was born.'

Milner then took a piece of paper from his pocket. On it were the two names found in the sleeve of one of DC Shipley's files: Lionel Tedman and Adrian Wolfe. 'Could you please take a look at these two names? Do you know either of them? Please take your time.'

'No. I don't know either of them,' she replied, almost straight away. 'Why? Do you think they were involved in Daniel's murder?'

'I've really got no idea. At this stage we are following up on every lead that we have.' Sensing that the time was now right to ask more searching questions, he went on. 'I'm sorry to have to ask you this, Mrs Melton, but it's important I find out as much as possible about Daniel's movements leading up to his death, as well as who he might have been in contact with. Do you have any idea who might have done this?'

'I told the other police officers everything I know. I think they thought I wasn't telling them something, but I told them everything. I just want those who killed Daniel to be caught and sent to prison.'

'I've read the report, and I can see you did tell them everything you knew,' said Milner. 'Sometimes, though, telling another person can help you remember things you might have forgotten.'

'I've got no idea who might have done this,' she immediately replied. 'I stopped asking him what he was doing a long time ago.'

'So he didn't seem upset or worried when you last saw him?' asked Milner.

'No. He seemed really happy.'

'And when was that?'

'A few days before he...' She tailed off, unable to finish.

Milner decided to pursue another line. 'But you saw much more of Daniel over the past few months.'

'A lot more. Especially after Daryl was born. He couldn't wait to show me the baby. He was so proud. I honestly thought he'd given up doing all of that crime and just wanted to settle down with his new family. Diana was good for him. Perhaps, though, that was just what I wanted to happen.'

'I know this is another very difficult question for you, but do you have any idea what happened on that day?'

'Not really, only what Clinton told me.' She paused. 'Look, I've told the police all of this. Why do you have to go over it all again?'

'I'm sorry, Mrs Melton, but if you could just tell me what Clinton said, I would be very grateful.'

She shook her head. 'He said Daniel had had an argument with some people the previous day. They said he owed them some money he'd borrowed to help buy things for the baby. He couldn't pay them back straight away, so he agreed to do some sort of work for them. Clinton said he later decided he wouldn't do what they wanted him to do.' She stopped speaking for a moment, apparently composing herself. 'It was just after that when he was murdered.'

'Do you know how Clinton knows all of this?' asked Milner.

'I don't know,' she quietly answered.

'Would Clinton know the names of these people?'

Mrs Melton's expression suddenly changed. 'What do you

mean? Look, I've just told you I don't know. Don't you believe me? You think Clinton was involved in this, don't you? I shouldn't have told you. I would like you to leave now.'

Milner, realising that any continuation would be counter-productive, stood and said, 'I'm very sorry for your loss, Mrs Melton, and I apologise if I upset you. I certainly didn't mean to.' He handed her a card showing his contact details. 'If there is anything I can do to help, please call me on one of these numbers.'

He offered his hand, but Mrs Melton was no longer in the mood to reciprocate and, instead, walked to the door and opened it for him so he could leave.

Chapter 9

As Milner drove back to the station, he reflected on his conversation with Mrs Melton. It was clear she had tried to raise her children, in very difficult circumstances, to the best of her ability, but, despite these best efforts, there was a sense of inevitability that one if not both of her sons would at some stage find themselves in trouble with the police.

Although he hadn't discovered any compelling new evidence, he nonetheless felt his visit had been very useful. He had found out, for example, that Daniel and his partner Diana had recently had a baby. Although the assumption was based upon what Mrs Melton had told him, it would appear Daniel had been trying to do what was best for his family. What that involved was difficult to say.

Probably more importantly, Milner now suspected that Clinton knew the people his brother had spoken to about the monies owed. He therefore determined it would be very useful to have a conversation with Clinton about who might have murdered his brother.

When he arrived back at the station, DC Grey was waiting for him.

'I'm glad you're back,' DC Grey said. 'There's a briefing in half an hour. Looks like we might be paying a visit to some of the dealers' houses tonight. We've been hoping this might happen, ever since DC Shipley's death. Anyway, looks like we had a tip-off that something out of the ordinary was happening tonight. I thought you wouldn't want to miss out on all the excitement.'

'So there haven't been many of these raids recently?' asked Milner.

'A few, but mainly very low-grade stuff,' he answered. 'Some were more successful than others. But nothing which brought us closer to the criminal network's involvement. It's been pretty quiet since he died. But you never know what you'll find on one of these. Sometimes it's the low-grade arrest which turns out to be crucial.'

'Were any of the people on the list I showed you earlier picked up on any of the recent raids?' asked Milner.

'Maybe one of them, if I remember correctly.'

'Can you remember offhand if it was Clinton Melton?'

'I don't think so, but you can find out from the files. Anyway, half an hour in Conference Room B.'

*

Milner was seated with DC Grey on his right and DC Turton on his left. DC David Turton was part of DS Foster's team. They'd first met each other in the station's canteen, on the first day Milner had joined, and had developed a sort of professional friendship since then. There were also a number of uniformed officers in the room, including what were clearly specialist armed officers.

'Have you been on any raids yet?' asked DC Turton.

'I have, yes,' Milner said. 'Well, I did in my previous job, but this will be my first one here. What about you?'

'I was on one a week ago. We'd obtained intelligence that a house was being used to cut crack. It was all a bit of a damp squib, though. We only found a bit of weed and a couple of small packs of coke.' He shook his head. 'We arrested the two guys who were there, but, surprise, surprise, they claimed it was for personal use and they were released with a warning. Still, you never know what you'll find,' he added, echoing DC Grey's earlier comment.

As he spoke, DCI Shaw came into the room, accompanied by DI Richards, DS Gordon and DS Foster. They all stood in front of a screen, on which were already displayed photos of various individuals. Everything was arranged in a clear, pyramid-shaped, hierarchical way, and under each photo was a name. At the very top was the name Ravon Shehu.

'Right, let's get started,' said DCI Shaw without any preamble. 'I think you all know by now why you are here. I'm sure the station's jungle drums have been working overtime.

Anyway, before I hand over to DI Richards to brief you on the operational issues, I'd like to say a few words. I know DC Shipley's death came as a real shock to everybody in this room. It was a tragedy, especially for him and his immediate family. Undoubtedly, however, it also set us back in our objective of shutting down the OCN which operates in our area.' He paused, momentarily, as he looked around the room. 'I also know how, in such situations, rumour and speculation become the common currency. I would strongly advise everyone, therefore, to let the ongoing inquiry run its course and not jump to unproven conclusions. Do I make myself clear?' When there was no immediate response, he repeated what he had just said, but this time in a louder and more assertive voice.

Milner, who was probably one of the few officers in the room who had previously worked with DCI Shaw, suddenly realised this was the first time he'd actually heard him speak in such an authoritative way. He couldn't help thinking about how DCI Stone would have reacted.

After his final words had elicited the desired response, DCI Shaw continued. 'Good. Okay, let's all get our game faces on. Tonight's operation is the start of a new era for Operation Deliverance. From now on we check and double-check everything we do, and that includes the boring stuff like paperwork, search warrants, written reports and all those legal niceties which sometimes seem to get in the way of catching criminals. We all know how lawyers love to find procedural errors. The last thing we want is for criminals to go free due to someone's sloppiness. From now on failure is not an option. The only end result which is acceptable is if this operation,' he said, pointing to the screen behind him, 'is totally closed down and those at the top are sent down for a long time. Right, DI Richards, if you could now carry on with the briefing.'

DI Richards took over. 'As DCI Shaw has just said, tonight we have the opportunity to take the fight back to the OCN. Let's just remind ourselves who these people are.' He turned to face the screen and shone his presentation light on the top name. 'They're all members of the Westie Crew gang, headed up by this man, Ravon Shehu. Underneath him is his second-in-command, and also his cousin, Amar Shehu. As far as we can tell they have been in London for about ten years, but it's only in the past two or three that they have emerged and become known to us as one of the main traffickers of drugs, particularly Class A drugs, in this part of London. There is also increasing evidence, albeit mainly circumstantial, that they are involved in people trafficking, as well as being responsible for a number of vicious robberies of high-value individuals. As you can see, just beneath them are the names of other members of the gang. We believe it's these individuals on the second level who carry out the orders of the Shehus. Those orders include violent robbery, abduction, torture and murder. They are truly nasty individuals.'

He clicked through to the next slide of the presentation, calling up an image of an obviously palatial house. 'This is where Ravon Shehu lives. It's in the Holland Park area. He bought it last year. According to the sales blurb, it has seven bedrooms, an indoor pool and a cinema in the basement. Unless he has won the lottery, I would suggest the only way he could pay that type of money would be due to the proceeds of crime. And, as you can see, there have been a lot of proceeds. This is no small-time, backstreet drug operation. We are talking about multi-millions being generated from the proceeds of crime.'

He clicked again, and the previous slide reappeared. He pointed at the lowest line of the hierarchy. 'The people down here are the foot soldiers. Their job is to cut the drugs, parcel them up and then sell them on: sometimes to other drug dealers, but mostly to users. It's highly likely these are the people who will be there when we hit their houses. But, of course, we might get lucky and net some of the bigger fish.

'We are sure this is the gang that is responsible for the massive increase in drug usage, as well as the recent spate of drug-related murders. The latest, of course, being this man.' He clicked again and a photo of Daniel Melton appeared on the screen, showing him lying lifeless at the foot of some stairs. 'As you'll know, his body was found a few weeks ago. He had been shot, but not before he had been systematically tortured. They are not averse to exacting their form of justice on their own, if someone steps out of line. Be assured that these are seriously dangerous people. They will stop at nothing to protect what they have.'

As DI Richards said this, Milner couldn't help thinking back to the difficult conversation he'd just had with Daniel Melton's mother, and he hoped she would never have to see this particularly graphic photo of her son.

'Tonight,' DI Richards went on, 'we will simultaneously be carrying out raids on two houses. Start time is 3am, so hopefully they will all be tucked up in bed. We will go in hard and fast. We don't want to give anyone the chance to dispose of any evidence. We will have people at the rear of each property to ensure no one tries to get away and to retrieve anything that might be thrown out of a window. DS Gordon will lead Team A, whilst DS Foster will lead Team B. DC Robins will be on comms, based here. All communications are to go through him, so make sure your radios are working and are tuned to the correct channel. DS Foster and I will provide a further brief to the rest of the entry, back-up and search teams at 11pm. Those of you who have done this before will know the drill. For those who haven't, this is your chance to learn.'

He paused briefly before continuing. 'As DCI Shaw said, it's important that all the paperwork, especially the search warrants, is legally watertight. Make sure you comply with any restrictions, read them their rights, and bag up and label all items seized. One final thing before I take any questions: search the properties thoroughly. We are especially interested in getting hold of any phones, laptops or external hard drives. These usually contain a treasure trove of information, which our techies can uncover. These people are experts at concealing stuff, so search everywhere, as we'll probably only get one chance to do this. Anyone arrested will be brought back here and checked in, and then we'll start the formal interviews sometime tomorrow morning. You'll be issued with a list of who you'll be interviewing later.' He looked around the room. 'Right, any questions?'

It was DC Grey who asked the first question. 'Is it likely that some of them will be armed?'

DS Gordon answered it. 'Probably unlikely, or at least that's what our intelligence source suggested. But we will take no chances. It all depends on who is there. If there are some of those second-level individuals in either of the houses, things might get nasty. Anyway, that's why armed officers will be in attendance. If it does all kick off, then get out of the way and let the trained officers deal with it.'

'How many are we expecting to be there?' asked one of the other officers.

'Again, not 100% sure. What we do know, though, is that today is usually the day of the week when they are at their most active, and so more of them are around doing the dealing. And more dealing means more drugs and more money.'

'Are we sure that our information is reliable?' asked DC Gregory. 'We've been here before, and the results proved to be disappointing.'

It was obvious to everyone in the room that this was a reference to DC Shipley's alleged involvement with the criminal network.

'We are sure this time our information is as reliable as it can be,' DI Richards said. 'For obvious reasons, I can't disclose our source, but we are confident enough in its reliability to mount this scale of operation.'

There followed a brief silence before DS Gordon spoke. 'Okay. If there are no more questions, we'll stop there.' He turned to face DCI Shaw. 'Unless, sir, you want to add anything?'

'Just this,' DCI Shaw said. 'It's true we've had some setbacks recently, but this is our opportunity to demonstrate that we are not just going to roll over and let these criminals control our streets. This is the start of our fightback. I'm sure there will be other disappointments and setbacks. That's the nature of this type of policing. But we are better than they are. I have absolute confidence in each and every one of you in this room, and I know that ultimately, due to your efforts, we will succeed in ridding the streets of West London of the Westie Crew and all of their murderous thugs.'

Chapter 10

It was their second day in Hanoi, and Tom and Mary were standing inside what remained of the Hanoi Hilton. This was the name given to it by American prisoners of war, shot down and then incarcerated there during the Vietnam War. In the early 1990s most of the original prison had been demolished and what remained had been converted into a museum, acting not only as an enduring legacy of its past use but also, nowadays, as a tourist landmark.

Not everyone had decided to go on this particular trip. This was no doubt due to the uncomfortable emotions it would surely generate, but also, on a more practical level, because the hotel's air conditioning was more attractive than enduring the day's forecasted furnace-like heat.

Just inside the entrance there was an exhibition stand on which was printed a brief history of the site, dating back to the time when it was a French colonial prison. Most of the visitors took their turn to read it before passing through the entrance and into the main part of the museum, where the air was significantly more humid, generating a dankness which was slightly unpleasant. Most of the walls displayed several black-and-white photos, which on closer examination showed some of the US prisoners who had been held there during the war.

A few people who had been at the front of the group were already taking advantage of the bench seats which were conveniently placed against some of the walls, whilst others took their turn to look more closely at the photos. Inside there was an eerie, almost reverential silence, with any talk being conducted in muted whispers. For a few it was proving to be a difficult experience and they had already become visibly overcome with emotion.

Yesterday, Tom had found himself talking to one of the

other American couples on the trip, Don Simpson and his wife Estelle. It was difficult to exactly determine Don's age, as he was clearly suffering health problems, looked very frail and had some mobility issues. Despite help from his more mobile wife and their son Brett, he still had to use a walking stick to get around. Notwithstanding his physical condition, it had been immediately obvious to Tom that he was still extremely lucid and engaging. As they had continued their conversation, Tom had begun to suspect Don was part of the small group of US airmen on the trip who had been shot down, captured and imprisoned here in Hanoi. Tom had been reluctant to ask him about it, though, and it wasn't until Don himself had mentioned it, almost in passing, that Tom's assumption had been confirmed.

In the museum, Tom could see that Don and Estelle were both paying particular attention to one of the photos on the wall, and Don would occasionally use his stick to point out something that he wanted to highlight. As they moved on to look at the next photograph, Tom noticed how Don had suddenly become much more agitated as he, once again, pointed out something that had clearly caught his interest. As he continued to do this, Estelle placed her right arm around his shoulder, and then handed him a tissue, which he immediately used to dab his eyes. His son, Brett, moved closer to his mum and dad and placed his arms around both of them as they all continued to look intently at the photo.

It was another forty-five minutes before everyone in their group had emerged from the museum's exit and into a long rectangular courtyard. The heat was ferocious, intensified by the suntrap shape of the courtyard as it bounced off the original concrete and brick walls into the faces of all those there. Even though almost everyone was wearing a cap or hat to protect them from the sun, for some of them the heat had still proved too much. Although they had found whatever shade was available, a few were now being attended to by some of the Mekong Cruises staff, who were handing them bottles of cold water. Tom could see Don was one of those, and so he and Mary went over to see if they could offer any assistance.

'Is there anything we can do to help?' asked Mary.

It was Brett who answered. 'That's very kind of you, but I think Pops just needs a couple of minutes to recover. He had a bit of a shock back there and, together with this heat, it's just been a bit too much for him. We're encouraging him to drink some water. Give him a few minutes and I'm sure he'll be okay.'

Tom looked towards Don. 'Do you mind if I ask you what that shock was?'

When Don answered, given the circumstances, it was in a surprisingly strong voice. 'I think I told you yesterday how I had been in Hanoi before. It was during the war. I was a Navy pilot and was shot down in June '68. I was captured soon afterwards and brought here.'

Brett provided more details. 'Pops was held as a prisoner for nearly five years. It wasn't until February 1973 that he was released and flown back to the States.'

'It wasn't long after Don had got back that we first met,' Estelle said, a little wistfully. 'Providence, I guess.'

'I did know he had been held here, but I had no idea that it was for such a long time,' Tom replied. He turned to face Don. 'I also noticed, back in the museum, you seemed to get quite upset looking at one of the photographs. I imagine it must have brought back all those memories again.'

For a moment Tom thought Don was about to become upset again. It was Estelle who answered for him. 'Don thought he'd recognised one of the men in the photo.'

'It was him,' Don suddenly said, now quite agitated. 'No "thought" about it. It was Rich, Rich Waters. We were here together for over two years. You don't forget something like that. Especially after what we went through together.'

Estelle squeezed his hand. 'It was a long time ago, Don. I don't know, but maybe that's what you wanted to see.'

'I know what I saw,' he replied, quietly but still defiantly. 'My body might have gone, but my mind is still sharp enough to remember a thing like that.'

Sensing the increasing tension between Don and Estelle, it was Mary who next spoke. 'Was he released at the same time as you?'

When Don spoke, it wasn't the reply she had been hoping for. 'He never made it. He died about six months before we were released. He just didn't have the strength to carry on any longer.' As he finished saying this, his eyes once more became teary, and both Estelle and Brett moved closer to console him.

'I'm so sorry,' said Mary. 'I didn't mean to upset you.'

'It's not your fault,' replied Don, in a strong voice which suggested he'd now, somehow, regained his composure. 'I thought I'd be able to handle my emotions, but seeing that photograph of Rich again just got to me. He suffered real bad just before he died. He wasn't treated well.' The understatement was obvious to everyone. He hesitated momentarily. 'Another six months and he'd have been back in the States with his family,' he added, more to himself than to the others, as Estelle gently squeezed his hand.

Just then they were interrupted by a now-familiar voice.

'Ladies and gentlemen,' said Lan. He pointed in the direction of a stone arch. 'Please make your way through there, where the coaches are waiting. If anyone requires any help, please come and speak to one of us.'

'Can we help you to the coach?' Tom asked Don.

'No, thank you,' answered Don. 'I might have needed help the last time I left here, but this time I'm going to walk out by myself.'

Chapter 11

After their visit to the Hanoi Hilton, and a few hours' rest back at the hotel, an evening meal in Hanoi City had been arranged for everyone. Although the meal was enjoyable, there was a noticeably subdued atmosphere amongst the guests when they first arrived, no doubt due to what they had experienced at the prison. After a few more drinks had been consumed, however, the noise levels started to increase. They all returned to their hotel at around 10.30pm.

'Why don't we have one final drink in the Sky Bar?' suggested Tony. 'It's unlikely we'll ever be back, so it would be a shame not to take advantage.'

'If you don't mind, I think I'll go up to our room,' Mary answered. 'I'm really tired. I think it must have been the heat.' She looked at Tom. 'But why don't you go with Tony?'

'So how about it, Tom?' asked Tony.

'I'm going to bed,' said Sue. 'It's quite an early start tomorrow.'

'Why not?' replied Tom. 'I won't be too late,' he added to Mary.

As they entered the Sky Bar it was apparent that quite a few more had also decided to head straight up to their rooms, as the bar was not as busy as the previous night.

'I thought you Brits would make an appearance,' said John, seated alongside Bob and Jim, and in exactly the same place as the previous evening. 'Come and join us,' he added, without waiting for any reply. 'Let's have another round of cocktails.' He held up his hand to get the attention of one of the bar staff.

'I'll just have a beer, thanks,' said Tom. 'Their cocktails are a bit too much for me. It's not something I would normally drink, so I think I'd better stick to beer. I'm less likely to have a sore head in the morning. We are travelling tomorrow for quite a while, and I don't want to be feeling the effects of those last cocktails sat on a coach.'

'But I thought you British cops were serious drinkers? Bottles of whiskey and vodka for lunch. Those are your favourites, aren't they?'

'That's just for television, I'm afraid,' answered Tom. 'I rarely drink spirits.'

'What about you, Tony?' John asked. 'Are you going to have one or, like Tom, are they a bit too much for you?'

Although Tom could tell this was just John teasing Tony, he doubted whether Tony, given his already voiced feelings regarding John, would see it that way. He was more than a little surprised when Tony answered, in an uncharacteristically measured tone, 'I'll have one with you. It's always considered unsociable to refuse a free drink where I come from.'

When they were seated, both of them now with a drink in their hands, Jim asked, 'What about a toast?' He raised his own glass and said, 'To the Brits and Yanks. Friends forever.' They all repeated it and then quite enthusiastically clinked each other's glasses.

'You mentioned, when we first met, how you were all here in 1969. If you don't mind me asking, where exactly were you based?' asked Tom.

'Most of the time we were up north, not far from the North Vietnamese border,' Bob answered.

'So, did you get into any heavy fighting?' asked Tony.

Suddenly John's usual bonhomie disappeared, almost as though a switch had been thrown. When he spoke, it was in a voice even louder than normal and with more than a hint of aggression in it. 'Are you kidding me? Why do you think we were there? It wasn't some sort of boy scouts' outing. Of course there was heavy fighting. We were fighting all the time. Did you guys never see the news reels, or weren't the Brits allowed to see them?'

Both Bob and Jim looked at John, with a hint of concern etched on their faces. Their concern was not misplaced.

'I suppose not,' John continued, 'as you chose not to get

involved in the first place. About two and a half million of us did our tour of 'Nam, and over 50,000 didn't make it home. At least the Aussies had the balls to help us. You Brits always expect us to bail you out, but when we need your help, you've gone AWOL.'

'Apart from Iraq and Afghanistan, of course,' Tony said in a contrastingly calm voice, although still loud enough for everyone to hear. 'Anyway, so much for friends forever.'

Tom, taken aback by the turn the conversation had taken, quickly said, 'Let's all calm down. It's been a long, hot day and I'm sure we're all a bit tired, and emotions are still running high after our visit to the prison.' He took a moment to collect his thoughts. 'Look, I'm sorry, John. I'm sure it wasn't meant to imply anything. It would just be interesting to know, that's all. We both respect the fact that you were there, and we weren't. But there's really nothing we can do about that.'

An uneasy silence followed John's outburst, before Bob once again broke the silence. 'I know. It's just that this trip is starting to bring back lots of bad memories for us. More than we had imagined, to be honest. We lost a lot of good friends here. Most of them just out of college. We saw things that no one should have to see. That's why emotions are a bit raw. But to answer your question, Tony, yes, we were involved in a lot of fierce firefights.'

Clearly having decided it might help ease the atmosphere if he provided more information, Bob went on. 'One time was when we had been tasked with a search and destroy mission. They'd named it Operation Resolve.' He glanced towards Jim and John, almost as though he were seeking their approval to carry on. 'Actually, it was our third such mission in two weeks. Each time we had been helicoptered into a different small valley close to the Cambodian border, and tasked with securing and then checking out the few villages there. Intel had told us that it was part of the Ho Chi Minh trail, which was being used by the North Vietnamese to resupply the Viet Cong in South Vietnam. A lot of villages in that part of the country were pro-VC and hid weapons and food for them as well as providing shelter. But, as was normally the case then, what looked straightforward to the planners holed up in their nice, air-conditioned hotel back in Saigon, no doubt drinking their martinis, turned out to be anything but.'

'So why come on this particular trip?' asked Tom. 'You must have guessed that it might bring those memories back to the surface.'

'That's true,' replied Jim, 'but we felt we had to do it, if only so we could pay our final respects to all our buddies who didn't make it home. None of us are getting any younger, and so this will almost certainly be the last chance we'll get to say our goodbyes.'

'Well, I hope you all get to do that,' replied Tom.

When Tom and Tony had finished their drinks, they both decided that it was time to turn in. Whilst there had been some efforts to lighten the mood, there had remained an uncomfortable, palpable tension in the air amongst the group, not helped by John's continuing and uncharacteristic silence.

As they made their way from the bar to the lift, Tony said, 'What a prat.'

Chapter 12

It was just after 3am and Milner was standing, alongside three uniformed officers, in one of the bedrooms of the house they had raided. The room was just large enough for the two single beds and camp bed that had been squeezed into it. The three young men who had been sleeping here were all now out of bed, handcuffed and having their rights read to them.

When there had been no response to the police's warning, the front door had been forced open. Despite this, the entry had been reasonably straightforward. They had not been met with any resistance, and all seven bleary-eyed young men found in the house had woken to find their bedrooms full of police officers. As soon as they had been detained, the specialist search team had commenced their work.

'What's all this about?' asked one of the young men. 'You can't just break into someone's house in the middle of the night.'

'Actually, we have a legal search warrant which says we can, and, anyway, I doubt very much that this is your house,' replied Milner. He paused. 'Is it your house?'

When no answer was forthcoming, Milner followed up. 'Is there anything on you which shouldn't be there or could injure me or any of the officers?' Once again, there was no reply, so Milner continued. 'Okay, this is what is now going to happen. You'll shortly be taken to West London police station, where you will be formally charged and taken into custody.'

The one who had previously spoke decided to do so again, this time in a more confrontational manner. 'So what? We'll all be out soon. You'll find nothing. You're wasting your time.'

'What are you doing here?' asked Milner.

One of the others now spoke. 'We'd heard there was going

to be a party and we decided to check it out. It was late when it finished, so we crashed out here.'

'Really? Just a coincidence, was it, how there was a room and beds for you to all crash out here?' Once again there was no response. 'We'll soon find out if the others in the house say the same thing when you're all back at the station being interviewed.'

Just as Milner was saying this, DC Grey came into the room and quietly spoke to him. 'You might want to come and see who is in one of the other rooms.'

When Milner entered the room, he saw two other young men, both just wearing boxer shorts, and who had already been placed in handcuffs. One of them he recognised immediately as Clinton Melton, Daniel's younger brother. Unlike those in the other room, Melton was proving to be less than physically compliant as he kicked out at the two officers who were trying to restrain him.

'Don't keep hitting me,' he shouted as loudly as he could. 'This is victimisation. I know my rights.'

'No one is hitting you,' replied DC Grey. 'And the body cams that the officers are both wearing will show that's not the case.'

This seemed to have the desired effect, as Melton suddenly stopped shouting.

'Is there anything here which shouldn't be?' DC Grey asked. 'I'm going to just take your first answer, so here's your chance to be cooperative.'

This simply had the effect of replacing his previous physical aggression with verbal aggression. 'Cooperate with the pigs? You must be joking.' He let out a snigger. 'I'd rather do a two stretch than be seen as a grass.' In a more controlled and slightly sinister tone, he followed this up with, 'You've got no idea who we are.'

'And who are you?' asked Milner, speaking for the first time.

'We are the Westie Crew,' he answered proudly, as if being a member was a badge of honour. 'It's us who run West London, not you scum. You're all just little men. We are the main guys now, and there's nothing you can do to stop us.'

Milner couldn't help thinking back to the discussion he'd recently had with Clinton's mum, Mrs Melton. Everything suggested she was right to be concerned about her youngest son.

Realising that any continuation of this conversation was unlikely to become civil, DC Grey turned towards the officers and said, 'Take them down to the station. They can get dressed when they are there.'

If this was meant to placate the two men, it had the opposite effect, and both of them started to kick out at the arresting officers as they were frogmarched out of the room.

As this was happening, DS Gordon walked into the room. 'Having trouble?' he asked, directing his question at DC Grey.

'Only to be expected. Zero cooperation, but maximum attitude.'

'Same as the room I was in. What about yours, DC Milner?'

'Pretty much the same. Aggressive, non-cooperative, aware of their rights. What concerns me, though, is how they are absolutely convinced they will soon be back on the streets. They're not in the least bit concerned about being arrested.'

'Well, let's see if they still feel that way after the search team have finished taking this place apart.'

Chapter 13

In total, eleven males and one female had been arrested at the two houses, and all had now been formally charged by the station sergeant. They had been locked up in individual cells, but, as there were more than expected, some had been transferred to a nearby station. The team had a quick debrief, mainly to ensure all the necessary paperwork had been correctly completed, and were then sent home to get some sleep.

It was 9am when the full team were reassembled in the main briefing room. Although the search was still ongoing, the team had already found evidence to suggest what the houses were being used for. As well as the inevitable personal drug-taking paraphernalia, there were lots of individual wraps of crack cocaine and heroin, in varying stages of completion. As expected, many electronic devices, mostly phones, had also been retrieved, and everything had been bagged and tagged in order to ensure that any DNA was not compromised.

A small number of notebooks had also been found, which, at least on an initial inspection, looked to show some type of payment record. What was of particular interest was lists of any monies paid and any monies outstanding, presumably from their dealings. Some cash was simply lying around, in open sight, on a table in the room where Milner had arrested the three young men. Of more sinister concern, however, were the numerous weapons that had been in the house, including a number of knives, a couple of machetes and a sword.

'Good morning, ladies and gentleman, and thanks for being here so promptly,' said DI Richards. DS Gordon and DS Foster were alongside him, together with the projector screen and laptop. 'I know you won't have had much sleep, but, hopefully, when we've finished searching both houses, it will have been well worth it. As our intel had suggested, all the evidence we have so far suggests they were being used as major hubs in the processing and selling of Class A drugs throughout this part of West London. I believe, due to this morning's action, we have seriously set back their operation by taking a sizeable quantity, together with a number of weapons, off the streets. We now have to make sure we put together watertight cases, based on real, compelling evidence – not circumstantial – so that the CPS will refer this onwards to trial. We need any jury to send each and every one of them down for a number of years.' He paused briefly. 'Okay, the first interviews will start at 11.30am. DS Gordon will now go through the interview list with you in a bit more detail. Thanks again, and good luck.'

DS Gordon pressed the slide change button on the laptop, and a list of names appeared on screen. 'These are the names of all the people who were arrested earlier today. Or at least these are the names they gave us. It's likely there are a few false ones there, and we are currently checking those. Nonetheless, we are confident most of them are bona fide. Needless to say, they have already been assigned a brief, so tread carefully. You've got a couple of hours to get your evidence together. Facts only, remember.' He looked pointedly around the room. 'The notebooks we found listing various names and amounts of money is another line of inquiry for us. It's unlikely we can pin this on any of those we arrested. It looks like they are mostly foot soldiers. Even so, they might have important information which will lead us to finally closing down the Westie Crew and putting away Ravon Shehu and his cronies for a long time. DC Gregory has a briefing paper for each of you, which provides background information for each of our arrests. Name, age, last known address, criminal record. That type of thing. If you need any clarification, I'll be in the ops room.'

Milner was handed his briefing sheet and immediately saw that he was slated to be lead officer in the interview of Dennis Farmer: one of the names mentioned in DC Shipley's file. Despite this connection, he was disappointed. Ideally, he would have preferred to interview Clinton Melton.

'DS Foster. Can I have a quick word with you?' he asked as DS Foster was walking past him.

'Sure. What is it?' DS Foster answered.

'Is it possible for me to interview Clinton Melton instead of Dennis Farmer? I know it means a bit of juggling around, but I really do think it might be a better use of our resources.'

DS Foster looked at him with a hint of scepticism. When he replied, that scepticism had turned into obvious annoyance. 'And what makes you think that? I'm sure you can appreciate how much work has gone into this over the past few hours. If we do this for you, then we might have to do it for some of the others as well. Before we know it, we won't know whether we're coming or going. We're up against the clock as it is without any last-minute changes.'

'I do appreciate that, sir, but I wouldn't ask if I didn't think it might be more productive.'

'Okay,' DS Foster answered, a weary annoyance still in his voice. 'Tell me why you think that.'

Milner briefly told him about his recent visit to see Mrs Melton and the fact that Daniel and Clinton Melton were both, on numerous occasions, mentioned in DC Shipley's files. 'So, you see, sir, there's already a strong connection there, and I feel that I could use that to our advantage. Of course, it might not result in anything, but you never know.'

DS Foster took a moment to examine the interview list again. 'Okay,' he said. 'Come with me.'

They both made their way to where one of the other officers was standing.

'DC Turton. Before you get too engrossed in your interview prep, there's been a slight change. Instead of interviewing Clinton Melton, I'd like you to interview Dennis Farmer.'

'Any reason, sir?' DC Turton asked, not unnaturally.

'DC Milner has already made a strong connection with the Melton family. It makes sense for us to capitalise on that.'

There was a slight shrug of DC Turton's shoulders before he replied. 'No skin off my nose. Happy to oblige if there's a better chance of putting him away.'

Milner simply nodded his appreciation. They exchanged

their interview briefing notes, and then he made his way towards his own desk.

'So, who have you got?' asked DC Grey.

'Clinton Melton,' Milner answered.

'That's a bit of luck. Didn't you visit his mum yesterday?'

'Yes, I did,' he simply answered. 'What about you?'

'Curtis Seton. He was one of the names you showed me. If there's anything you think I should know about him, I'd appreciate the heads-up.'

'Will do, although at the moment I only know what's on file.' He hesitated, then grabbed a piece of paper and wrote down two names: Lionel Tedman and Adrian Wolfe. He handed the paper to DC Grey. 'Could you ask him if he knows these people?'

'Who are they?' DC Grey asked, unsurprisingly.

'They are a couple of other names I came across in DC Shipley's files,' Milner replied, reluctant to reveal that he'd found them hidden in the sleeve.

'Okay. I'll see if he knows anything about them.'

Milner felt a little guilty about not being totally honest with him, especially as he'd been so helpful. At this stage, though, he felt it important to reveal the details of the hidden names to as few people as possible until he had made more progress regarding their identity.

He carefully started to read through the briefing notes that had been prepared for him, whilst at the same time making a note of any other information he felt would be important. His earlier introduction to Clinton Melton had suggested that any interview was unlikely to be of a cooperative nature. The short time he had spent with Clinton was enough to convince him to expect a very aggressive and confrontational interview.

Perhaps that was something he could use to his advantage.

Chapter 14

By mid-morning the following day, Tom and Mary were seated on their coach, travelling to the place where they would embark on their ship, the *Mekong Voyager*. According to the tour itinerary they would be based on the ship for the next five days, before arriving at their final destination in Ho Chi Minh City.

Tom was still thinking about John's outburst in the Sky Bar. He'd decided not to tell Mary about what had happened, as it might prompt her to act out of character when they all next met. He knew, through the long period he'd spent working in the police, how different experiences affected people differently. Sometimes it was the more sensitive ones who, during times of stress and anxiety, showed the most fortitude, whereas those people who outwardly appeared strong and seemed unable or unwilling to display any human emotions could sometimes be the first to break down. Whilst Tom didn't place John in this category, there was clearly something deep inside which was troubling him. Understandable, Tom mused, given what he had almost certainly experienced during the war.

'Are you looking forward to getting on the ship?' asked Mary, interrupting his thoughts about John. 'I can't wait to start cruising down the Mekong.'

'I am,' he answered. 'Although five days on a ship does seem like a long time, especially as it's not especially big.'

'But I thought that was one of the things that attracted you to this trip? You said it was much better than being on one of those huge ocean liners. You could get to know people.'

Tom suddenly remembered saying this. 'I did, you're right, but everything is relative.' Not wanting to dampen her enthusiasm, he added, 'I'm sure it will be a great experience, and, of course, we'll then have our final two days in Ho Chi Minh

City. I'm probably looking forward to that more than the cruise. It will be really interesting to see how it compares with Hanoi.'

'I still can't get used to the name Ho Chi Minh City. For me it will always be Saigon,' she replied. 'Many years ago, quite a few of us from our am dram society went to see *Miss Saigon* in London. I suppose that's one of the reasons why the name will always stick in my mind.'

'Well, we'll soon see what the locals call it,' said Tom.

A short while later the two coaches pulled into a rest area, and everyone got off to stretch their legs, buy a drink or use the restrooms. Tom joined the queue for a small building which was selling refreshments. It was only partly shaded, and so open to the sun's heat. He found himself immediately behind Jim.

'Man, it's hot,' said Jim, turning to face him. 'I hoped I would meet you. I just wanted to apologise for yesterday. John shouldn't have reacted that way. But I know he didn't mean it. He tends to get a bit excited sometimes.'

'That's really not a problem with me – although I can't speak for Tony,' Tom said. 'I can only imagine what it must have been like for you all, especially as I've never been in the military.'

'Yes, well, it wasn't a picnic, that's for sure, but, nonetheless, he shouldn't have taken it out on you. If it's any consolation, I know he's not feeling great about it himself.'

'Do you mind me asking what you are looking for on this trip?' Tom asked. 'I get the impression there are a lot of conflicting emotions. Is it some sort of closure?'

Jim didn't immediately answer Tom's question, as though he were collecting his thoughts. Eventually, he said, 'It's a question I've asked myself many times since I decided to come on this trip.' Once again, he paused, and his voice was wistful when he spoke again. 'I doubt whether I will ever get full closure. I suppose the most I can expect would be some peace or, at least, to be able to try and make some sense of it all.'

Tom gave him a little more time with his thoughts before speaking again. 'Maybe it would be better if John spoke with

Tony. I did detect a bit of friction between the two of them, so it's probably just the two of them who could sort it out.'

'Well, yes, John can get a bit worked up at times. That's his nature. Usually, though, it's just hot air. I think we should give him a bit of space and time to calm down. He'll come around eventually,' he said, with a degree of confidence that suggested it was a common occurrence. 'He usually does.'

'I think the problem is that Tony is cut from the same cloth,' said Tom. 'I've only known him for a few days, but I suspect he's not one to take a backward step. Probably something to do with him also being ex-military. I think he told you all, when we first met, how he joined when he was seventeen and then spent the next twenty-five plus years in the army. That's bound to have a huge impact on formulating your character and personality.' He paused. 'Tell me, Bob said there were five of you from the same company on this trip. I've noticed, though, that I've only ever seen the three of you together, not all five. Is there a reason for that?'

It took Jim a moment to answer. 'Yes, we were all in the same company, but we were in 3rd Platoon, while they were part of 1st Platoon. We tended to keep ourselves separate. We did know Gene and Bill, but we all hung out with different guys. That's pretty normal in the military.'

'So how come they are on this particular trip with you?' asked Tom.

Jim shrugged. 'We didn't realise they were also on the trip until we spotted their names on the list Lan gave us. It's been over fifty years since we were here with them, and none of us are young men any more.'

'That must have been a great surprise for you all,' said Tom. 'Have you spoken with them yet?'

'Well, we've had a few brief conversations, but, like I said, we didn't spend much time together anyway. We might have been in the same company, but there's always competition between platoons.' He paused. 'Sometimes it's healthy competition and other times it's not.'

Just then Ruth joined them. 'How y'all doing here? Do you want me to take your place in the line?'

'Shouldn't be too long now,' Jim replied. 'You go and sit back in the shade. I'll bring the drinks over.'

Ruth walked back to where some of the others were still seated.

'Were Gene and Bill with the ones in the Sky Bar who all seemed to be enjoying themselves?' asked Tom.

'They were,' Jim replied. 'Well noticed. I suppose that's why you were a cop,' he added, with a slight laugh.

By now Jim was at the counter, and he ordered some drinks and snacks. After he had paid for them, he picked up the tray and said, 'Nice speaking with you Tom. I'll see if I can persuade John to speak with Tony.'

*

Three hours later, Tom and Mary were busy unpacking their clothes in their cabin aboard the *Mekong Voyager*. Much to Tom's surprise, the onboard check-in had gone smoothly, and even their luggage had already been waiting for them in their cabin when they had got there.

'It's bigger than I thought,' said Mary, in her usual cheerful tone. 'I didn't expect it to be quite so spacious.'

'Well, we did pay extra for the room, and to be on this level.' Tom immediately regretted his words. 'But, yes, there is a lot more room than I had imagined,' he quickly added, hoping his previous comment might be forgotten.

'And look at the view.' Mary had pulled back the curtains to reveal the greenish-brown expanse of the Mekong River alongside them. She slid back the full-length windows and stepped outside onto the veranda. 'Come and look, Tom,' she said with increasing excitement. 'I can't believe we are actually *on* the Mekong River. It's so wide.'

When he stepped outside, even Tom was taken back by the panorama that greeted him, and all he could manage in response was, '*That* is special.'

Their cabin was located on the upper guest deck of three, which gave them the spectacular view that they were both currently admiring. As they stood there, a familiar voice said,

'Stunning, isn't it?' It was Don, who, along with Estelle, was also looking across the wide expanse of the river. 'What a coincidence that we are in the cabin next to you.'

'Yes, we were both just saying how wonderful it is,' answered Mary. 'I'm so glad we chose this deck.'

'How are you feeling today?' Tom asked, without mentioning the specifics of yesterday's visit to the prison.

'Much better, thank you, Tom,' Don replied. 'It is Tom, isn't it?'

'It is, yes,' Tom confirmed.

'Our son Brett is in the cabin next door,' Estelle said. 'We asked for an upper deck cabin so that Don didn't have to go up and down all the stairs. Anyway, we're still unpacking. We want to finish before the welcome drinks at six. No doubt we'll see you there.'

After Don and Estelle had gone back into their cabin, Mary sat on one of the two chairs which, together with a table, were placed on the veranda.

'Mary, why don't we have a glass of wine while we are enjoying the view?' Tom suggested. 'I saw there was a bottle in the fridge.'

Not for the first time on this trip, Mary was surprised by his apparent change of personality, as if he had suddenly become someone who didn't feel too self-conscious about enjoying himself. 'That would be nice.'

After he had opened the bottle and poured two glasses of wine, Tom placed them on the table and sat beside her. For a while neither said anything as they continued to look out, almost hypnotised by the serenity and quietness of the river.

It was Mary who broke this silence. 'Just think, Tom: if you were still in the police, we wouldn't be here, and you would no doubt be involved in some horrible murder investigation. Aren't you glad that's now all behind you?'

As he sat there, alongside Mary, in this environment, Tom found it hard to disagree with her. Unfortunately, though, murder, as he was soon to find out, had a habit of interrupting even the most serene of situations.

Chapter 15

Milner was in Interview Room 3, immediately opposite Clinton Melton. Seated alongside Clinton was his legal representative. Seated next to Milner was DC Paul Robins, whilst standing behind them both was a uniformed officer. Milner and DC Robins had spent the preceding hour or so reviewing all the available evidence and agreeing what their interview strategy would be.

After Milner had started the recording equipment, he introduced himself and DC Robins and then informed Clinton of the reason for the interview.

'Your name is Clinton Melton, and you are twenty years old. Is that correct?' Milner asked whilst looking down at his notes.

'No comment,' Clinton replied, in his characteristically cocky manner.

'You were arrested earlier today at 25 Melrose Street, Greenford.'

Although Milner read this as a statement of fact, Clinton repeated, 'No comment.' The slightly supercilious expression on Clinton's face suggested this wasn't the first time he had been formally interviewed by the police, and so he was perfectly aware of the format and was happy to play the game.

'What were you doing there, Clinton?' Milner asked.

He yawned and placed his hands behind his head. 'No comment.'

'Okay. If you won't tell me, then I'll just have to tell you,' Milner said. He proceeded to list the items they had found at the house. 'We believe that you are part of an organised crime network called the Westie Crew. The house was used to cut, wrap and distribute Class A drugs. We have CCTV footage of you entering and leaving the house on numerous recent occasions, including last night.'

DC Robins then read out a list of the various times and dates when this had happened.

'We also took possession of your mobile phone, which is currently being analysed,' Milner said. 'Are we likely to find anything on it which will incriminate you further? Will there be anything that links you to other crimes? If there is, here's your chance to tell us.'

When the inevitable 'no comment' was repeated, Milner closed his file, paused momentarily, and then, looking directly at Clinton, said, 'How do you think your mum will feel when she finds out what you have been doing, especially after Daniel's murder?'

For the first time, Clinton's expression changed. He moved his hands from behind his head, leaned forward and said in a menacing tone, 'You leave my mum out of this.'

'Do you think she will be proud of you or, as I suspect, very upset? How do you think she will cope with all of this? She's still struggling with what happened to Daniel. Do you know why I'm so certain?' Milner asked. Without waiting for an answer, he carried straight on. 'That's because, less than twenty-four hours ago, I was with her in your flat in Shepherd's Bush, and she told me how worried she was about you and how you'll end up.'

'You are lying,' Clinton angrily replied.

'I noticed the photograph of you and Daniel, on the wall, when you were much younger. Both of you were in your QPR shirts. It was then she told me she was so worried that you would end up dead, like Daniel. Or don't you care about her or your sister, Shannon?'

Clinton suddenly lunged across the table and tried to grab hold of Milner. Fortunately, the uniformed officer, briefed earlier on how there might be a violent reaction, quickly intervened, restrained him and sat him back on his chair.

Clinton's legal representative then placed a restraining hand on his client's shoulder and said directly to Milner, 'I strongly object to your line of questioning, and particularly your deliberate provocation. My client is within his rights to refuse to answer any of your questions. If you continue in this vein, I will be forced to insist this interview be terminated.'

Although Clinton was by now less agitated, nonetheless, he suddenly said, 'I've told you, pig, leave them out of this ... or else.'

'Or else what? Are you threatening me?' asked Milner. 'It certainly sounded like a threat. What do you think, DC Robins? Did it sound like a threat to you?'

'It did, yes, and it's all being recorded.'

'If you threaten Mum, you will be taking on not just me but all of the Westie Crew,' Clinton said. 'We look after each other.'

'What? Like they looked after your brother?' said Milner, defiance now in his voice. 'And I wasn't threatening your mum. I was simply telling you how she was very worried about you.'

Once again Clinton lunged forward, trying to get hold of Milner, but, again, the uniformed officer had anticipated this. It was almost as if simply the mention of his mother triggered the same physical, aggressive response.

After a brief pause, Milner, this time in a more friendly tone, said, 'As I mentioned, no one is threatening your Mum, Clinton. She is a lovely lady who was trying her best to provide for her two sons and your younger sister Shannon. You might not believe this, but I have great respect for what she's trying to do.'

The mention once more of Shannon's name clearly affected Clinton, as this time, when he spoke, it was in a far less aggressive and confrontational manner. 'Mum and Shannon aren't involved in any of this. Just leave them out of it.'

Taking his lead from Clinton, Milner responded in an equally conciliatory tone. 'I know that, Clinton, but she's scared of what you've got yourself into. That's how any mum would feel. She's already lost one son. She frightened that she might also lose her remaining one. Who do you think will look after them if you're not around?'

An extended period of silence followed, before Clinton spoke, once again in a quiet voice. 'Just leave them out of it, that's all. I've told you already, this has nothing to do with them.'

'What has nothing to do with them, Clinton? What do you mean? Is it that you are involved in the distribution of Class A drugs and possibly murder?' asked Milner.

'Murder?' Clinton repeated. 'What's murder got to do with it? There were a few drugs at the house. So what? I've told you already, it was a party and everyone was using.' He paused before adding, 'Everybody uses them, including lots of cops, or don't they count? I heard one of your lot was a user but died because he couldn't handle them.'

Milner chose not to respond. 'A number of men have been murdered recently, including your brother Daniel. We know what the house was used for. Let me ask you again. How will your mum react when she finds out you've been arrested?'

Once again, Clinton's legal representative intervened. 'This is not acceptable. You cannot keep provoking my client in this way by using his mum as a tactic. I insist this interview now be terminated.'

Immediately afterwards, Milner concluded the interview and Clinton was returned to his cell.

'What do you think?' asked DC Robins. 'He's certainly cocky.'

'Probably had lots of experience of that,' Milner said. 'It's what he and the others thrive on. But I think we definitely rattled him and made him think about the impact of his actions on his mum and sister. Whether it will make him change his behaviour or, better still, prompt him to provide us with information, I somehow doubt. I think he's in too deep for that, but you never know.'

Chapter 16

Later that afternoon, the team were once again assembled in the operations room.

'Okay, listen up, everybody,' said DCI Shaw. 'I just wanted to give you an update on what, so far, we've been able to find out from the raids on the houses. Whilst it's true we didn't find the large quantities of cash and drugs we were hoping to discover, all the phones, iPads, laptops et cetera will, I'm sure, provide us with a wealth of information. We are also reviewing all the CCTV footage in the area, just to see if there were any unusual movements prior to our raids. Anyway, once the techie team have done their stuff, I'm hopeful it will implicate Ravon Shehu and the other family members.'

He paused before continuing. 'I've heard some feedback that some of you are disappointed because you were expecting more. Well, to be frank, so was I, especially given the information we had regarding the importance of those houses. But that doesn't mean it was a waste of time and resources. Most of you here have been involved in major crime investigations during your time with the force – that's why you've been selected to be part of this team – and so you know there are always disappointments and setbacks along the way. They don't just progress in a straight line. If they did, they would all be solved in double-quick time and there would be no need for our type of specialist operation. Also, it's often the case that the seemingly inconsequential, boring stuff turns out, ultimately, to be the most important. My strong advice to you all is that you see this as a vital stepping stone in achieving our ultimate objective of bring the Shehus to justice.' Once again, he momentarily paused. 'As a team, we now need to double down on our efforts to make this happen. It's not going to be easy, but, trust me, we *will* be successful.'

After he had finished speaking, he handed over to DI Richards.

'I know you are disappointed we had to release everyone,' DI Richards said, 'but it was to be expected and, in fact, it would have been a huge surprise if we hadn't. They have all been bailed, with investigations continuing. It's important you now use the evidence we obtained from the raids to put together a strong case against those you arrested.

'As DCI Shaw just said, we are very hopeful that information contained on their personal devices will make that task a bit easier. There is a dedicated team reviewing all their social media communications. We all know how these types of people like to brag to their mates about what they've just done or what they've got. They might think they are using secure apps, but, if they've sent it, our techies will be able to retrieve it. I'm sure we'll find something that further incriminates them.

'In the meantime, we stay close to these people. They now know we are on to them, but it's my experience that that's when they start to make mistakes. They get cocky and provocative and think they are untouchable. We need to be there when they make those mistakes.

'To help with that: you will, no doubt, have already noticed that most of the young men arrested had similar hairstyles and trainers. Here's what I mean.' He called up a slide that showed four of the men. 'All have a skin-cut hairstyle and are wearing white trainers. This is clearly a bit of a status thing for them, and one of the ways they tell everyone they are now members of the Westie Crew. Make sure to keep your eyes open for anyone fitting that description, as they could be of special interest to us and lead to other contacts.

'I know it's been a long day so, finally, remember what DCI Shaw said about this being a marathon and not a sprint. It might take a bit longer than we hoped, but we'll get them; of that I'm certain. Anyway, thanks again for all your efforts.'

After the meeting had ended, DS Foster approached Milner. 'DC Milner, could I have a word? I've taken a look at the footage of your interview with Clinton Melton. It was very impressive. Well done.' When Milner didn't immediately reply, he carried on. 'The mention of his family certainly shook him. What do you intend to do next?'

'I did consider going to see his mum again, to tell her Clinton had been arrested, but that's probably not a good idea right now, especially as I was only there yesterday. She might just think it's victimisation. Anyway, I don't think it will be too long before we have enough evidence to pull him in again. I think that's the time to apply a bit more emotional pressure, as well as evidential pressure. I have a feeling the relationship with his brother will be key.'

'Well, whatever you decide, I'd appreciate it if you kept me informed.'

Milner then made his way back to his desk with the intention of rereading DC Shipley's files, just to make sure he had not missed anything of importance. It wasn't long before his attention, not for the first time, was drawn back to the two names he had found hidden in the sleeve of one of the files: Lionel Tedman and Adrian Wolfe. But the more he studied them, the more blank his mind went, so he decided to forget about them for a while and return later with a fresh mind.

Just then his mobile rang. He could immediately see it was Jenny calling. He pressed the green receive button.

'Hi, it's me,' she said. 'Are we still on for that dinner tonight?'

Whilst he hadn't exactly forgotten about their date, it had not been at the front of his mind.

'Definitely,' he answered enthusiastically. 'How about if I pick you up at seven thirty?'

'Look forward to it. You can tell me all about your day.'

It was good that Jenny was interested in his work, but sometimes trying to forget all about it, however fleetingly, was more appealing. He hoped this occasion would give him the opportunity.

Chapter 17

Tom and Mary were seated in the lounge area of the ship, on the middle deck, each with a glass of wine on the table in front of them. A pianist was playing, with a guitar placed just behind him. Earlier, at the formal welcome, all the senior staff on board had been introduced, from the captain to the chief engineer, after which everyone had moved one deck down into the restaurant for their first dinner on board the *Mekong Voyager*.

It was a very informal arrangement, with no reserved seating places. Inevitably, people had once again gravitated into their own national and friendship groups, and some had even kept places available for any latecomers.

'Well, that was something special,' exclaimed Sue. 'I don't think we've ever been offered such a choice before.'

'Definitely, but I couldn't bring myself to try the crispy tarantula,' said Mary. 'Although you seemed to enjoy it, Tony.'

'Compared to some of the things we had to eat when I was in the army, it was delicious,' Tony said. 'Tasted just like crunchy chicken.'

'Where was that?' asked Tom.

'I can't remember, to be honest. It was a long time ago.'

'And they kept bringing the wine,' said Shelley. 'I'm not used to drinking so much. I don't know how much I drank, but the waiters kept filling up my glass.'

In fact, as so often happens when on holiday, they had all already had more than they would normally drink, and this was reflected in their increased garrulousness.

'I think we should all go back on deck when the boat starts to sail,' Mary said. 'Didn't Lan say it would be at ten thirty?'

'Good idea,' answered Shelley, clearly now in the holiday spirit. 'It's not every day you get the chance to do this.'

Tom looked around the room. Whilst he now recognised some of the others on the trip, there were still more than a few he could not put a name to. He could see John and Joany, together with the rest of their group, seated on the opposite side of the lounge.

Since his earlier discussion with Jim, Tom had been hoping for an opportunity to speak with Tony about it. Unfortunately, that hadn't happened. Given the alcohol that had already been consumed, Tom decided to wait for another opportunity tomorrow, as he didn't want to take the risk of finding out whether Tony and alcohol were a combustible combination.

A short while later, Lan announced the ship would shortly be beginning its cruise down the Mekong and towards Ho Chi Minh City. Most people decided they didn't want to miss this, and so they took their cue from Lan and headed to the upper sun deck. As Tom and Mary waited their turn to exit the lounge, they passed close to where John, Joany and the others were still seated.

'Are you going to watch it?' asked Tom.

'We might go up later, when things are a bit quieter and the ship is on its way,' replied Joany.

'Come and join us later in the bar on the upper deck for a couple of beers,' said John. 'I owe you all an apology anyway.'

'We might just do that,' Tom answered, slightly wrong-footed by his frank admission, but determined to reciprocate. He couldn't help noticing, however, that Tony, who was immediately behind him and had listened to this conversation, had ominously remained silent.

An hour or so later, and the novelty of feeling the ship's forward movement on its journey down the Mekong had largely worn off. This was especially the case as, in the dark, there wasn't much to see, apart from a few lights along the riverbank and the occasional passing boat. Most people, therefore, made their way to their cabins, whilst a few went back into the lounge area to listen to the resident musicians.

When Tom had suggested trying out the upper deck bar to the others, Mary had said that she wanted to get back to the cabin to complete their unpacking. Most of the others did the same, and so it was just Tom, Sue and Tony who entered the bar.

The room itself was surprisingly large, with the bar at the front end of the ship, and most of the tables and chairs placed at each side. At first glance it looked more or less full, but it wasn't long before John's unmistakeable voice made itself heard above the general noise level.

'You made it then,' he said, seated between Jim and Bob. 'Come over here. We'll make room for you.'

It was soon clear that Sue was the only woman there. If she felt at all uncomfortable with this, though, it was far from obvious, as she said, 'Budge up so that I can sit down.'

Tom wasn't sure if they appreciated Sue's directness, although they all dutifully did as they were told to make room for her.

What was different from previous occasions was the presence of Lan. Tom could see that he, unlike the others, had a soft drink in front of him.

'What do you think about our ship?' Lan asked, directing his question to no one in particular.

'It's lovely,' Sue answered. 'There is so much room. Much more than I imagined, and the food tonight was just great. So much choice.'

'Do you get time off, or are you always on duty?' Tom asked, once he was seated.

'We do get a little downtime, but it's important we are always seen to be around for our guests,' Lan answered.

'Even here in the bar,' said Bob, with a slight laugh.

'Does that also apply to Sang?' Tom asked, indicating where he was seated with some of the other guests.

'Yes, it does. As I said, we try to be around at all times.'

Just then, a young-looking man, wearing a Mekong Cruises branded white polo shirt and black trousers, appeared to take their drinks order.

'How long have you worked for Mekong Cruises?' Tom asked Lan, after the barman had left to get their drinks.

'This is my fourth year. Before that, though, I worked for another international travel company here in Vietnam.'

'You speak excellent English,' said Sue.

'Thank you. I studied English at university, including spending a year in the States, but working on these trips with mainly English-speaking guests has helped the most.' With a slight laugh, he added, 'I do sometimes, though, find it difficult to understand some of the British accents. They are so different. It always amazes me how such a small country has so many different accents.'

Tom, suspecting that this might be the perfect opportunity for Tony to mention Yorkshire, quickly carried on. 'Where in Vietnam were you born?'

'In the north.'

'What? North Vietnam?' asked Tony.

'There was no North Vietnam when I was born,' he replied. 'Vietnam had been reunified by then and was just one country.'

At that moment the barman returned with their drinks.

'What time does this bar close?' Tony asked, directing his question at the barman.

'When the last guest leaves, sir,' he replied. 'Until then, the bar is always open.'

'Sounds like my kind of bar,' said John, prompting a few chuckles from some of the others.

'I'll drink to that,' added Tony, raising his glass in salute, before taking a generous sip.

After the barman had left, everyone, and not for the first time, formally raised their glasses in a sign of holiday friendship. This time, however, Tom noticed that Tony was a bit reluctant to go through the formality of clinking glasses with everyone. In the event, and without any great enthusiasm, he simply raised his glass once again and made no attempt to clink anyone's glass.

It was Jim who next spoke, directing his question towards Lan. 'If you don't mind me asking, I'm interested to know how you feel, given our history, when you meet lots of Americans, like us, in your country.'

It was a question Tom had thought about asking on a few occasions during the trip, but he had never felt the time was right to ask it. In a way, it seemed appropriate that it was Jim who asked it. At least as far as Tom was concerned, Jim had struck him, from the outset, as being the most sensitive and diplomatic of their small group.

'The war was a long time ago,' Lan answered. 'Vietnam is now a completely different country from when you were last here. We always welcome our foreign guests, wherever they come from.'

Whilst Tom considered Lan's reply to be very diplomatic, at the same time, he couldn't help thinking that it was well rehearsed and almost certainly not the first time he'd given the same answer.

Tom was still considering whether or not to pursue this line of conversation when the decision was made for him by Tony, albeit not exactly in the way Tom would have done it.

'What do you feel now about your country's involvement in the war?' Tony asked, directing his question at Jim. 'I know from my own experience in Iraq, sometimes it just makes the situation even worse. Afterwards, you just wonder if it was worth it and what you were fighting for.'

'Well, it's a question I've asked myself many times since then,' Jim answered. He took a sip from his glass before continuing. 'I can't speak for the others, but I certainly doubted myself by the end.' He paused momentarily. 'I read somewhere that the US had tried to fight a rich man's war in a poor man's country. Looking back, there's no doubt it was a mistake for the US to even get involved in the way it did and think it could win. But at the time, especially in the early days, that wasn't so obvious. The world was much different then. The Cold War was at its height, and we were almost paranoid about stopping the spread of communism throughout the rest of southeast Asia. By the time we got here, though, things had started to change back in the States. The anti-war movement was growing, and to most people it was clear the US was never going to win, so they were asking why more young men were still being sent there to die. By the time the US withdrew, Vietnam seemed to be back to where it was before we first arrived. That's when you ask yourself if it was worth all those people – on both sides – being killed.' He fell silent for a while, before quietly saying, with a nod to Tom, 'Anyway, I'm hoping that, by the end of this trip, I'll have a better answer to that question.'

Just as Tom was considering Jim's reply, John suddenly began to speak. 'Jim's always been a bit of a dreamer, even back when we were together in 3rd Platoon. I've always seen things differently. We were here to fight the commies and preserve our way of life. I've got no time for those bleeding-heart pinkoes who protested against the war. As far as I was concerned, they were all traitors, especially those conchies.'

Not surprisingly, and not for the first time, John's comments had completely changed the atmosphere at the table. Tony, though, with a few red flags now starting to flutter, seemed determined not to let the subject drop.

'What about all those innocent civilians who were killed? How did that help preserve your way of life?' Tony's manner could have been construed as confrontational, although to Tom it seemed a very reasonable and restrained question, especially coming from Tony. 'When I was in Iraq, all it did was turn more people against us. As far as I am concerned, it finished up having exactly the opposite effect to what we hoped would happen.'

Despite the increasing tension between the two of them, Tom had taken an interest in how John's opinionated bravado would play out against Tony's Yorkshire directness. He was about to get another hint as to the answer.

John looked directly at Tony and said in a quiet, considered tone, 'That's always happened in wars. It was just that our war was the first time it had been shown every night on the TV news bulletins.' His voice became much louder and angrier, and the whole bar suddenly fell silent. 'Do you think we just went round all the time deliberately shooting at civilians? Did you, when you were in Iraq, or are you telling me you Brits never shot innocent people? We weren't all like that. Some did, that's for sure, so you should ask those people why they did it, not us.'

After his outburst John drained the rest of his beer, stood

and simply said, 'Goodnight. I think it's time I left before I say something I'll regret.'

'You hit a raw nerve there, Tony,' said Jim, after John had left the bar. 'John sometimes comes across as the tough guy, but I can assure you he does have sensitivities and feelings like everyone else. John was our platoon sergeant and, despite his young age at the time, took great care in looking after all his soldiers. We lost quite a few, and I know John took those losses personally.'

As Tony didn't reply, it was left to Tom to try to get the conversation back onto more of an even keel. 'Perhaps, as you've said previously, Jim, people who were in your position have different ways of dealing with these things. I'm sure you did as well, Tony. I've seen it throughout my career, although not to the extent you all did. Do you think he will be okay?'

'As I've said before, with John, his outward manner is not always the same as what might be going on inside him.' Jim seemed to hesitate. After a moment, he continued in a very subdued voice. 'We all experienced some things, during the war, which aren't easily forgotten. Most of the time, when we were here, we were bored out of our minds. When we were back at base, some of the guys played baseball, football or other sports to pass the time. Others decided smoking pot was their way of handling it. Then we would be briefed on a mission and sent out on patrol, which we all knew might end in a firefight with the VC, and some of us wouldn't be coming back alive. It played tricks on your mind and nerves.'

The noise in the bar had returned to its previous level as the different groups there resumed their own conversations.

Tom suddenly looked at Lan. 'I'm sorry, this must be really difficult for you. It'd maybe be best if we discussed something different.'

'I'm used to discussing the war,' Lan answered. 'We've had lots of other groups on our tours which included men who had been here in the sixties or early seventies. It's true that sometimes it can be quite difficult, especially for those of us whose parents and grandparents were here in Vietnam at the time, to have to hear them talking about the war and, in some cases, what they did. But it was a long time ago.'

Jim, taking his cue from Lan's comment, stood up. 'I think it's past my bedtime as well. Good night to you all. I'll see you tomorrow.'

'I think it's the same for me,' added Bob. He made a slight detour to where one of the other groups were seated, said something Tom couldn't make out, and then walked out of the bar.

Chapter 18

It was just after seven thirty in the morning, and Milner was already back at his desk in the station. He had enjoyed his time with Jenny, but, despite his best efforts, his mind had kept drifting back to his interview with Clinton.

He was sure Clinton held one of the keys to making a breakthrough in the case. During his journey to the station, he had therefore decided to focus on him, pulling together as much evidence as possible, so that he had the justification for interviewing him again. Just like DS Foster, Milner had the strong impression that Clinton was vulnerable to more questioning, particularly whilst the memory of his last interview was still fresh in his mind. It might also be useful if he could find out more about Clinton's background, information which wasn't available from simply reading his police file.

He had already called up Clinton's police record on his computer screen when he saw DC Grey walking towards him.

'You're an early bird,' DC Grey said, as he sat down and fired up the computer on his desk. 'You'll be getting a bad reputation with the rest of the team, especially as you weren't there last night.' There had been an informal get-together at a nearby pub the night before, involving some of the others from the team. They had been there, ostensibly at least, to celebrate the raids on the two houses.

'I'd already made other arrangements, unfortunately,' Milner replied. 'Was it a late night?'

'Not for me, it wasn't,' said DC Grey. 'I just showed my face, had one drink and then left. I have a wife and three young kids and, if you're not careful, you can start to put them second to the job. I've seen quite a few relationships destroyed already and don't want ours to add to that list.'

Milner was reminded of a similar conversation he'd once had with DCI Stone, who had told him how exactly what DC

Grey was now concerned about had happened to him. 'It's difficult enough for someone like me, who doesn't have a family, so I can't begin to understand what it's like for you and the others with young families.'

'I guess it helps if you have an understanding wife,' replied DC Grey. 'Anyway, have you made any more progress trying to make sense of DC Shipley's files?'

Milner shook his head. 'Not yet, unfortunately, but, as you know, it can happen at any time. I just need to be able to spot it when it does happen. What about you? Weren't you interviewing Curtis Seton?'

'Nothing that you could describe as a major breakthrough,' DC Grey said. 'Although the social media history is promising. I'm always amazed how much they give away when they use it. It's almost like an addiction for them. It's all showing off, of course, but it gives us a window into their world.'

'Did you have any luck with the two names I gave you?' Milner asked, fingers metaphorically crossed.

'Sorry,' DC Grey replied. 'He claimed not to know them. For what it's worth, I believed him.'

'Thanks anyway for asking,' Milner answered in a level tone that suggested it wasn't unexpected, belying his inner disappointment.

Milner spent most of the rest of the morning reading through everything there was on the system relating to Clinton and Daniel. As he did this, he made a separate note of anything that he felt was either of special interest or of an unusual nature. After a while, when he felt he'd done as much as he could without simply rewriting the files, he sat back in his chair and stretched out both arms behind his head.

'Anything interesting?' DCI Shaw asked abruptly from behind him.

'Sorry, sir. I didn't see you there,' Milner replied, slightly uncomfortable he hadn't noticed DCI Shaw's presence.

'Yes, you looked as though you were fully engrossed in something or other.' He looked down at Milner's handwritten notes. 'I see you have inherited some of DCI Stone's methods,' he said with a light laugh. 'No matter how many times I tried to persuade him to make use of the latest technology, he still continued to use pen and paper.' As if to make it clear that this wasn't intended as a criticism, he quickly added, 'Mind you, it seemed to work much better than all the other things we now have available to us. Well, at least for him.'

Before Milner could respond, DCI Shaw spoke again. 'Incidentally, how is DCI Stone? Have you heard from him lately? It still amazes me when I hear myself saying this but I do miss him – even the occasional acerbic comment.'

'I'm sure he would be equally surprised to hear you say that, sir,' Milner said, with a laugh. 'He and Mary are on holiday at the moment. Believe it or not, they are in Vietnam.'

From DCI Shaw's slightly startled expression, it was clear that he was just as surprised as Milner had been when he had first been told. 'Really? Well, good for him. I just hope Vietnam is ready for him. Has anyone warned them?' After a momentary pause, he continued. 'Anyway, how are you settling in? I haven't had the chance to speak with you since you started.'

Milner, conscious that he was in an open office, was hesitant to say anything that could be construed as critical of his new colleagues. 'I feel I'm just starting to understand what's going on. To be honest, it's not been easy picking up DC Shipley's caseload. It would have taken much longer, though, without DC Grey filling me in on some of the background stuff.'

'I heard about your interview with Clinton Melton. Sounds as though that might be promising.'

Milner was surprised DCI Shaw, given everything else that had happened over the past twenty-four hours, should be aware of this. After all, his interview with Clinton was just one of many that had been carried out. 'Let's hope so, sir.'

'The real goal, however, is to take down Ravon Shehu and his associates. It's important that any piece of information that might get us closer to achieving that, however seemingly inconsequential, is followed up. Anyway, good luck with your leads. I know you'll be a valuable member of the team.'

'Thank you, sir,' Milner answered, doubting that the other officers currently felt the same.

*

Later that afternoon, Milner was seated in a small flat in Acton, occupied by a member of the Melton family. Milner had come across a contact telephone number in Daniel's murder case file. He'd called it and spoken with Daniel's partner Diana. Just like Mrs Melton, she had been very suspicious about the reason for the call, and doubly so when he had asked if he could visit her. Notwithstanding this, she had reluctantly agreed.

'You can't be here long,' Diana said. 'I'm expecting Daryl to wake up soon. He'll want feeding.'

The flat occupied the ground floor of a multi-storey Victorian building and consisted of a small lounge diner, bathroom and single bedroom. Milner was sitting on a two-seater settee, whilst Diana was in the solitary armchair. The room was full of baby-related paraphernalia, and Milner could see a pushchair to one side of the small electric fire. A large television screen was mounted on one of the other walls and dominated the small room.

Diana looked to be in her early or mid-twenties. The dark lines under her sunken eyes suggested that being a single mother was taking its toll on her.

'I won't take long,' Milner said. 'I can see you are very busy. It must be very difficult bringing up a young child by yourself.'

'I'll manage,' she answered, clearly still wary about Milner's motive for being there.

'You really don't have to answer, but I wanted to ask what you can remember about the days leading up to Daniel's death.'

'I've been through this already with those other policemen,' she said. 'Don't you ever speak to one another?'

'I know, I'm sorry, but I've just taken on the inquiry from one of my colleagues and I wanted to at least meet with you. If you ask me to leave, though, I'll go.'

She didn't immediately answer, but then said, 'Okay. I'll tell you what I know, but if Daryl wakes up, you'll have to leave.'

'Thank you,' replied Milner. 'How was Daniel at the time?'

'What do you mean?' she asked.

'Well, I spoke to his mum a couple of days ago, and she told me Daniel was really enjoying being a dad. She felt he was taking his new responsibilities seriously and determined to put the past behind him.'

'You spoke with his mum?' she asked, with a look of surprise on her face.

'Yes, I did. She told me how proud she was of you all. I could tell just how much she loved being a grandmother to Daryl.'

'She has been really good to us since Daniel died, and she does what she can to help out. But she doesn't have much to spare.' She pointed towards the bedroom, where Daryl was sleeping. 'It's so expensive trying to bring up a kid when there's just one of you. What she doesn't know, though,' she suddenly announced, 'is that I'm pregnant again. We were going to tell her, but then ...' She started to cry. 'Then Daniel was murdered.'

Milner suddenly felt genuine sorrow for her, thinking of how difficult it was likely to be for her in the years ahead. 'Are you getting help from social services? I'm sure you're eligible and would be entitled to lots of different things.' As he said this, he suddenly felt a pang of guilt as he realised just how little he actually knew about these things.

'A social worker comes to visit every week and helps me fill in all the forms. I have trouble understanding some of them. I'm sure she only comes to see if I'm looking after Daryl properly, though. I'm scared they'll take him away.'

'Do they know you are pregnant? That must qualify you for extra support.'

'I haven't told anyone yet, apart from you, just now.'

Milner took out one of his cards and handed it to her. 'If you need any help, please just call me on this number. I can't guarantee I will be able to get you everything you are entitled to, but I'll definitely at least try.' He paused, thinking. 'Do you mind if I mention your circumstances to someone I know? They might also be able to help.'

She looked at the card and read out his name. 'Detective

Constable Milner.' Her tone was suspicious. 'Why are you doing this? Is it because you think I'll tell you other things about Daniel?'

'It's not, but I can understand why you would think that. I just wanted to try and help, that's all. I know about Daniel's previous criminal offences. It's all on his record. I just want to know how he was just before he died.'

Milner stopped talking, adopting DCI Stone's proven tactic of using silence to encourage a reply. It worked, as Diana then began to speak. 'He really was trying to get away from all of that. I'd told him if he didn't then he could forget about me and Daryl, and now, of course, the new baby.'

'Mrs Melton mentioned that Daniel owed money to the gang he had been a part of. Is that correct?'

'How did she know that?' Diana immediately answered, clearly now even more suspicious.

'Clinton told her,' Milner simply replied.

'Clinton?' she repeated, anger now replacing the previous suspicion. 'He's one of the reasons why Daniel is now dead.'

Milner was unsure whether she had intended to say this. Not wanting her to clam up, he responded in a quiet voice, hoping she might continue. 'Why was that? What had Clinton done?'

Despite Milner's matter-of-fact tone, Diana, now recognising that she had said something she hadn't meant to, just said, 'Nothing. I don't want to say anything else and end up dead, like Daniel.'

'But why would you end up dead?' Milner asked, taken aback. 'You have nothing to do with whoever killed Daniel.'

'You don't know what these people are like. They will kill anyone who crosses them. We thought Daniel could get out, but they will never let anyone leave. I know that now.'

Just then a baby started crying.

'You'll have to leave now,' Diana said. 'Daryl will need feeding.'

Milner stood up and offered his hand to her. Unlike Mrs Melton, she shook it, albeit in a perfunctory manner.

'Thank you for seeing me,' he said. 'Remember, if you need

any help, please call me. You have my details.' He made his way to leave.

As he approached the front door, Diana suddenly said, 'Have you taken over from John?'

Milner stopped and turned to face her, surprised. 'Do you mean DC Shipley?'

'Yes,' she simply answered.

'Well, yes, I have,' he replied.

'Just watch out, then, or you might end up like him.'

Milner was about to ask her a follow-up question when Daryl's crying became much louder.

'I have to go,' she said, and she entered the bedroom.

Chapter 19

After breakfast, Tom and Mary spent a leisurely morning on the sun deck, gazing out over the river as the ship slowly continued to make its way down the Mekong. It was proving to be an almost hypnotic experience as their attention remained focused on the surface of the river.

Although it was not yet midday it was promising to be another hot day, although the river breeze, together with the plentiful shaded areas on the sun deck, provided some welcome relief. Mary and Sue were both lying on loungers, a small table between them on which were a placed a couple of large glasses of orange juice. Mary was busy trying to solve the next crossword from the book she'd bought at the airport. Tom could see she was already partway through the book and wondered if it would last her until the end of the holiday. As long as he'd known her, Mary had always started her day by trying to fill out a crossword. If she wasn't able to do this, she would return to it later in the day until either it was finished or she reluctantly gave up on it.

Tom had begun the morning lying alongside her, reading the book on Vietnam that his ex-colleague had loaned him in anticipation of the trip. It hadn't taken long, though, before he had become restless, and so he had announced he was going to take in a different view. Tony had joined him, and they were now both standing on the uppermost point of the ship, at the very front of it. This gave them an almost perfect view of not just where they were heading, but also both sides of the river.

Although the river was wide, the banks on either side were surprisingly high. In some places, parts of the bank had recently been washed away, leaving a dark scar where fresh earth and soil had been revealed and hadn't, as yet, been bleached by the sun. On the most stable parts of the riverbank there was a very distinctive line indicating the height to which the river had previously risen when in flood. Despite the ship taking a middle course down the river, it was still possible to spot people moving around the occasional small hamlets dotted along the sides.

Although the Mekong was now a popular cruise destination, it was still essentially a busy working river, and this was most apparent as they passed those parts of the river where extensive dredging was taking place. Alongside each of these dredges were long barges, some of which were already completely laden with what looked like gravel and sand, whilst others were currently being loaded by the nearby cranes which were mounted on separate boats. They also occasionally passed a few slower-moving cargo boats, transporting mainly bricks, which were making their way down the river towards Ho Chi Minh City. All this activity was probably a factor contributing to the river's distinctive greenish-brown colour, as river silt was disturbed and washed up towards the surface.

Another common sight was the number of clumps of water hyacinth, some quite large, floating down the middle of the river. Some of these had other river detritus, often manmade, caught up amongst them, and this created a strange contrasting sight.

Although there were fishing boats of varying sizes, most were very small and occupied by just a single person. They were clearly used to having to share the river with the large cruise ships and barges and seemed very skilled at giving them a wide berth, in order to avoid the ship's wake. Notwithstanding this, it was still possible to hear the rhythmic *chug-chug* of their small diesel engines as the ship passed them.

Very occasionally they would pass beneath a large, modern concrete bridge. This gave a contrasting, almost incongruous image when compared to the immediate surroundings. As the ship got closer to these bridges Tom could see that lots of people had taken the opportunity to gather there, waiting for the bigger ships to come into view. As the people on the bridge began to wave to those on the ship passing underneath, the captain responded by sounding the ship's horn, which just made the children on the bridge wave even more.

'I know you were a police officer,' said Tony, 'but you never told me exactly what your role was.'

Tom had long ago made it a personal rule not to talk about his job outside work, or at least, if he did, to provide the absolute minimum of information. This was doubly so now he had retired. He decided, though, on this occasion, to make an exception for Tony, not least because he wanted to find the right moment to discuss his and John's acrimonious relationship. 'I was a detective chief inspector in the Met. My patch was in West London.'

'Detective chief inspector? Wow. You kept that quiet,' he replied, genuinely surprised by Tom's answer.

'I'd like to keep it that way, if at all possible.'

'You can trust me not to advertise it.' He fell silent momentarily. 'I imagine you must have been involved in some juicy murder cases.'

'One or two, but mostly it was fairly mundane stuff,' Tom answered, reluctant to mention how one of those had, for a short while, captured the entire nation's interest just a couple of years ago.

Tony evidently realised he wasn't going to divulge anything case-specific. 'I also noticed you've got a slight limp. Is there a reason for that?'

'Well spotted,' Tom replied. 'It was the result of a slight disagreement with a family member of someone I'd recently put away. He seemed to take exception to it.'

'Did he stab you?' Tony asked.

'No. He shot me,' Tom replied, in a low-key manner. 'Fortunately, he wasn't that good and missed all the main arteries. A few weeks' treatment and physio and I was, more or less, back to normal.'

'And I thought my job was dangerous,' Tony replied with a slight laugh.

Tom decided this was as good an opportunity as he was likely to get to discuss Tony's deteriorating relationship with

John. But, rather than simply asking him outright, he thought a less obvious way might prove more fruitful. 'I was going to ask you about your time in the army. You mentioned how you'd completed tours of Northern Ireland and Iraq. You must have had your fair share of dangerous situations. I got the impression you didn't want to elaborate on them.'

'Is that your police training at work?' Tony asked.

Tom didn't reply, hoping his silence would work to his advantage.

'Just like you, it's not something I go around advertising,' Tony said. In an obviously disapproving tone, he added, 'Unlike John, who always seems to want to discuss his time here in Vietnam.'

'I'm not sure that is actually the case,' Tom said, taking Tony's comment head-on. 'I get the impression he's quite tormented and is holding a lot back. You heard what Jim had to say about him last night.'

'Hmm. Well, maybe, but I'm not convinced.'

'For what it's worth, I think you two have more things in common than there are differences,' Tom said, now trying to get to the bottom of why Tony felt such animosity.

'Maybe,' Tony admitted, although not in a manner which suggested he entirely agreed with Tom's reading of their relationship.

'As an outsider I can see how, despite some obvious personality differences, your lives, and probably your perspective on the world, have been heavily influenced by your time in the army. Or have I got that wrong?'

Tony shook his head. 'I just don't like the way he keeps slagging off us Brits. During the first Gulf War, I spent a lot of time working alongside US forces. I have a lot of respect for them and would never slag them off the way he slags us off.'

'I'm sure he doesn't mean it. He's clearly angry about something and he's just taking it out on whoever is nearest at the time. Unfortunately, because he knows you have a military background, it tends to be you.'

'So are you suggesting I should be more tolerant and less confrontational when he's around?'

'I'm not sure that would work. After all, you are from Yorkshire,' Tom answered, trying to inject a little humour into the discussion.

'That's true,' Tony answered, in a similarly jocular tone. 'Anyway, he doesn't even know where Yorkshire, let alone Sheffield, is. Probably thinks it's somewhere near Big Ben.'

'Probably. All I would say is try and see it from his perspective. I know it's difficult, but it might just take the heat out of your relationship with each other.'

'I'll see what I can do,' Tony replied, although, less promisingly, he quickly followed this up with, 'but I can't promise anything.'

As they were making their way back to Sue and Mary, they were approached by Brett, Don's son. 'I just wanted to thank you,' he said, speaking to Tom, 'for looking out for Pops when we were at the prison. Mom and I appreciated that.'

'I'll see you back at the girls,' Tony said, realising that the conversation related to just the two of them.

'You don't have to thank me,' Tom told Brett, making his way back towards the side of the ship. 'Anyway, it was a privilege to meet him. You must be very proud of him.'

'I am,' Brett replied, before saying, 'although I'm not sure about some of the others on the trip.'

'Really?' answered Tom, in a slightly quizzical tone. 'What makes you think that?'

'There has always been a bit of tension between the army boys and those in the air force.'

'Isn't that just natural rivalry?' asked Tom.

'According to Pops, some of the GIs blamed the pilots for bombing the wrong targets and, in some cases, even bombing their own people. He told me how yesterday he heard some of the ex-army guys, even after all these years, still badmouthing the pilots. It's really upsetting him.' He paused and then, more to himself than to Tom, said, 'They had better not say that when I'm around, especially after all he's been through.'

Tom, still puzzled by what Brett had just told him, simply said, 'Well, let's hope they don't.'

They both focused their attention on the river as the ship

continued on its way downstream towards Ho Chi Minh City. After a short while Brett spoke again. 'Pops is a very sick man – although you probably suspected that already.' When Tom didn't respond, Brett continued. 'The doctors say he's got less than six months to live. That's why he wanted to come on this trip. As he's got older, and I suppose closer to the end, all he could talk about was wanting to come back to this country again for the last time.'

'I'm not an expert in such matters,' said Tom, 'but maybe his experience during his imprisonment affected him in a much deeper way than anyone could imagine. I'm sure it would, if it had been me in his position. I think we saw some of that yesterday at the prison.'

'Maybe,' Brett answered. 'Well, anyway, thanks again for the kindness you showed him.'

Chapter 20

After his brief discussion with Brett, Tom joined the others. Mary and Sue were still lying on their loungers, whilst Tony was leaning on the railing, his back to the river.

'I thought you'd left us,' said Mary. 'I was wondering where you'd gone. Anyway, if you ask Huan, he'll bring you a drink.'

'Good idea,' said Tony. He looked at his watch. 'A bit early for a beer, but, then again, we are on holiday.'

Huan suddenly appeared alongside them, as though he had an extra sense that told him when he was needed. 'Can I get you something to drink?' he asked.

Huan looked to be in his early thirties and, rather than the red polo shirt that Lan and the other more senior cruise personnel wore, his shirt was white, although it still had the prominent Mekong Cruises logo stitched onto it. The top two buttons on his polo shirt were undone, revealing a thick cord on the end of which was a distinctive carved, wooden symbol.

'Weren't you working in the bar last night?' asked Tom. 'What time did you finish? It must have been late.'

'It was just after 2am, sir, I think, when our last guests left,' he answered.

'Which guests were those?' asked Tom.

'It was a few of the Americans in Sang's group, sir.'

'You poor man,' said a clearly sympathetic Mary. 'So what time did you start again this morning? I hope it wasn't too early.'

'It was at 7am, ma'am,' Huan replied. He immediately added, 'But it is not a problem. I am used to it.'

'Is this your first year working on the ship?' asked Tom.

'No, sir. This is my third year.'

'Do you enjoy your work?' asked Sue. 'It must be hard to be away from your family.'

'Yes, ma'am, I do miss my wife and children, but there are not many jobs in my village. It's only a small village and was damaged during the war. Today, most people still work in the fields. This job means I can send money back to them. Without that, things would be more difficult. Sang is actually my older brother, so that is good.'

'Yes, that must help,' agreed Sue. 'Has he been with Mekong Cruises longer than you?'

'Yes, ma'am. Sang has been working for five years. My dream is, one day, to be a cruise director. But it is hard to learn to speak English correctly.'

'Your English is very good already. I'm sure you'll achieve your dream,' Sue said, as encouragingly as possible.

'Where is your village?' asked Mary.

'As I said, it is a small village, ma'am. It is in the middle of the country. My family have lived there for many years.'

Huan took their drinks order and then stopped to do the same for another group who were seated nearby.

'What a nice young man,' said Sue, after he had disappeared into the bar. 'It's good that his brother is here so they can support each other.'

Mary, though, was clearly still thinking about his late finish. In her most disapproving voice, she said, 'That's so inconsiderate of them, staying in the bar until two in the morning. They must have known he couldn't leave until they had left.'

'I suppose he knew that when he took the job,' Tony said, in his usual matter-of-fact manner. 'Don't forget we've all paid to be on this trip.'

'Even so,' Mary said, not wanting to let the matter drop. 'I do think they should have left earlier.'

Tom, realising this was exactly the type of cause that Mary could take on with an almost evangelical fervour, quickly changed the subject. 'Are you looking forward to the visit to the village this afternoon?' he asked, directing his question at Sue.

The afternoon's itinerary involved a visit to what Lan had described as a perfect example of the many small villages that could be found dotted along the side of the Mekong. As one of life's confirmed cynics, Tom did wonder just how typical it really would be, given that this cruise ship and others had probably made this stop every week during the six months of the season. Notwithstanding this, he wasn't about to spoil everyone's sense of excitement.

Fortunately, Sue had not attended the same school of scepticism as Tom. 'I can't wait. According to the schedule, we'll visit a family's house. I hope it will be more like the real Vietnam than what we saw in Hanoi.'

Just then Huan returned with their drinks. He placed them on the small table and picked up any empty glasses.

'Excuse me, Huan,' said Mary.

Tom looked at Mary, wondering what she was about to say. Knowing her, he suspected she hadn't yet moved on from their previous brief discussion.

'I hope you don't mind me asking,' Mary said, 'but do you work on board for the full six months of the season?'

'Yes, ma'am,' he replied. 'Afterwards I then go back to my family.'

Mary, Tom sensed, was now in full flow. 'That must be awful for you and your family.'

'Yes, ma'am, but I try to speak to them every day on FaceTime. So that way I do get to see them as well.'

'But do you have to work every day?' she asked.

'Not every day, ma'am. I have one day's rest each week.'

'But what can you do then, if you are on the ship?'

'I mainly sleep, ma'am,' he replied. It was unclear whether he was being serious or not.

Now it was Sue's tune to quiz him. Pointing to the wooden carving around his neck, she said, 'What's that you're wearing? It's very unusual.'

Huan immediately touched it. 'It's a bamboo tree, ma'am. The bamboo tree is very special to everyone who lives in the countryside. It reminds me of where my family come from.'

Tony interrupted before Sue could continue the conversation. 'I think the group over there are trying to get Huan's attention.'

Mary waited until Huan was out of earshot and then said, 'It can't be much of a life for all those who work on the ship. How can they cope with being away from their families for so long? I feel quite guilty now about making them have to do this.'

Once again, it was Tony who provided the counterargument. 'You shouldn't feel guilty, Mary. No one is forcing them to do this. Huan is one of the lucky ones. There must be thousands of young Vietnamese men and women who would love to have his job. Where else is he going to earn the amount of money he does? If there weren't any tourists, then he wouldn't have a job and he wouldn't be able to take care of his family. Well, not the type of job that pays what he gets here.'

Tom was glad it had been Tony, and not him, who had made these points. Nonetheless, he knew Mary would continue to fret about this, and it would resurface every time she saw Huan.

Mary went uncharacteristically quiet for a while. This was a sign that Tom recognised as her being in one of her contemplative moments, and this was confirmed when she eventually spoke. Looking directly at him, she said, 'Tom. I think we should give Huan a large tip when we finish this trip. It's the least we could do.'

Predictably, once again, Tony put in his opinion. 'Don't forget that all onboard tips are included in the overall cost of the trip. They made a big thing about that in the brochure. And, anyway, if you give a tip to Huan, what about all the others? They are just as deserving, even if you don't see them all. There are over thirty crew on board. Are you going to tip them all?'

Mary didn't immediately reply, but, after a few seconds, said, 'Well, I'll be tipping him anyway.'

Chapter 21

After everyone had finished lunch, the normal quiet hum of the ship's engines suddenly changed to a much deeper, more violent and less rhythmic sound, and it began to noticeably reduce its speed. Most people had come up onto the upper deck to watch as the captain, skilfully using the ship's bow thrusters, carefully manoeuvred the ship alongside what seemed like a very tight and rudimentary landing area.

As the ship got closer, a couple of the crew jumped down from the rear onto the dry ground and tied ropes around some heavy metal poles. Another couple repeated the same procedure towards the front. Although this was not for the faint-hearted, the young crew members were clearly well practised in this, and within a couple of minutes the ship was secure and the engines had stopped completely. Another two crew members released a section of the guard rail and then pulled out a metal gangplank, which was soon secured and ready for the passengers to use for disembarking.

They all patiently waited their turn to get off the ship. As they got to the gangplank, they handed over their cabin key and, in exchange, were given a numbered tag, corresponding to their room number. This, they were told, would enable the captain to know which guests had left the ship, and they would exchange the tags for their keys when they returned. At both ends of the gangplank there was a crew member ready to offer help to any of the less mobile passengers.

After they had got off the ship, they all lined up in their normal groups, with each group led by their nominated Mekong Cruises guide. Tom's group was the second to get off and, led by Lan, soon began to move off down a narrow, hard-packed track, all the while keeping the same distance from the group ahead.

Almost as soon as they had all got off the ship, groups of

children mysteriously appeared alongside them, hoping to sell cold drinks or steer them towards a particular shop. This part of the village, a short walk from the ship, had many small, open-fronted shops selling the sorts of items you would find in any tourist area. Some of the items had been intricately carved or woven and, in a few places, an elderly woman could be seen at the back of the shop working on something new. In contrast, however, most of the things on sale were mass-produced gifts and, when Tom examined one such item, he was quietly amused to see the 'Made in China' sticker had been left on it. Despite this, most of the shops seemed to be doing a brisk trade, at least based on how many plastic bags the tourists were already carrying.

After they had walked for a while, the number of shops started to thin out, and they increasingly found themselves amongst the places where the villagers actually lived rather than where they worked.

'Ladies and gentlemen,' said Lan. 'We are now going to visit the house of a family. You are all welcome to enter and see any part of the house. If I could ask you, though, to show respect to their home. Please try to speak as quietly as possible as, quite often, there are babies there. You can take photos, but it is tradition that you ask whoever is there if they are happy with that. If you simply point at your phone or camera, they will understand.' He paused, allowing his instructions to be fully understood. When no follow-up questions came, he continued. 'Guests always ask if it is okay to give money and what the usual amount would be. Mekong Cruises takes care of all such costs, but if you do feel you would like to show your gratitude then please go ahead. The usual amount would be a US dollar.'

As they walked around a small bend, they arrived at the house, although in truth it more resembled a large wooden shack. It was set back about twenty metres from the track and raised off the ground by large, sturdy-looking wooden props, supplemented by a few strategically placed concrete blocks in each of the corners. Although most of the house was made from wood, the roof was protected by metal sheeting and the solitary entrance was accessed via a slightly inclined, narrow wooden plank. On one side of the house was a small plot where a few rows of vegetables were growing. A large pole near the main track carried a tangle of wires, and a few of these disappeared into the house.

They waited a few minutes, until the group ahead had all left the house, and then Lan spoke again. 'Please make your way inside. Be careful, though, walking up into the house. As you can see, the plank is very narrow. If anyone needs any help, just ask me.'

Tom's small group of Brits made their way into the house, closely followed by John's group. They found themselves in the main, largest room, which also included a tiny cooking area in one corner. Two smaller rooms were at the rear, both separated from the main living area by a brightly coloured curtain. A small television was precariously placed on a narrow shelf fixed to one of the walls.

There were two people in the main area. An elderly woman was busy preparing food, whilst an equally elderly man was seated on a well-used chair, a cigarette in his mouth as he continued weaving a large basket. On the floor behind him were a number of already finished smaller baskets. He was wearing a short-sleeved white shirt and black trousers. He wasn't wearing anything on his feet. What made his task even more special, though, was that his right arm was missing.

On one of the walls were a few photographs of various family members, and these were already being studied closely by some of the other guests.

'It's very small,' said Mary in a hushed tone. 'I wonder how many people live here?'

'Why don't you ask Lan?' replied Tom, who had been watching the old man, using just his left hand, expertly manipulate a new length of cut reed onto the frame of the basket.

Lam was standing at the rear of the house, just as a maître d' would in a fancy restaurant, carefully taking in everything that was happening. Tom and Mary both walked a few paces to where Lan was standing. 'How many people live here?' Mary asked.

'There are actually seven in total,' Lan replied. 'Mom, Dad and three children. Mom and the kids are busy working at the shops. Dad will still be out fishing. The lady and gentleman here are the grandparents.'

'Seven,' Mary repeated, clearly astonished that that many people could live together in such a small area.

'It's normal in Vietnam for grandparents to live with their children and grandchildren. The family will have lived here for quite a few generations. It's becoming more common, though, for the children to leave and try to find work in the cities. I expect, in a few years, what you are seeing here will almost be a thing of the past,' he said, real regret obvious in his voice.

Just then John, Joany, Bob and Ruth came to join them, together with Jim.

'This is like some of the houses we came across,' said Bob. 'I guess it's off the ground in case of flooding.'

'Exactly,' said Lan. 'As you can see, we are not far from one of the Mekong's small tributaries. Although they also give a bit of protection against wild animals and snakes.'

John was looking at the old man. 'Do you know how he lost his arm?' he asked Lan.

'Do you want me to ask him?' asked Lan.

'So long as he doesn't mind.'

'I'm sure he's been asked that many times,' said Lan. He went and spoke to the man, who responded quite readily and enthusiastically, with even the hint of a thin smile appearing on his face. The man also quite theatrically raised what remained of his right arm, as if to add to his explanation. Eventually he stopped speaking and drew on his cigarette.

'He says he lost it a long time ago, during the war,' Lan said, returning to the group. 'It was a grenade which went off in his hand as he was about to throw it. They had to amputate his arm to save him.'

'Oh, my goodness,' said Ruth. 'Poor man.'

There followed a brief silence before John spoke again. 'Which side was he on?' It was a good question and one which a few of the others were, no doubt, interested to know the answer to.

'He said he was in the South Vietnamese army, fighting the North Vietnamese.' Lan paused. 'It was after the Americans had left and just before the Viet Cong took Saigon. He says it was not a good time. They didn't have much ammunition. When the Americans were here, they had everything, but when they left, they had nothing.'

All the Americans in the room were aware of how, after the peace agreement had been signed between the US and North Vietnam, it hadn't been long before most aid, despite assurances to the contrary to the South Vietnamese government, had dried up. Lan's last sentence, whether intentionally or not, had the effect of almost instantly creating a palpable tension amongst the group.

It was Jim who broke the tension. 'Could you please tell him that we would be honoured if we could have our photograph taken with him?'

After Lan had translated Jim's request, a wide smile suddenly appeared on the man's face and, with his left hand, he beckoned them towards him.

Jim whispered something to John and Bob, and then they took their places at either side of him. As Lan took a couple of photos, all three suddenly stood ramrod straight and then turned to face him and saluted. The previous tension within the group instantly changed to pure emotion, which affected everyone watching.

They each thanked him afterwards. This time, though, there was no need for Lan to translate.

Jim asked Lan if the old man would accept a small payment from them. The man replied in Vietnamese, whilst simultaneously pointing down at the group of finished baskets.

'He says he doesn't want any payment,' Lan said. 'Instead, he would like to give each of you one of his baskets, so that you will remember him when you get back to the United States, and that he fought alongside American soldiers.'

As the group left the house, no words were exchanged between them.

Chapter 22

'What are you looking at?' asked Mary, in a slightly quizzical manner. They were back in their cabin, resting before dinner and the evening's onboard entertainment. As soon as they had returned to the ship and everyone had been accounted for, the *Mekong Voyager* had left its docking position and, once again, had begun making its serene way down the Mekong.

'It's an email from Milner,' Tom answered, looking up from his tablet. He was seated outside, on the veranda. The sun was now much lower, creating a softer light than at the height of the day. This, together with the stillness of the early evening and the first hint of a mist appearing on parts of the river, helped to create an almost mystical vista. 'I mentioned to him that I would be interested to hear how his inquiry was progressing.'

'Please tell me you're joking,' she answered quite brusquely.

Tom had hoped Mary hadn't noticed what he was doing, but, on reflection, he should have known that would always be unrealistic. 'It's not as though I'm likely to be getting involved.'

'Really?' she asked, in her most disbelieving voice. 'You know that's not true. Why can't you forget about it? You don't work there any more. I thought we were here to enjoy our time together.'

'We are,' he replied. 'Come and sit out here with me, whilst there's still some daylight.' He looked towards the eastern horizon. 'That sky looks a bit ominous. I think we might be in for a storm later. Lan told me they're very common at this time of year and can be really spectacular.'

Mary sat down. If she was impressed with the view, she wasn't about to mention it. 'Don't try and change the subject. I know what you're doing.'

Tom was silent, suspecting that anything he might say would only add to the tension.

'Look,' Mary said, 'I understand how the police have been your life and how it must be difficult for you to completely forget it. All I'm asking is, just for these few weeks, you try to put it to the back of your mind. Surely that's not too much to ask.'

'It's not,' he answered, taking hold of her hand. 'You're right. It's not as though I can do anything anyway. I'm sorry. I promise I'll try.' He leaned forward and kissed her gently.

'Wow,' she said, surprised. 'I'm just wondering if this is the same Tom Stone who flinches when I try to hold his hand.' She moved closer and kissed him in return, this time with increased urgency and feeling.

Tom set down his tablet, took hold of her hand and led her back into their cabin. 'It would be a shame not to take advantage of such a beautiful evening. I'm sure Milner can wait.'

'And they say romance is dead,' she replied, with a quick laugh.

*

Later, as they were both getting ready for dinner, Mary suddenly, and to Tom's surprise, said, 'What was it that David wanted? Was it anything important?'

Tom resisted the temptation to mention their earlier conversation. 'He inherited some case files from the detective constable who had previously been in that role,' he said, declining to mention the exact circumstances in which he'd inherited them. 'There were a few names in the files which kept cropping up, but, apart from two brothers, he's struggling to make any connections. There were, however, two other names, which he found apparently hidden in the sleeve of one of the files. He thinks these might be important, but, as I say, he can't work out why or even if there's a connection.'

Milner's earlier email had summarised the current status of the case. Whilst he had been careful not to reveal anything that might compromise the investigation, Milner's frustration had been obvious.

'Did he send you those names?' Mary asked.

Milner had indeed listed the names, presumably in the hope it might provide some sort of inspiration. Tom was reluctant to admit this to Mary, not least because it might simply confirm her earlier suspicions and take them back to their earlier conversation. Notwithstanding this, he decided that trying to keep anything from her was probably doomed to failure, and so he simply said, 'He did, yes. That's what I was looking at before you distracted me.'

'Distracted you? Well, at least you got your priorities right,' she said, squinting briefly. Before he could respond, she asked, 'Am I allowed to take a look?'

'I can't win. Now you're encouraging me to get you involved,' he said, laughing. 'Okay. Let me just open up the document.' He opened the file attached to Milner's email, then turned the tablet so she could see the list of names. 'See what you can make of them.'

All the names were listed, with Daniel and Clinton Melton at the top of the list. At the bottom of the list were the names that had been hidden: Lionel Tedman and Adrian Wolfe.

Tom continued to get ready whilst Mary looked intently at the names. After a short while, she walked to the small table, where she picked up an A4 sheet of notepaper and pen, both embossed with the Mekong Cruises logo. She copied all the names onto the sheet of paper and started to cross out letters, replacing them with new ones.

Tom left her to it as he finished changing. After a while he looked over to her. 'Making any sense of it?' he asked, not expecting much progress, especially in such a short period of time.

'Well, there are a couple of obvious connections I can see straight away.'

'Oh, you mean the Melton brothers. Yes, I thought I mentioned that connection.'

'Tom,' she replied, 'I can see they have the same surname. You don't have to be Poirot to spot that. No, what I mean is that Lionel Tedman is an anagram of Daniel Melton. Adrian Wolfe, though, doesn't fit any of the other names listed. All I can get from it at the moment is Diana Fowler, although I'm sure there must be other anagrams.' She handed him the sheet of paper. 'Anyway, I hope it helps David. Are you nearly ready? We said we'd meet Sue and Tony in five minutes.'

'How did you make that connection so quickly?' he asked, impressed.

'Doing lots of crosswords, I suppose,' she answered simply.

Tom, with an imperceptible shake of his head, said, 'I'll just quickly email Milner with what you've found, so he gets it while he's still at work.'

'Do you think it's important?' she asked.

'If it's not, then it's a hell of a coincidence, and I've never really believed in coincidences.'

Chapter 23

Tom's email had arrived in Milner's inbox, coincidentally, whilst he had been meeting with Diana, and it wasn't until he'd got back to the station that he had been able to read it. To say it had been a surprise – albeit a welcome one – would have been a huge understatement.

One the one hand, Milner was delighted that this particular puzzle had been solved. His immediate thought had been that it could move the inquiry on, although the direction in which it might move still wasn't immediately obvious. On the other hand, though, there was a part of him that wished he had made the connection before DCI Stone had.

What made it worse, and in truth slightly unnerved him, was the briefness of his email. Under normal circumstances DCI Stone would have followed such a breakthrough with a detailed brief as to what should happen next or, at the very least, a request for follow-up information. Perhaps this was simply because he was on holiday and had other things on his mind. The more Milner thought about this, though, the more out-of-character his behaviour seemed. Nonetheless, whatever the reason, this information could only help.

During his earlier drive back to the station, Milner's mind had been busy trying to make sense of Diana's parting comment: the warning that he might end up like DC Shipley. Mainly due to the way she had said it, he suspected she knew more than she had been willing to say. The good news was that she had not said it in any threatening way. If anything, her tone had almost suggested genuine concern for his safety. He had determined, therefore, that he would speak to her again and see if she would elaborate on her warning. This information from DCI Stone simply reinforced that decision.

The other thing that troubled him was Diana's current personal situation. It was clear to him that she desperately needed help, and not just financial, although that was probably her immediate priority. He didn't claim to be an expert on such matters, but even he could see that she also needed practical and emotional support, especially now that she was pregnant and would soon have two very young children to look after.

As soon as he had returned to the station, and even before he'd fired up his computer, he'd contacted one of the police welfare support officers, who he knew from a previous case. After he'd explained Diana's circumstances and provided as much information as he was aware of, the officer had promised to follow up with the relevant social services departments immediately to see what was possible. Although he felt better for having initiated this, he remained very concerned about her current emotional state.

The news that both Daniel's and Diana's name had been hidden, and, even more significantly, deemed to be important enough for both names to be converted into code, simply reinforced his concerns. What was perhaps of even more concern, however, was that fear for her physical safety had now been added to that list. There must have been a reason that DC Shipley had tried to protect their names. One of those individuals was now dead, whilst the remaining one was clearly very frightened about her own safety.

As he reflected on all of this, during the immediate aftermath of receiving DCI Stone's email, the outline of a plan had begun to emerge in his head, and this was the reason he was currently back at Mrs Melton's flat in Shepherd's Bush.

'Thanks for seeing me again,' he said, seated in the same place as the last time he was here. This time though, Mrs Melton had been more welcoming, and this was confirmed by the cup of tea she had offered him as soon as he had arrived.

'You said you wanted to speak about Diana and Daryl. Are they okay?' she asked, concern palpable in her voice.

'Yes, they are both fine,' he answered reassuringly, albeit slightly disingenuously, not wanting to immediately put her on edge. 'I went to see them yesterday as part of our ongoing investigations into Daniel's death.' He paused briefly, allowing her to react. When there was nothing forthcoming, he continued. 'Diana confirmed that becoming a father had seemed to change Daniel for the better, and that he seemed determined to leave his previous life behind.'

'That's what I told you,' Mrs Melton said, 'but you didn't believe me.'

'Yes, I'm sorry for that,' he said, even though he hadn't exactly used those words.

They both fell silent for what seemed like an extended period of time, before Milner broke the silence. It was the subject he had been least looking forward to discussing, and one which had the potential to completely erode any trust he might still have with Mrs Melton.

'I'm sorry to have to tell you, Mrs Melton, but Clinton was arrested a couple of days ago.'

'Oh my God,' she said immediately, the pitch of her voice rising to reflect her sudden concern. 'Why was he arrested? Did it have something to do with Daniel's murder?'

Milner explained the circumstances of his arrest and then described most, but not all, of their subsequent interview.

Mrs Melton shook her head. 'I knew this would happen. I haven't seen him for about a week now. I always worry when that happens. Where is he now?'

'He has been released while we continue our inquiries. If it's any consolation, he was genuinely concerned about the impact his arrest might have on you and Shannon.'

'Will he go to prison?' she asked, ignoring Milner's attempt to provide some reassurance.

'I honestly don't know. We found a lot of evidence to suggest he was involved in producing and selling drugs, some of them what we call Class A. In other words, the most serious ones.'

This proved too much for her and she began to sob quietly. 'What have I done wrong?' she said, between sobs.

'Please don't think it's your fault. There's only so much you can do,' he replied, immediately regretting the banality of his words.

Her reply, though, surprised Milner. 'I'm glad,' she said,

now in a very determined voice. 'At least if he's in prison he's away from all the others and so he can't end up like Daniel.'

'Well, anyway, I just wanted to make sure you knew before you heard about it from someone else. If you want me to, I will keep you updated on developments. Of course, if you'd rather I didn't, then I totally understand.'

'Thank you. It'd probably be better if you did keep me informed, even though I might not like what I hear.' She paused. 'Tell me, Mr Milner, as you're a policeman: is there anything I can do to keep Clinton from getting into even more serious trouble?'

Her question was unexpected and certainly not something to which he had a definitive answer. 'Well, as you say, him not mixing with those he's currently mixing with would help.' Even as he said this, he realised just how difficult it would be. Clinton seemed to be totally under the spell of the Westie Crew and everything it stood for, and this manifested itself in the total disrespect he had for any type of authority, but especially the police. 'The other thing which might help would be to somehow get him back here with you. As I said earlier, he seemed genuinely concerned about your and Shannon's welfare. Maybe he would see himself as the man of the house and take care of you both, without getting involved in any crime.' Having met Clinton, he doubted even his own words. 'You have my contact details. Please call me if you think I can help in any way.'

'Thank you, I will,' she answered, in total contrast to the last time he had made the same offer.

Milner had one more thing to discuss with her, and now seemed as good a time as any to mention it. 'When I was with Diana yesterday, she told me something that I thought you should know.'

Not for the first time, Mrs Melton's changed expression betrayed her anxiety. 'What is it? She isn't in any trouble, is she? Or is it Daryl?'

'Well, not exactly,' he replied. 'She's going to have a baby.'

It was clear this was not what Mrs Melton had expected, confirmed by her silence as she tried to take in what she'd just been told. Eventually she simply said, 'Poor girl. How is she going to cope?'

'I think this is where you can help,' answered Milner. He had thought carefully about this very subject and how it could work to everyone's advantage. 'It was obvious to me yesterday that, whilst she is doing everything possible to be a good mum, she is finding it very difficult, especially now she's by herself. I think she is really worried she won't be able to cope when the new baby comes along. I have to say, having seen her circumstances myself yesterday, she is definitely struggling to cope.'

'But she isn't by herself,' Mrs Melton said, rather indignantly. 'I'm here to help.'

'I did tell her that, but I don't think she's in the frame of mind to see it.'

'Why didn't she tell me?' she asked, not unreasonably.

'As I said, she's not in the right frame of mind yet. She and Daniel were looking forward to telling you, but then ... well, circumstances changed.'

'So what do you think I should do?' she asked, a touch of helplessness in her voice.

'Someone I know will be contacting her to make sure she is receiving everything she's entitled to, and I'm sure that will help. But, right now, I think it's more important she receives your emotional support. I'll do what I can, but she needs the company of someone she trusts.'

Mrs Melton gave a determined nod. 'I'll go to see her as soon as I can sort something out for Shannon.'

'I think that will be really good. If you need any help from me – even if it's just taking you there – please just ask.'

'Thank you,' she said. 'I might ask you to do that.'

Chapter 24

Later that same day, back at the station, DCI Shaw held another meeting, involving the full team. Detective Inspector Richards was alongside him.

'I just wanted to update you all on where we are right now.' DCI Shaw paused momentarily before continuing. 'I'm afraid it's not good news. The CPS have come back and said there is insufficient evidence to pursue the convictions.'

There were the inevitable and immediate audible responses, some heavy with expletives, from some of the people in the room. DCI Shaw held up both hands in an attempt to call for silence. It took a while, but eventually his patience was rewarded.

'I know you are all disappointed, and in my opinion you have every right to be, but I'm sure this is not the first time it's happened to you. In an inquiry as complex as this, we have to be as near dammit one hundred percent sure we will get a conviction. At the moment the CPS doesn't think we are anywhere near that point. We will only have one chance to get convictions, and so we can't take any chances. In the long run this may prove to be a blessing in disguise.'

'But what about all the drugs and money we found in the houses?' asked DC Grey. 'Surely there's enough there for the CPS to act?'

'Not in the CPS's opinion, I'm afraid, and that's what matters. None of those items could be directly and unequivocally linked to anyone there.'

'So all the work we did has been wasted. Is that what you are saying, sir?' asked DC Turton in a tone of increasing anger, reflecting the general mood of everyone.

'No, I am absolutely not saying that,' DCI Shaw answered, in a contrasting calm voice. 'This just means that we have to double down on what we've been doing and be smarter than they are.'

'But surely they'll all know now that we're on to them, so they'll be extra careful,' suggested DC Turton.

'That's always possible,' answered DCI Shaw, 'but this might also work to our advantage. They might now feel they are invulnerable. If that's the case, then I can guarantee they will make mistakes and, when they do, we need to be there. That way the CPS will have to accept the evidence.' He went into his final rallying call. 'If they think this is the end of the investigation, and that they now have full licence to continue causing murder and mayhem on our streets, then they will soon realise they have seriously underestimated the determination of everyone here. We don't just give up after the first setback.' There was a slight pause before he said, in an uncharacteristically emotionally charged voice, 'I can promise everyone here that we will eventually put these murderers and their thugs away for a very long time.'

There was no immediate reaction to what DCI Shaw had just said, each person no doubt with their own thoughts as they took in the full implications of what they'd just been told. After a short while, though, some in the room began to clap, and soon everyone had joined in, either clapping or just banging on a table near them.

DCI Shaw, visibly moved by their response, could only manage a 'thank you' as an acknowledgement of their obvious support.

*

After the meeting, Milner was back at his desk when DS Gordon approached him.

'I'm sure you're as disappointed as everyone else,' DS Gordon said, as he pulled up a chair and sat down.

'Well, of course,' replied Milner, slightly puzzled as to exactly why he was there.

'But, as DCI Shaw said, this just stiffens our resolve to put them all away.'

Milner, now even more unsure what DS Gordon wanted, deliberately didn't respond.

'What's the situation with Clinton Melton?' DS Gordon asked. 'Are you making any progress?'

Milner had already decided it was too early to mention the two anagrams. He needed to work out what the best next course of action would be, and until he'd done that he was reluctant to discuss it with anyone else, including his immediate boss. All else aside, he didn't want to falsely raise any hopes amongst the senior detective team. Given what they'd all just been told, it was important to keep a cool head, at least until he had further information which would move the investigation forward.

He also couldn't help thinking about what DCI Stone would do in such circumstances. His strong feeling was that DCI Stone would also want to obtain more information before he finally decided on any particular course of action. 'Check and double-check' had been one of his many mantras.

It had even crossed Milner's mind to contact DCI Stone just to see what he would suggest he should do now he had this information, especially as it was DCI Stone who had provided the connection. However, he'd quickly dismissed this thought. There would be a danger of DCI Stone taking this as a green light to involve himself, albeit unofficially, in the investigation. It wouldn't make any sense for DCI Stone to be involved when he was over 6,000 miles away.

Milner was also conscious of the fact he'd shared information with a person, albeit a recently retired DCI, who was not involved in the investigation. This, by itself, could be viewed as compromising the overall inquiry, and, given his recent disciplinary charge, he was already on thin professional ice. If things went wrong. it would almost certainly be the final nail in his career coffin.

'It's a bit slow, I'm afraid, sir,' he answered, in a noncommittal tone. 'I'm still certain he could be crucial to our investigation, and a way of getting at the Shehus. But, given what DCI Shaw had to say, I think it's now a case, unfortunately, of starting all over again and examining what evidence we do have.'

'Could be,' DS Gordon replied. 'But don't throw the baby out with the bathwater. I looked at your interview with him, and both DS Foster and I think he knows more than he's letting on. My suggestion would be to keep the pressure on him and see where that leads you.'

'Thank you, sir,' answered Milner, who had already decided that was exactly what he intended to do anyway.

Chapter 25

After dinner, Tom, Mary and the rest of the group had made their way to the main lounge, where the evening's entertainment would take place. It had already become a bit of a holiday tradition, allowing everyone to wind down and relax after the day's activities.

Tonight's entertainment was based around the two musicians who had joined the cruise at the same time all the guests had boarded. It was apparent from the various musical instruments assembled behind the piano that they were very versatile performers. The entertainment was to begin at 10 pm, and this left plenty of time beforehand for most of the guests to take full advantage of their gold drinks package. The noise levels had gradually but perceptibly increased as the evening wore on, and by the time the entertainment started, the bar staff were at their busiest.

The music reflected the profile and nationalities of the guests, mainly comprising American and British songs from the 1960s, and it wasn't long before the small dance floor was fully occupied. Even Tom, who was not known for his willingness to exhibit himself so publicly, had eventually been encouraged by Mary to do so.

Whilst the two musicians were taking a break, everyone saw this as an opportunity, once again, to top up their glasses. Tom and Tony, both with drinks in hand, had made their way to the upper deck and were now looking out into the near distance, where dramatic sheet lightning was briefly, but spectacularly, lighting up the sky. This was followed by a deep, menacing crack of thunder. Although, at this stage, there wasn't any accompanying rain, it was clear they would soon be experiencing the full effects of the coming storm.

'I think we are definitely in for some bad weather,' said Tom. 'It sounds as though it's coming directly towards us.'

'Yep, looks that way,' Tony replied. 'Although you can never quite tell with the weather. When I was in Iraq, sometimes, when we were in the desert, there was lightning and thunder all around us, but the rain never came.'

As they both continued to stare in the direction of the storm, Tom asked, 'What was it you did during the Gulf War? You mentioned briefly how you worked closely with the US military. Were you in special forces?'

Tony, continuing to stare into the distance, said, 'I was part of a team looking for Scud missiles.'

'Did you find any?' asked Tom, now totally engaged in the conversation. Like lots of other people, he'd seen programmes and read about the exploits of special forces during the first Gulf War. But, unlike the vast majority of those people, he now had the opportunity to hear about it from someone with firsthand experience. Or, at least, that was what he hoped.

'Not really,' Tony said quietly. 'More like they found us.'

Tom, sensing now that Tony, for whatever reason, was reluctant to provide any fuller details, decided, reluctantly, not to pursue the matter. This was a shame, because he would have been genuinely interested to hear what Tony had to say. Their thoughts, however, were suddenly disturbed by the sound of raised voices coming from the bar.

'Looks like something is kicking off in there,' said Tony, nodding towards the bar. 'Sounds as though my friend John is in the middle of it. No surprise there,' he added, with a slight laugh.

Tom, also hearing the raised voices, could even pick out John's amongst them. He could also just about make out Jim's voice, sounding as though he was, as usual, acting as a peacemaker.

'Should we go in?' asked Tony. 'It might be fun.'

'I'm not sure we would be able to do anything,' said Tom. 'I think it's best if we leave them to it. Anyway, the girls will be wondering where we are.'

'That's a shame,' Tony said, reluctantly following Tom down the stairs and back into the lounge, where the musicians were busy preparing for their next session.

'Where have you been?' asked Sue, after they had returned to their seats. 'We were worried you might have fallen overboard.' It wasn't obvious whether she was being serious or not.

'Sorry,' said Tom. 'We were just admiring a storm which looks like it might be coming our way.'

Before anyone could respond, the music started again, making it difficult to hold a proper conversation.

As the musicians were finishing their first song, Tom noticed John and Bob, followed closely by Jim, entering the lounge and taking their seats next to their wives. Almost immediately afterwards, another small group of men entered and took their own places, sitting on the opposite side of the lounge to where John was seated.

As the evening progressed, the noise levels increased even further, and every song had now turned into a general singalong. After a while some people started to make specific requests for songs that they wanted to sing, and this quickly turned into a sort of karaoke, albeit without the words being displayed to help. The two musicians did their best to accommodate any requests, providing the backing music as well as occasionally helping out with the vocals. The standard was variable, usually based upon how much the singer had already drunk. Unsurprisingly, John had joined in, and he sang an Elvis number which seemed to go down well with the room, certainly based on how many others helped him out.

Suddenly Tony stood up and walked towards the musicians.

'Oh, no,' said Sue, rolling her eyes. 'I knew he couldn't resist. I wondered how long it would be before he put his name down.'

'I didn't know he could sing,' said Mary.

'He thinks he can, but I'll let you decide if he can or can't,' she answered.

A few minutes later, Tony was called up, and he took his place behind the microphone. It was obvious to everyone that he wasn't entirely steady on his feet, which was not surprising given how much he had already drunk. Tony's version of Neil

Diamond's 'Sweet Caroline' was, however, especially given his condition, more than half-decent. Whilst he seemed to forget a few of the lyrics, this was overlooked by everyone, who enthusiastically joined in every time he got to the chorus.

'That was very good,' said Mary, after he had returned to his seat. 'Is it your favourite? It looked like you'd sung it a few times previously.'

'A few times?' answered Sue. 'He always sings it. Some of our friends are fed up with him singing it. It doesn't stop him, though. In fact, a few years ago, he started to keep a record of all the places where he's sung it. You'd be surprised just how many different countries there are on the list. When we're away, he usually spends the first few days looking out for places where he could sing it. It's become a sort of ritual over the years. The problem is, he doesn't know when to stop. We've had massive arguments about it, but he doesn't listen.'

'It's all about timing,' Tony suddenly interjected, clearly still basking in the praise from his latest performance. 'I'm glad I sang it after John's attempt.' His words were slightly slurred. 'I think it went down better.'

It was well past midnight when the musicians ended their session. This, however, didn't end the entertainment, as one of the guests started to play the piano. Whilst some of the guests took this as their cue to go to bed, the majority stayed. After a while, though, it was Mary who decided it was time they left. It had been a long day, and even longer night, and it was well past their usual bedtime.

Sue and Tony tried to encourage them to stay, but Mary was insistent. She had encouraged Tom to embrace everything about the trip and, in truth, was more than a little surprised and pleased by just how much he had taken her advice. She knew Tom, whilst liking the odd glass of red wine and pint of beer, was not, by nature, a big drinker. She was starting to realise just how easy it was to totally underestimate how much you'd had to drink on a trip such as this, when drinks were available throughout the entire day, and with the staff always on hand to serve generously sized beverages. So, with common sense prevailing, they left the others to it and went back to their cabin.

Along with everyone else, however, they were woken just before it started to get light again, when the Tannoy in their room suddenly burst into life.

'Good morning, everyone,' said Lan, concern etched in his voice. 'I'm sorry to have to wake you so early, but it's important you all assemble in the lounge in twenty minutes. This is not an emergency, repeat, not an emergency,' he added, presumably to reassure everyone they were not about to have to abandon ship. Just in case some people had slept through his announcement, he repeated it twice more, five minutes apart.

'What do you think it is?' asked Mary.

'I've no idea,' replied Tom, 'but I can't think it's going to be good news. We wouldn't be woken at this time just to announce it was going to be a beautiful day. Anyway, we'll soon find out.'

They quickly finished getting dressed and, along with everyone else, made their way to the lounge. Despite the previous evening's entertainment and the late finish, the room had already been cleared of the night's detritus and had been returned to its previous pristine condition.

There were already a lot of bleary-eyed people there when they arrived, all of whom, despite the general low-level noise they were making, had the same concerned expression on their faces. This concern was only compounded by the fact that alongside Lan were some of the other senior tour staff, including the captain. Of even greater significance, however, was that John's wife, Joany, seated nearest to Lan and the other staff, was obviously in a lot of distress. Although she was being comforted by her friend Ruth, her attention didn't seem to be having any effect on her emotions.

After another few minutes, Lan decided he couldn't wait any longer for any latecomers to arrive. He took hold of the microphone and started to speak. 'Ladies and gentlemen, thank you for getting here so promptly.' He seemed to take a deep breath before continuing. 'I'm afraid I have to inform you that one of our American passengers, Mr John Fisher, is missing. The crew have been carrying out a search of the ship for a few hours now, ever since Mrs Fisher reported that he hadn't returned to their cabin. At the moment we cannot confirm what has happened to him or where he is.'

The silence that had immediately followed Lan's announcement was suddenly broken when one of the guests asked, 'So what happens now? Is there anything we can do?'

It was the ship's captain who answered. Taking hold of the microphone, he said, 'There are clear rules for every ship when this happens in Vietnam. We will be docking at the next main town on the river. We should be there in about one hour. Regional police will then come on board to start their investigations. I'm afraid I cannot tell you how long these will take or what they will involve.'

Chapter 26

Unsurprisingly, the atmosphere on board for the rest of the morning was extremely subdued, with any conversations taking place in hushed tones. An earlier-than-usual breakfast had been prepared by the ship's chefs, after which most people either returned to their cabins, to sit on their verandas, or just sat around on the upper deck or in the lounge.

The ship, even to the untrained eye, appeared to have increased its speed as it travelled towards its new destination. Rather than the usual hypnotic sound of the engine, it had now altered its pitch into something more urgent.

Tom and Mary were on the upper deck, standing against the ship's port side rail.

'What do you think will happen next?' asked Mary, rephrasing the question she had already asked a couple of times.

'I'm really not sure,' Tom replied. 'I guess it depends just how thorough the police will be when they get on board. No doubt they will want to interview all those who John was last in contact with.' He paused. 'And of course they'll want to speak with Joany.'

'How awful for poor Joany,' said Mary. 'I can't begin to imagine what she must be going through.'

Tom decided not to respond, not least because he couldn't think of anything positive to say.

Just then Jim walked by. 'Hi, Tom. Mary,' he said, in a distinctly downbeat manner, before stopping and taking his place alongside Tom.

'Is there anything we can do for Joany?' asked Mary, turning to face him.

'I don't think so,' he answered. 'Bob and Ruth are with her right now. The staff are all being incredibly helpful, especially Lan, but there's only so much they can say or do to console her.'

'Were you with him when he left?' Tom asked.

'The first time, yes. We all – that's me, John and Bob – left together. As I think you know, John has a cabin on one of the upper decks, and so we left him up there as we walked down the stairs to our cabins. He said he wanted to get some fresh air before he turned in. The storm had passed by then and the air was a lot fresher.'

'So he was still upstairs when you last saw him?'

'He was, yes, but apparently, according to some of the others, he then went back into the bar and ordered another drink.'

'Do you know who else was in the bar when he returned?'

'According to what Joany was told, apart from a couple of the crew, the guys from our old company and Brett, Don's son, were there. Oh, and Tony, your buddy, was also there. I heard that John left soon after 2am. As far as I know, that's the last time anyone saw him.'

'So you weren't there?' asked Tom.

'No. I'd already decided to turn in,' he answered.

Like John, Tony had had a lot to drink. That had been quite obvious when, earlier in the evening, he had been singing. If he had then, later, gone to the bar, that would only have added to his condition. In addition, and presumably relatedly, Sue and Tony had not been seen since the early morning announcement, as they had immediately returned to their cabin.

Everyone fell silent, each with their own thoughts relating to John's disappearance. Finally, Jim broke the silence. 'I can't believe he's gone,' he said, a few tears now appearing on his cheeks. 'Who would have thought this would be the way he would go, especially after surviving everything he'd gone through in this country?'

'What do you think happened to him?' asked Tom, in a quiet, respectful tone.

'I don't know,' he replied. 'Maybe he slipped and fell and ended up going over the side. That's what everyone seems to think. You might have noticed how, like the rest of us, he'd had a lot to drink last night, even before he went back into the bar. Anyway, I'm sure the police will soon be able to tell us.' He added, in a much quieter voice, 'I just hope it was a quick ending.'

He leant against the ship's rail and stared across the river.

After a short period of this strained silence, Tom began to speak. 'Earlier, just before the music restarted, Tony and I came onto the upper deck. We heard some shouting coming from the bar, as if there was an argument going on. Were you there when it was happening?'

Jim looked at him with a hint of suspicion on his face before answering. 'It wasn't really an argument. Just some of the guys getting a bit rowdy. A lot of people had drunk quite a lot, even by then.'

'So who was there?' asked Tom.

'Mainly the guys from our old company.' Before Tom could ask anything else, Jim said, 'Anyway, I must go. I want to be with Joany and the others.'

After he had left, Mary turned to face Tom and said, in her most disapproving tone. 'Did you have to ask Jim those questions? The poor man has just lost one of his best friends. It was almost as if you were interrogating him.' Before Tom could respond, she continued, her earlier critical tone now absent. 'Do you think we should go and see how Sue and Tony are? We didn't get the chance to speak with them this morning.' Sue and Tony had arrived in the lounge just as Lan was beginning to speak, and so had stayed near the entrance to the lounge and then disappeared immediately afterwards.

'I was just thinking that myself.'

A short while later, and Mary was knocking on Sue and Tony's cabin door. Sue opened it, and it was immediately obvious that she had recently been upset about something. Her eyes were red, with dark shadows beneath, and her face a bit blotchy, suggesting a lack of undisturbed sleep.

'We were just wondering if you were both okay,' said Mary. 'You left straight after the meeting this morning.'

'We were both still tired,' Sue answered. 'It was a late night.'

'Is Tony okay?' Tom asked.

'He's out on the veranda. Why don't you come in?' Sue asked.

She led them through the cabin and out onto the veranda. It was tight, with four of them there, and so Tom and Mary remained standing.

'How are you?' asked Tom.

'I've felt better, that's for sure,' Tony replied, a cup of black coffee on the small table in front of him. He then turned to face them, revealing a nasty-looking cut on his right cheek and a swelling above his right eye.

'Looks like you've been in the wars,' said Tom. 'They look quite nasty.'

Tony touched his cheek. 'I've had worse.'

'How did you do it?' asked Mary.

'I must have bumped into something and then stumbled when I was coming back to the cabin last night. I'd had a skinful and must have lost my footing. To be honest, though, I can't remember.'

'He was in a right state when he got back here,' Sue suddenly said, with no sympathy apparent in her voice. 'I told him it was time to leave but, no, he insisted on going to the bar to carry on drinking. God knows how many he'd had.'

Tony didn't respond, although it was unclear if this was because he'd accepted what Sue had said or simply thought it was a battle he was never going to win.

'So what time did you get back?' asked Tom.

Tony simply shrugged his shoulders. It was left to Sue to provide the answer. 'It was seventeen minutes past two, according to my phone. He woke me when he was trying to unlock the door. I had to get out of bed to let him in. I could see he was in a state, but I just left him to get on with it. He suddenly made a noise and then tripped and fell against the wardrobe. I put the light on, and that's when I checked the time. I couldn't get any sense out of him then, so I pushed him to his side of the bed and left him there, still fully clothed. You can see where he slept.' She pointed at the bed. 'There's some blood from his face on the pillow.'

'Sorry,' said Tony, genuine contrition in his voice. 'I haven't been like that for a long time. It must have been the shots we were drinking in the bar. I vaguely remember having a drinking competition with some of the others there. I can't even remember who won.'

'Who was there with you?' asked Tom.

Tony looked at him with a hint of suspicion. 'Why all the questions?' he asked, a degree of tetchiness now apparent in his voice. 'You're not on duty now.'

'It's just that Jim told me how a few people, including you and John, were all there together, and that John left after 2 am. I was just wondering if you saw John leave, that's all.'

'I can't even remember me leaving, never mind anyone else,' Tony answered, clearly unable or unwilling to provide any meaningful information. 'I don't even know how I found my way back here.'

'What's the latest news on John?' Sue asked, either out of genuine interest or simply because she wanted to move away from a conversation she felt was starting to get a bit strained.

It was Mary who provided them with the latest update, after which she and Tom left the cabin.

'Tony was a bit rude, don't you think?' Mary asked. 'After all, we were only trying to help.'

'It's just his personality, that's all,' answered Tom, downplaying any possible hostility. 'I think he's the type of person who doesn't like to be checked up on. Can't say that I blame him.' Somewhere at the back of his mind, though, his well-honed copper's antenna was starting to spring into life.

Chapter 27

Later that day, Tom and Mary were on their veranda. The ship had arrived at its rescheduled destination a couple of hours earlier and been stationary since then. Mary was once again concentrating on completing a crossword puzzle whilst Tom was reading his book about Vietnam. Suddenly this peaceful scene was interrupted by the intrusive sound of someone pressing their cabin doorbell.

Mary went to see who it was, and when she opened the door she was confronted by a very distraught Sue.

'They've arrested Tony,' Sue burst out.

Mary quickly ushered her into their cabin and sat her down on the edge of the bed.

'They say he murdered John, and I don't know where they are taking him,' Sue managed to say, between deep sobs.

'Why did they say that?' asked Tom, having now joined them in the cabin.

'Apparently, it's on CCTV. Tony was seen fighting with John at the side of the ship, and so the police have arrested him.'

Mary put her arm around Sue and tried to offer some words of comfort. 'I'm sure it's a mistake and he'll soon be released.' She looked at Tom and, with a nod of her head, said, 'Why don't you go and see what you can find out?'

Tom looked suspiciously at Mary before heading for the cabin door. 'I'll see what I can find out,' he said, without any great enthusiasm.

Tom knew that, with a murder investigation ongoing, particularly one which had only just started, it would be very difficult to obtain any hard information. As he made his way to the upper deck, he could see that parts of it had already been cordoned off and a couple of forensic officers were there, concentrating their attention on a section of the railings on the port side of the ship. He could also see that the bar was now out of bounds. Those guests who were in the area were on the starboard side, mostly standing together in small groups. One or two were even trying to record what was happening on video. Tom could see Jim amongst one of the groups.

'Have you heard?' Jim demanded, in an uncharacteristically aggressive tone. 'Your buddy has been arrested. They think he killed John.'

'Do you know what evidence they have?' Tom asked. 'I understand there's some CCTV footage.'

'Apparently so, although I probably only know as much as you do.' There was rising anger in his voice. 'I thought you were going to speak with him and ask him to back off.'

Tom could sense that, if he wasn't careful, this could rapidly develop into a blame game. 'I did,' he simply replied, feeling it unnecessary to add anything else.

After a few seconds Jim spoke again, this time in his normal, non-belligerent tone. 'I'm sorry. I didn't mean to blame you. It's just that I'm still struggling to come to terms with him not being around any more. We go back a long way.'

'I know you do. It must be difficult for everyone who knew him,' replied Tom, as sympathetically as possible.

Just then Lan appeared at the top of the upper stairs and turned to walk by them.

'Lan?' asked Tom, turning to face him. 'Do you have a minute? I'm sure you are fully occupied, but I need to ask you something regarding Mr Young's arrest.'

Lan stopped in front of them. 'How can I help?' he asked, in a surprisingly stress-free tone of voice, given the circumstances.

'As I'm sure you can imagine, Mr Young's wife is extremely worried. She doesn't know what's happened to her husband, other than that he's been arrested, or even where he is now. Are you able to tell me so that I can let her know?'

'I'm afraid he's been arrested on suspicion of murder,' Lan confirmed. 'The police have taken him to the local station. He'll be held there until the national police arrive from Ho

Chi Minh City. I guess then he'll be taken there for further questioning.'

'What's the procedure regarding him having legal representation?' asked Tom.

'I believe the British consulate there have already been contacted. My understanding is that they will visit him when he arrives.'

'Do you know when his wife will be able to see him?'

'We've already passed Mr and Mrs Young's full details to the police, including their passports. They will liaise with the consulate and then contact us as soon as they can. I'm afraid I won't have any more information until that happens. When it does, we will arrange for Mrs Young's transfer to Ho Chi Minh City.'

'Thank you,' Tom replied, impressed by the sympathetic and efficient way Lan was handling the situation. 'Do you know if a body has been found yet?'

'Not as far as I know,' Lan answered. 'Although it is still early in the search.'

Lan then explained that, once John's disappearance had been reported by his wife, and after the subsequent onboard search had failed to find him, the Mekong River authorities had been alerted and a search of the river had commenced at first light. 'Losing someone in the Mekong is not that unusual. This is the first time, as far as I know, it's happened on one of our ships, but losing fishermen or those working on the dredging rigs and barges is quite common. The river authorities, therefore, have lots of experience in rapidly carrying out the searches. They know where the main channels and eddies are for each part of the river and are able to focus their searches there first.' He quickly followed this up. 'I'm sorry, but I have to leave now to go to a meeting involving the captain and the local police chief. I'll be speaking to all our guests sometime after that.'

'Just before you go, Lan, one other quick question, if you don't mind.' Tom immediately went on, not giving Lan the opportunity to leave. 'What, in the meantime, now happens to Mrs Young? Does she have to stay on board in her cabin? I assume, at some point, the local police will want to talk to her.'

'I'm sorry, Mr Stone, but I'm not able to answer those questions yet. We will, of course, make sure she receives her meals, and anything else she needs, but I just don't know the answers to your questions beyond that. I will find out, though, and let you know. I'm sorry,' he added, this time with a greater degree of urgency and assertiveness, 'I really do have to go now.'

After Lan had left, Tom turned his attention back to Jim. 'Do you know exactly who was in the bar with John, just before he disappeared?'

'I've told you this already,' Jim replied, a bit testily, before answering in a very deliberate manner. 'I'm not one hundred percent sure, as I wasn't there, but from what Joany was told it was John, Brett – the son of the captured pilot – Gene and Bill from our old company, and, of course, your buddy. Sang, one of the tour guides, was also there. You'll need to talk to one of those who were there if you need any more information.'

They both remained silent for a short while before Jim spoke again. 'Anyway, why are you so interested? I know you were once a cop, but it's obvious what happened.'

Tom had learned, long ago, that things were rarely obvious where murder was involved.

Chapter 28

Milner was once again in Diana Fowler's flat.

'I had a call from social services first thing this morning,' Diana said. 'Someone is coming round to see me later today and help me fill in all the forms. She said I should be entitled to more than I'm getting and she'll make sure I get it quickly.'

'That's good,' he replied.

'Did you have anything to do with that? It seems strange this has happened almost straight after we met.'

'I simply spoke to someone I knew,' he answered. 'That's all.'

'Well, whatever it was you did, thanks for doing it. At least, hopefully, that's one thing I won't have to worry about.' She paused momentarily, before continuing. 'Sharnia, Daniel's mum, also called. She's coming round to see if she can help. She said it was you who told her that I was pregnant.'

Recognising that her tone had not been aggressive or confrontational, Milner felt confident enough to reply in a similar vein. 'I did. I'm sorry if that upset you, but I could see when we last met that you needed some help. Please don't take that the wrong way. You are a very good mum with Daryl, but, with a new baby on the way, you will need as much help as possible. Having spoken with her, I know Mrs Melton is only too happy to help. In fact, I got the impression she can't wait. I'm not an expert, but I've got a feeling it will help both of you.'

'You said you wanted to talk to me again. What is it you want?'

'I wanted to speak to you about DC John Shipley. I keep thinking about what you said when I was leaving, the last time I was here. You said I should take special care of myself. Could I ask you why you said that?'

Diana began to play with the thin chain she was wearing

around her neck, betraying her sudden nervousness. After a short while, in a quiet voice, she said, 'I shouldn't have said that, but I wanted to warn you.'

'Warn me about what?' asked Milner.

When she answered, it was in a much faster and more worrying manner. 'You don't know what you're getting into. The people who killed Daniel don't care who they kill. All they're bothered about is making money. If they think you're getting close to them, then they'll kill you as well.'

'But that's what might happen every day when you do the job I do. What's so different about them?'

Diana continued to look directly at him, but this time in a more pitying manner. 'You really don't know, do you?'

A strained silence followed, before Milner, now choosing to play his trump card, asked, 'Does the name Adrian Wolfe mean anything to you?'

He could see from her changed expression that she was startled by the mention of the name. Milner gave her a while for her to consider what she had just heard, before continuing. 'It's a code name I found in DC Shipley's files, which he used instead of using your name, Diana Fowler. He also used another code name, Lionel Tedman, instead of Daniel Melton. It looks, for some reason, like he was trying to protect your real identities. Why would he do that?'

'Oh, my God,' she said, genuine fear now in her voice. 'Which other police officers know?'

'No one. It's just me,' he answered, trying to offer her some reassurance.

'Are you sure?' she asked, her right hand now visibly shaking.

'I'm certain. I'm the only one,' he answered, judging it prudent not to mention how DCI Stone had provided him with the key to the code names. 'Can you tell me why DC Shipley was protecting your names?'

There followed an extended period of silence, which Milner, perhaps a little unkindly, was determined not to break. He could see that Diana was in a state of mental turmoil as she tried to work out the consequences of what

Milner had just told her. Nonetheless, he suspected this was his best, and possibly only, chance to make a significant breakthrough, so he was determined not to waste the opportunity.

It was almost as though she took a deep breath before finally saying, albeit somewhat cryptically, 'We were giving him bits of information.'

'Do you mean you and Daniel were passing on information to DC Shipley?' Milner asked.

She nodded. 'That's right. Although it was mainly Daniel who did it, as he knew what was happening.'

Suddenly a raft of additional questions were now bouncing around in Milner's head. Nonetheless, he knew the importance of asking the most important questions, without scaring Diana to the point where she refused to answer any more. If he overloaded her with follow-up questions, given her current state of mind, it was highly likely she would simply refuse to answer any of them. Eventually he settled on, 'What type of information was he passing on?'

'The names of some of the dealers and where their drugs were kept. That sort of stuff.'

'But why would he do that?' Milner asked, struggling to fully take in what he was hearing.

'We were scared. We had a new baby and we wanted to get away from all of this. I told Daniel, if he didn't stop what he was doing, I'd leave and take Daryl with me.' She fell briefly silent before carrying on, in a heightened manner. 'But Daniel wanted Clinton to get out of it as well, and Clinton didn't want to. He's young and likes the lifestyle and glamour you get being in a gang as big as the Westie Crew, and the clothes and shoes. I told Daniel it was too risky to involve Clinton, but he just said he had to as he knew his mum was really worried about what might happen to him if he mixed with others in the gang.'

'That must have been really scary for you both, especially after Clinton refused to go along with you.'

'That's why I didn't want him to say anything to Clinton.' She suddenly began to quietly sob. After a short while her sobbing had abated, and she was able to continue. 'And Daniel would still be alive.'

'So, what made you go to DC Shipley?' asked Milner, desperate now to know what the connection was.

'I knew John from school,' she answered, and Milner tried to hide his amazement. 'We weren't in the same year – he was a year older than me. We sort of dated for a while. Nothing serious, just more like hanging out together. We lost contact after school, but I could see on his Facebook page that he'd joined the police. After Daryl was born, and I'd told Daniel that we'd leave him unless he got out, he said he'd get out. I thought John might be able to help us. It was then that I messaged him and we met up.'

'When was this?' Milner asked.

'About six months ago,' she answered. 'At first it was just me who met him, as Daniel was scared that he might be seen with a cop. Then, after we'd met a couple of times, Daniel went with me as well. But soon after that he started to get nervous again and didn't want to carry on. He said, if they found out he was talking to the police, they'd kill him. But I persuaded him to carry on.' She broke off abruptly, unable to continue. Her silence was more telling than any additional words.

Milner suddenly, and not for the first time since they'd first met, felt an overwhelming sense of both pity and compassion towards her. He was struggling to come to terms with how someone who had only tried to do the right thing for her family was now suffering so terribly. 'What did DC Shipley say to try and reassure you both?'

'Daniel was worried about Clinton and what he'd got into. John promised to let Daniel know if a drugs bust was planned, so that he could keep Clinton away from it. But when Daniel told Clinton to stay away, he just wasn't interested, and it just made him more suspicious. He kept asking Daniel how he knew when to expect a bust. As I said, he'd got too used to the lifestyle by then. That's when I knew it was dangerous for us.'

'So Clinton didn't know about DC Shipley and where the drugs bust information was coming from? Is that right?'

'Daniel said he didn't, but I don't think he was telling me the truth – probably so I wouldn't get scared.'

'You mean Daniel might have told him about DC Shipley.'

Diana nodded her head in agreement. 'They were brothers, after all. I think Daniel might have bigged up his relationship with John so as to impress Clinton.'

Milner had not intended to raise the nature of DC Shipley's death with her, but, given what he'd just learned about their relationship, it now seemed the most opportune time. 'Do you know why DC Shipley would kill himself? It's said he was on the payroll of the Westie Crew gang and was passing important information to them in return for drugs and cash, and that he was a user himself.'

Diana looked at him with a mixture of incredulity and shock. 'John wasn't on the take, and he definitely wasn't a user. He was murdered by the gang, and it was set up to look like suicide. I've told you. They will do anything, including killing a cop.'

Chapter 29

After Diana's shocking revelation, Milner was suddenly totally lost for words, trying to process what he'd just been told. Given what he knew – or, at least, thought he knew – about DC Shipley's death, this had come as a bolt out of the blue. If it was true, and at the moment the accusation was based only upon the word of the partner of a career criminal, then this would have a seismic effect on Operation Deliverance. It would negate or compromise almost everything that had so far been achieved.

Eventually Milner's usual equanimity returned, and he was able to articulate some follow-up questions. He started with the most obvious one. 'How do you know this? It's not the sort of information that is widely shared.'

'Daniel told me. The Westie Crew had somehow found out that someone in the gang was an informer. The message then came back from the top men to kill John and make it look as though he'd died from a drugs overdose. They also placed cash and drugs in his house to make it seem he was on the take.' She fell briefly silent. 'That's why I warned you. If they can do that to John, then they can also do it to you.' She paused momentarily before adding, 'And me.'

'Did Daniel say why he thought they'd found out?'

'Clinton had told him. He'd heard rumours from another gang member who was in contact with one of the top men. Clinton also told Daniel they had someone on the payroll who was a police officer, working in the same team as John. I've told you, these people will stop at nothing to keep what they've got.' She then added, with genuine concern for his safety, 'If I was you, I wouldn't tell anyone what I've just said. Don't trust anyone.'

If Milner's brain had previously been working overtime, it was now in danger of complete overload. Outwardly, he tried to maintain an air of calm and composure. Inwardly, though, he suddenly felt a deep, leaden sickness in the pit of his stomach. Within a very short time, he had first heard how DC Shipley, the officer whose role he had taken over, had been murdered and totally discredited, and now he'd been told there was an informer within the Operation Deliverance team. According to Diana, someone in the team was on the payroll of the Westie Crew and passing high-level operational information to them.

If all these things weren't bad enough, there was also now the small issue of his personal safety. He didn't for one moment doubt that, if they had to, the gang would have absolutely no qualms about murdering him as well.

'I'm sorry to ask you this, because I know how painful it must be for you, but I have to ask.' He hesitated briefly, trying to interpret Diana's facial expression before continuing. 'Do you know who killed DC Shipley?'

'Someone from the Westie Crew,' she answered. 'Isn't that obvious? Daniel thought it was someone who was close to the gang leaders, but he didn't know who.'

'Did he tell you who the gang leaders were?' Milner asked.

'Don't you even know that?' she asked, as though it were common knowledge. 'It's the Shehu family.'

When Milner didn't immediately respond, she went on. 'Then they somehow found out that Daniel had become an informer. They tricked him into meeting with them and then killed him as well.' She began to cry again, with real grief and anguish, but somehow she still managed to say, 'But they didn't just kill him, did they? They tortured him and then just left him lying there like a piece of meat.'

Despite having more questions to ask, Milner just couldn't bring himself to do so. In any case, he desperately needed time to process everything Diana had told him.

Eventually, though, she had composed herself enough to say, 'I think you need to go now. I've already told you more than I should have. I don't trust the police no more. You seem a nice man, but so was John, and look what happened to him. I don't think we should meet any more. It's too dangerous.

I've told you, if they find out I've been talking to a police officer then they will kill me as well.'

Milner stood up and walked towards the door before turning back to face her. 'I know how difficult it must have been for you to tell me all of that, and I appreciate your concern for me, but it's the job I've chosen. I'm sure it's no consolation, but I think you have been incredibly brave.' He continued, in an almost pleading voice, 'Just promise me that you will contact me if you need any help, day or night. I think it's the least I can do for you and Daryl.'

After he'd left, he just couldn't face going back to the station. He needed more time alone to reflect on, and try to make sense of, everything he'd been told, especially Diana's impassioned warning about his safety. DCI Stone's comment when they had last met up, about taking care of himself, suddenly seemed extremely prescient.

As this came back to Milner, he realised that he desperately needed someone to discuss all of this with. Someone who he could totally trust, and there was only one person he knew who could provide that.

Chapter 30

After his impromptu discussion with Lan, Tom returned to Sue and Tony's cabin in order to update Sue. When he knocked on their door it was Mary who opened it, whilst Sue was seated outside on the veranda.

'Did you find out anything?' Mary asked him, almost whispering.

'A bit,' he replied. 'It's probably best if I tell you both at the same time.'

Sue had now stood up and stepped back into the cabin. 'What's happening, Tom?' she asked, concern etched on her face. 'Can I see Tony?'

Tom recounted his brief conversation with Lan and how Tony was now being held at the local police station, waiting to be transferred to Ho Chi Minh City.

'So does that mean I can't visit him?' Sue immediately asked, her voice heightened with fear and anxiety.

'I think the best time will be when Tony has been transferred. The British consulate have been notified and are likely to contact you as soon as they have seen Tony. In the meantime, though, I'm afraid it's just a case of waiting until that happens.'

He could see that his attempt to break the news to her as painlessly as possible had only partly worked, as she now began to quietly cry once again. What he was about to tell her next was hardly likely to decrease her apprehension and anxiety levels. Nonetheless, he judged now was probably the best time. Sometimes, he thought, it was better to get all the bad news out of the way in one go.

'There is one other thing, Sue, which you should be prepared for. It's highly likely, at some point, the police – either the local or national police – will want to speak with you. This is normal procedure in such situations, but I just wanted to forewarn you.'

As he'd predicted, this didn't help Sue's current state of mind. He also noticed how Mary had looked at him, her eyes narrowed, clearly wondering whether, at this particular time, it had been really necessary for him to tell her.

'But I can't tell them anything,' Sue cried out, 'except that Tony couldn't have done it. What am I supposed to say?'

'As I said, it's just procedure, that's all,' he replied as calmly as possible. 'Just tell them what you know.'

'We'll be with you. Won't we, Tom?' Mary suddenly announced.

Tom could sense that his involvement was now beyond the point where he could simply step back and allow the investigation to run its course. But, even if he wanted to, he knew Mary wouldn't let him. Her natural kindness and compassion, when mobilised, was a powerful emotional driving force.

'I hope so,' he answered, not wanting to promise something he subsequently wouldn't able to fulfil. 'We will have a better idea when the consulate contacts you.'

'That's very kind of you. But that will spoil your holiday,' Sue answered, still quietly sobbing.

'That's not important,' Mary said, taking hold of Sue's hand.

'I don't know what I would do without you two,' she said.

'What's important is that we are here for you and Tony. Isn't it, Tom?'

Before he could answer, however, the cabin's announcement Tannoy sounded, and this was quickly followed by Lan's distinctive voice. 'Ladies and gentlemen, could you please assemble in the lounge in fifteen minutes' time? I would like to update you on what is happening regarding the rest of the scheduled itinerary. Please make your way to the lounge. Thank you.'

'Oh my God,' Sue exclaimed. 'He's going to tell everyone. They will all know Tony has been arrested for murder.'

Mary put her arm around Sue, trying to console her. 'You don't need to go. I'll stay here with you whilst Tom goes.'

In a way, this was a relief to him. Whilst the cabin was perfectly comfortable for two people, it was a bit claustrophobic when three people were in it, and, anyway, there wasn't much else he could tell Sue which might provide her with any comfort, let alone any cause for optimism.

Tom made his way to the lounge, where most of the available seats were already taken. He decided to stand, and so walked to the side of the room, where he could get a better view. He noticed that there was a definite divide between the Brits and the Americans, and any previous fraternising was now absent. He also noticed that Joany, Bob and Ruth were not in the room.

As with the previous meeting, when they all had been called to assemble, the ship's captain was standing alongside Lan. This time, though, there was one new addition, as a police officer had taken his place beside them.

With his usual punctuality, Lan began to speak exactly fifteen minutes after he'd made his announcement. 'Thank you for getting here on time. When I spoke to you last time, I informed you how one of our guests, Mr John Fisher, had not returned to his cabin, and that we were carrying out a search for him.' He paused briefly, suggesting he wasn't about to impart any good news. 'I'm sorry to have to tell you that the Mekong River authorities, earlier this afternoon, retrieved the body of a man. It has not been officially confirmed as that of Mr Fisher, but that is the assumption. Formal identification is happening right now.' It was easy to assume that John's wife, Joany, was the person identifying the body, explaining her absence.

There was an audible gasp, followed by a general increase in noise levels within the room. Lan waited patiently and then finally held up his hand for silence.

'I'm afraid I also have to tell you his death is now being treated as murder.'

Even though the news of Tony's arrest on suspicion of murder had quickly spread throughout the ship, it was still a huge shock, and made a bigger impact when communicated in this more formal manner. Predictably, the raised noise levels instantly returned. The noise now, though, was interspersed with some of the guests shouting out questions.

Lan simply ignored them and waited for the general din to subside, before he resumed speaking. 'I understand you want to know what is happening, and so, if you please give me the chance, I will tell you what I know.'

The room was suddenly completely silent, and Tom realised just how impressive Lan was, especially in his ability to retain an assertive but cool head, despite the seriousness of the situation and the undoubted pressure he was under.

'Thank you,' said Lan. 'You will see that we have a senior police officer with us. Captain Bao Ninh has been leading the investigation ever since Mr Fisher was reported missing. But this is now a murder inquiry, and so, until further notice, this ship is now classified as a murder scene. This means that, unless it is specifically agreed with Captain Bao Ninh, no one is allowed to leave.'

This time his words resulted in an immediate uproar, with many in the room shouting, all at the same time. Some people had stood up to make their voices heard, and there was a noticeable and worrying increase in raw anger within the room.

Lan, in his usual calm, phlegmatic manner, remained impassive, waiting for the anger to burn itself out. Finally, when he considered that point to have arrived, he held up both hands. 'At the moment, we don't know how long that will be the case. It's probable that the police will need to take statements from some of you.' Before anyone could respond, he quickly carried on. 'This is exactly what would happen in your own countries. What is different, of course, is that the deceased died in a foreign country. For that reason, the US consulate general in Ho Chi Minh City has already been notified, and their representative is currently on their way here. In the meantime, and I know this will be difficult, I suggest you continue to use the ship's facilities. Meals will be available at the usual times, although, out of respect, all onboard entertainment has been cancelled and parts of the sun deck bar closed.' He waited for that to sink in before continuing. 'Rest assured we are doing everything possible to speed up the process, but, as you will understand, a lot of things are out of our control. I will, of course, continue to update you as soon as I have any new information.'

The earlier chaos having completely disappeared, Lan judged that he could now take a few questions. Most questions that were asked related to practical issues, such as medication availability, missed return flights and potential refunds, and he provided reassuring answers as best he could.

Once the meeting had finished and Tom was making his way out of the lounge, he noticed Jim heading towards him.

'Can I have a quick word?' Jim asked quietly. 'Probably best if it's somewhere a bit more private.'

Jim's body language, together with the tone of his voice, immediately increased Tom's sense of foreboding.

When they were out of earshot of everyone, Jim said, 'I just thought I should warn you. A few of the guys are getting very angry about John's death and are looking for someone to blame. In Tony's absence, I'm afraid that someone is you.'

Chapter 31

As Tom returned to Sue's cabin, he could only wonder just how things had turned out this way. What was supposed to have been an enjoyable, relaxing post-retirement holiday, where he and Mary could share some quality time together, had rapidly spiralled into anything but.

It only seemed like yesterday when they had first met John, sharing a beer alongside that bustling road in Hanoi City. Now John was dead and one of the other Brits on the trip, Tony, had been arrested on suspicion of his murder. Mary had taken it upon herself to provide what now increasingly seemed like continuous support and comfort to Tony's wife. Bit by bit, sometimes at Mary's behest, Tom had found himself being dragged deeper and deeper into all of this.

But, as if that wasn't enough to contend with, he now found himself to be the possible target of some type of revenge. He wasn't unduly worried about this, but, the way things had so far developed, he couldn't be absolutely certain and so would need to be extra careful.

After his return to the cabin, he recounted the basics of the meeting, although he did leave out just how much anger had been generated after Lan had confirmed John's murder. He also, mainly to protect Mary, did not mention Jim's subsequent warning.

'What do you think I should do?' asked Sue. 'I want to call our son and daughter to let them know what's happened, but I know that will just make them really worried. If I get upset, that will only make things worse for them.'

'Do you want one of us to call them?' suggested Mary. 'Tom could do it, Couldn't you, Tom?'

'I think it would be better if someone from the British consulate did it,' Tom said. 'That would be the normal procedure.'

'But they don't know anything about what's happened. They don't even know Sue and Tony,' said Mary. 'I think it would better if one of us did it.'

Whilst Mary had a point, Tom could see how doing this would involve him even more than he was already. Whilst he was still considering Mary's suggestion, the decision was made.

'Are you sure?' said Sue. 'That would really put my mind at rest. I really couldn't do it myself.'

There was another consideration which Tom had not mentioned. It was inevitable that the press would get hold of the story, especially given the circumstances of John's death, the exotic location and the nationalities of the people involved. No doubt the papers would have a field day thinking up their Poirotesque headlines. It would make sense for Tony and Sue's family to be forewarned about this.

A more personal concern suddenly hit him. It was equally inevitable that, given his high profile in the British media over the past couple of years, the press would quickly find out his own involvement and, no doubt, name him as being a friend of the suspected murderer. Ironic, really, he mused, allowing himself a wry smile. It would be almost as if the wheel had turned full circle. Notwithstanding this, he knew he was now committed and, anyway, Mary was right to try to do everything possible to help Sue, especially at a time when she most needed it.

'If you give me their number, I'll call them,' he said.

Sue took hold of her phone and opened up her contacts list. 'I think you should phone David first. He's usually at home today. Maybe he could let my daughter Gemma know.' She handed her phone to Tom, who, before he could change his mind, pressed the call button.

After a few rings, the phone was answered. 'Hello, David speaking.'

Tom introduced himself and, as succinctly as possible, and without any undue emotion, told David what had happen to Tony.

After the initial shock, predictably David started to ask lots of questions, and Tom did his best to answer them. He soon realised, however, that they were quickly moving into areas, relating to what might happen, where Tom didn't feel qualified to give answers, and besides he didn't want to offer David any false hope. After a while he felt as though he had done as much as he could and handed the phone back to Sue. Whilst Sue and her son were talking, he and Mary went out onto the veranda.

'I'm so proud of you,' Mary suddenly said, giving him an affectionate hug. 'You didn't have to do that.'

'What do you think we should do with Sue?' Tom asked. 'It's obvious she's struggling to cope with what's happening, and I suspect things will only get worse.'

'Yes, I've been thinking about that as well. Why don't I stay with her until we have a better idea of what's happening?'

Tom hadn't thought of that option and, whilst it wasn't something he would normally suggest, he did concede that there was a certain logic to it. 'Good idea,' he answered. 'Let's see what Sue thinks. She might feel she wants to be alone.'

'Really?' Mary asked, clearly doubting Tom's thinking. 'If it was me, I wouldn't want to be alone. I'd want to be able to talk to someone.'

Tom, resisting the urge to say that, if it were him, he would certainly want to be alone, simply said, 'Good point.'

They could hear Sue becoming increasingly upset as she spoke to her son. Finally, though, they heard her say, 'See you soon. Love you,' and then put her phone on the bed.

Tom and Mary took that as their cue to come back into the cabin, and Mary, not for the first time, put her arm around Sue, who was now quietly sobbing. It was at times like this that Tom realised just how fortunate he was to now have someone like Mary, who could read the situation and then provide this type of empathy and compassion when it was most needed.

As he didn't quite know what to do whilst this was happening, Tom stepped over towards the spot where, according to Sue, Tony had fallen when he had returned to their cabin. He took a closer look, and indeed could see what looked like dried blood on a part of the wardrobe. Instinctively, he took out his phone and took a couple of photos. He did the same where there was some blood on one of the pillows.

'I just need to do a couple of things,' he said, as Mary continued to comfort Sue. 'I'll be back soon.'

Mary looked at him suspiciously but didn't say anything.

He made his way to the upper deck, hoping to find Lan. He was in double luck, as Lan was there speaking with the police captain Bao Ninh.

'I know you are very busy,' Tom said, 'but I wanted to speak with you both, if that's okay?'

Lan translated for the police captain, who, although looking suspiciously at Tom, gave a quick nod of his head.

Tom quickly recounted what Sue had told him and Mary about the events when Tony had returned to their cabin. How he had fallen against the wardrobe, injuring his face, and how there were bloodstains still on the wardrobe and the bed. After he had finished, the police officer said something in response.

'He asks why are you telling him this and what is it you want?' said Lan.

'Mr Young has been arrested on suspicion of murder, and I understand this ship is a potential crime scene. I think the blood in his cabin should be analysed to confirm it's his, and not anyone else's, before it degrades or is cleaned away.'

Once again Lan translated. When the captain responded, he was now visibly agitated and speaking noticeably quicker than previously. After he had finished speaking, the captain immediately turned around and walked away, towards the side of the ship that had been cordoned off.

'I guess he was not happy with my advice,' suggested Tom, not even waiting for Lan to translate.

'More or less,' answered Lan. 'Basically, he said this was a job for the police, not a foreign tourist. Sorry.'

'Thank you, though, for asking him anyway,' said Tom, wondering briefly if he could have handled the situation more diplomatically. It was now apparent he was unlikely to get much cooperation from the police captain. 'Is Mr Young still being held by the local police?'

'Actually, he is now on his way to Ho Chi Minh City. That was what Captain Bao Ninh was just telling me. I was just about to inform Mrs Young. Perhaps you could pass on the information to her. I will let her know when she can be transferred there to see her husband.' He then hesitated, and Tom, sensing there was something else he wanted to say, decided to help him.

'What is it? Is there anything else?'

'When Mr Fisher's body was found, it was obvious that he had been stabbed a number of times,' Lan replied. 'This means there can now be no doubt. It wasn't an accident. Mr Fisher was murdered.'

Lan's latest information completely stunned Tom, and he was almost unable to respond. In the event, he didn't need to, as Lan immediately carried on.

'This means the *Mekong Voyager* is now officially a murder scene. Captain Bao Ninh was also informing me that he will be commencing the interviews of those people he feels are the most important witnesses. They include Mrs Young. I believe this will happen later today, before she is allowed to travel to see her husband.'

'I will pass on that information to her. I think it will be better coming from someone she knows.' Even as he said this, Tom realised how they had only met less than a week before, but here he was talking as though they'd known each other for years. 'Thank you, Lan, for all your help. I know Mrs Young is very appreciative. I'm sure you must be under a lot of pressure.'

'Thank you. Yes, not just me but the whole crew,' he replied. 'But it's when things go wrong that we all earn our pay. It's easy when everything is going well.'

Tom took this as his cue to let Lan go. Just as he was leaving to head back to Sue and Tony's cabin, he spotted Brett emerging onto the upper deck.

'How is your father?' asked Tom. 'All of this delay must be quite unsettling for him.'

'He's fine, all things considered,' Brett said. 'Our main concern is to ensure he has enough medication. We only brought enough for the trip, plus a few extra days, but Lan has been very helpful and has arranged for more to be delivered to the ship for him.'

'Do you mind if I ask you a question?' said Tom.

'Sure. Go ahead,' he replied, in a laidback manner that struck Tom as typically American.

'I understand you were in the bar with a few others, including John, on the night he died. I was a bit surprised to hear that, given what you'd previously told me about how there was no love lost between soldiers and pilots.'

'Yes, I was. It surprised me as well. I couldn't sleep and decided to go up on deck. When I got there, I could hear there were some people still in the bar. I looked in and they called me over to join them. I knew instantly how that was likely to be a mistake. It's always uncomfortable when you're the only sober person among a group who've had a lot to drink, and I could straightaway tell they'd all had more than a few. To be honest, I didn't feel I could say no.'

'Who was there?' Tom asked.

'Just a few of the guys. Gene and Bill were there, along with Tony, the Brit, Sang, and of course John.'

'Tony mentioned something about a drinking contest. Were you there when it happened?'

'I sure was. To begin with, it was lots of drunken toasts, but then someone mentioned a drinking contest and there was no stopping them then. For old guys, they were really going at it, drinking bourbon, and they kept asking the barman to bring them more and, after that, different drinks – some of them quite exotic-sounding ones – until they couldn't drink any more. I took a few photos and a video, to show them when they'd all sobered up, but ... well, somehow it didn't seem right after John's death.'

'Sounds like you managed to avoid the drinking competition. That was a piece of luck,' said Tom.

'As I said, by the time I got there they were all well into it anyway,' he answered. 'Not that I could have kept up with them. I got the impression, though, that earlier there had been some strong words between a few of them, and the toasting was a sort of kiss-and-make-up.'

For a brief moment Tom remained silent before asking, 'Can you remember what time everyone left the bar?'

Brett's eyes narrowed slightly, a hint of suspicion on his face as he looked at Tom. 'Why all the questions? Pops said you were a retired cop.'

'I guess that's what thirty years as a detective does to you. You just can't get it out of your system.' Tom said this in as lighthearted a manner as possible, hoping it would help to reassure Brett that his question was no more than natural professional curiosity.

It appeared to have succeeded, as Brett began to provide some details. 'I'll tell you what I just told that police captain. I can't be one hundred percent certain, because I left before some of them. But I'm pretty sure that Gene left first. That must have been a few minutes after 2am. Next to leave was Bill, a few minutes later, and then I left a couple of minutes after him. You could ask the tour guide, Sang, as he was still there when I left.'

'Did you hear anything that Tony was saying?' Tom asked.

Brett considered his question for a short while before answering. 'It was difficult because, as I said, he was quite drunk by the time I got there.' He hesitated briefly. 'Also, to be frank, I couldn't make out what he was saying anyway. He has such a strong accent.'

Tom, inwardly smiling, and resisting the urge to try to explain the Yorkshire accent, instead just said, 'I appreciate your openness. And thanks again for indulging me.'

'No problem. As they say, once a cop, always a cop.'

Tom began to walk away but suddenly turned back to face Brett. 'Sorry, one last thing. You mentioned you took a couple of photos and a video. Would it be possible to send them to me?'

The earlier look of suspicion suddenly reappeared on Brett's face, but, after the briefest of hesitations, he said, 'I guess so. What's your cell phone number?'

Chapter 32

Not for the first time that day, Tom returned to update Sue and Mary, although he deliberately didn't mention that John had been stabbed. He then tried to ease Sue's concerns regarding her impending police interview.

'But what if I get Tony into more trouble?' she asked, clearly not entirely calmed by Tom's words.

'All you have to do is to tell the truth, that's all,' he replied, realising as he spoke that it would be difficult for Tony to be in any more trouble than he was in right now.

'Will you be there with me?' she almost pleaded.

Both Sue and Mary were now looking intently at Tom, waiting for his response. Although he wasn't exactly sure whether it would be possible, he nonetheless tried to sound positive and reassuring when he answered, 'Of course, if that's what you want, although I will have to confirm with the police if it's allowed.'

Both of them seemed to be content with his reply, as neither of them asked any follow-up questions. Instead, it was left to Mary to update him on developments whilst he'd been away from the cabin.

'Sue's son David called back to say he'd already booked a flight and is hoping to be in Ho Chi Minh City sometime later tomorrow. So at least Sue will have some family with her then.' She turned to face Sue, reached out and took hold of her hand. 'I've also mentioned that I'm happy to stay with her as long as she wants me to.'

'That's good. At least you won't be by yourself,' Tom said, trying to reinforce Mary's practical suggestion.

Sue, though, once again tried to seek reassurance from Tom. 'You do think Tony will be released, don't you?' she said, almost pleading for his confirmation.

'I'm sure he will,' he replied, considering that any other

response would be counterproductive, given Sue's already very fragile state of mind.

'I still can't believe he would have done that,' Sue said. 'I know he can be a bit bolshie at times, but he would never murder someone.'

'If it's any consolation, that's exactly how I feel as well,' Tom answered, once again trying to reassure her.

There followed a brief period of silence, and so Mary took this as her cue. 'I'll just go and get a few things first,' she said. 'I'll be back soon. Tom?'

Tom and Mary left Sue and went back to their cabin. As soon as they were there, Mary said, looking intently at Tom, 'It's bad, isn't it?'

He again chose not to mention the apparent cause of John's death. 'Well, all the evidence – such as it is – points to Tony being the person responsible. But, as far as I can see, the only real evidence they have is the CCTV footage, where he and John were allegedly having a fight. As I haven't seen it, I can only assume they are confident it is incriminating. Other than that, though, there doesn't seem to be anything else which would implicate him.'

'But what about their disagreements? You told me yourself how they'd had a couple of arguments in public.'

'That's true, but if everyone who'd had an argument with someone was accused of murder, the prisons would be more crowded than they already are.'

'So what are you going to do now?' she asked.

Tom, slightly startled and then annoyed by Mary's question, could only manage, 'What do you think I *can* do? I have absolutely no jurisdiction here. It wasn't too long ago you were complaining that I should forget everything about work, so that we could enjoy our time together. Now you seem to be encouraging me to get involved in a murder investigation over which I have no authority.'

An extended, strained silence followed before Mary spoke again. 'I'm sorry. I didn't mean it to come out that way. I know you're doing everything you can. It's just that I feel so helpless.'

Tom's earlier sharpness had now dissipated and he, too, realised that a little contrition was perhaps needed. 'You don't have to apologise. I shouldn't have been that sharp with you. I know you're only trying to help Sue and Tony.' He paused momentarily. 'The reality is, whether we want to be or not, we are now involved. For what's it's worth, until I'm presented with any irrefutable evidence to the contrary, I will continue to believe Tony is innocent. He can be a bit hotheaded at times, and isn't the type of person who naturally takes a backward step, but that doesn't make him a murderer.'

'What do you think will happen next?' Mary asked, now in her usual level tone.

'The forensics team will continue their work. How long that will take, and how extensive it becomes, is anyone's guess. Presumably a post-mortem will be carried out to determine the cause of death. The police will want to speak with other people here on the ship, especially those who were there with John in the bar. In the meantime, the national police in Ho Chi Minh City will start interviewing Tony.'

'Do you think they will be rough with him?' she suddenly asked, real concern and worry in her voice.

'I don't think things work that way here in Vietnam. Tough? Probably. Rough? Unlikely,' he answered. 'And anyway, knowing the little I do about him, I suspect Tony is not the type of person who is easily intimidated.'

Mary, now seemingly more assured, continued to put the things she'd selected into a small bag. 'What are you going to do for the rest of the day?' she asked as she was closing it.

'I'm not too sure what I'm going to do. I might see if I can have another word with Lan. He seems to know what's going on. If I get the opportunity, I'd also like to speak to a few of those who were in the bar. Anyway, keep your phone with you. If there's anything either of you needs, just call me.'

Mary leaned forward and kissed him on the cheek. 'Thanks for doing what you can, and I'm sorry again for getting at you earlier.'

'Just do what you can for Sue,' he replied. 'I think things are likely to get a bit worse before there is any chance of them getting better.'

After Mary had left, he poured himself a glass of wine, got his iPad, went outside and sat down. The sun was just setting, and he optimistically hoped that, together with the idyllic river setting, it might provide some much-needed inspiration or eureka moment.

He powered up the iPad and opened his emails. He could see that most were of an inconsequential nature, having somehow evaded his junk box. One, though, immediately stood out. It was from Milner and headed 'URGENT'. With increasing trepidation, he opened the email and quickly read it.

> *Sir,*
>
> *I apologise for disturbing you whilst you are on holiday. It's the very last thing I wanted to do, but, frankly, you are the only person I can trust. I have just received some information which, if true (and at the moment I have no reason to disbelieve it), would totally compromise Operation Deliverance in a shocking way. If you could call me when you get this message, that would be much appreciated.*
>
> *Regards,*
> *DC Milner*

Tom reread the email a couple times more, then placed his iPad on the table and took another sip of his wine.

His earlier comment to Mary, about things getting worse before they would get better, suddenly seemed particularly prophetic. Well, at least the first part.

Chapter 33

'Thanks for calling, sir,' said Milner. 'I'm really sorry for having to interrupt your holiday, but, as I said, you are the only person I can trust.'

After he had read Milner's email once more, Tom had immediately gone back inside, closed the doors to the veranda, and phoned Milner. Despite reading his email numerous times, he still didn't know what to expect. What he did know, however, was that it could only be bad news. Milner wasn't the type of person who would interrupt his former boss's holiday just to ask if he was enjoying himself.

'Well, I don't think I had a choice after the tone of your email,' Tom said. 'Why don't you take your time and tell me what has happened?' He quickly added, with a touch of concern, 'Where are you now?'

'I'm at home, sir. I couldn't go back to the station. I needed time to think.' He hesitated, as if trying to find the right words. Finally, he said, 'I just don't know what to do and, if I'm being totally honest, I'm now afraid for my own safety.'

Tom, sensing the rising tension in his voice, simply said, 'Why don't you take a deep breath and just slowly tell me?'

So Milner told him. He told him about how he'd first met with Diana and how she had ended his visit with a thinly veiled warning about his own safety, although, at the time, he hadn't given her warning much credence. After DCI Stone had informed him that the code names were anagrams of her and Daniel's names, he'd visited her again and confronted her with this new information, and it was then she had made some truly shocking allegations. For instance, that DC Shipley was not an informer for the Westie Crew, and had not committed suicide. He had, in fact, at least according to Daniel, been murdered to protect another unnamed police officer, who was the actual person providing key operational information to the gang. Then, as if this wasn't bad enough, Diana had given a far more overt and chilling warning that Milner should trust no one if he wanted to remain alive.

There followed a long period of silence, as Milner reflected on what he'd just said and Tom on what he'd just heard. Finally, it was Milner who broke the silence. 'Are you still there, sir?'

'I am, yes,' Tom answered, albeit in a subdued manner. 'Are you sure you trust her? After all, she is the partner of a known criminal, who had no love for any kind of authority.'

'I've asked myself that question repeatedly since she told me. I can only say, unless she is a great actress, then yes, I do believe her. To be honest, sir, I don't think I can afford not to believe her.'

Again, Tom didn't immediately respond, and Milner, knowing him as he did, had the good sense not to interrupt his silence. Eventually, Tom spoke again and, when he did, it was with some degree of assertiveness.

'I think the first thing you should do is document everything you've found out, when you found out, and the evidence to support it.' To emphasise the seriousness with which he was now taking this, he added, 'But make sure that none of this is recorded on anything that could be intercepted or retrieved. Ideally, that includes your own personal PC or laptop.' His mind was now totally focused on the problem. 'It's very important, though, that you try and act as normal as possible when you are around any other team members. Continue to follow up on some of the other leads you have. Ones which can't be directly linked with what you've just told me. Also – and I think this is the most important suggestion – at least for the next few days, resist the temptation to go back to see Diana. It's likely, at some stage, they will start watching her, trying to spot who she's meeting. As for who you can trust, I have a suggestion for you.'

'Who's that, sir?' asked Milner.

'Well, I don't personally know most of the others and so, for the moment, it's probably wise to exclude them. The only person who I do know personally, and can trust, would be DCI Shaw.'

This time it was Milner's turn to remain silent, and it was Tom who finally spoke. 'And one other thing. Make sure you keep a low profile and, more importantly, are very careful.'

Chapter 34

After his conversation with Milner, Tom sat back in his chair and reflected on their discussion. There was no doubt Milner was very worried about this dramatic turn of events. The fact he had asked Tom to call simply confirmed his level of concern.

To make matters worse, being so far away from what was happening just increased Tom's sense of helplessness. Although he was no longer part of the Met, he still had a strong feeling of personal loyalty to the service, and particularly towards Milner: a feeling which, to his great surprise, went beyond normal professionalism. They had only known one another for a few years, but, during that short period, Tom had found himself worrying about Milner's professional and personal wellbeing, and this had at times taken him outside his usual controlled emotional comfort zone.

In a way, albeit irrationally, he also felt he was personally responsible for placing Milner in this danger. If he'd been there, perhaps he would have been able to help Milner handle it in a different way, which would have increased his safety. Nonetheless, regardless of where he had been at the time, he understood that it would have been almost impossible to foresee how things had turned out.

The one comfort he had was knowing that DCI Shaw was a person who Milner could trust. Despite their initial disagreements and character differences, Tom knew that DCI Shaw was the best officer to provide Milner with the advice and protection he now needed.

It was at this moment that his attention was brought back to more immediate issues, as his phone suddenly beeped. It was a text from Brett and, when he opened it, he found a couple of photos and the video Brett had taken during his time in the bar. The first photo showed four men raising their glasses in a toast: John and Tony, plus who he now knew to be Gene and Bill from the other platoon. Brett's evocative photo perfectly captured the slightly drunk, almost childishly excited appearance of all the participants, even though they were over seventy years old. The other photo also included all four, although this one showed them having their glasses recharged by Huan, whilst Sang was seated behind them, looking on.

Tom opened the video and could straight away see and hear just how drunk they had actually been. He immediately played it again, trying to make out what was being said. Even after playing it for a third time, it proved to be almost impossible to understand what they were saying. He did notice that Tony had said something, but his exact words were lost against the general background noise, as everyone seemed to be speaking at the same time.

As Tom played the video for a final time it suddenly crossed his mind how, despite the apparent atmosphere of holiday bonhomie, one of those men would, just a few minutes later, be dead, whilst one of the others would be charged with his murder.

He closed the video and placed his phone on the bed. He suddenly had an idea, and so immediately picked up his phone again and started to scroll through his contacts list. Just as he'd finished doing this, his phone started to ring. He could see that it was Mary.

'Tom,' she said, without waiting for him to acknowledge it. 'Could you come here to Sue's cabin? There are some policemen here who want to ask her questions. They also want to carry out some investigations within the cabin and have already started taking away some of Tony's clothes. She's really upset.'

A few minutes later Tom was standing outside Sue's cabin, speaking via a new interpreter with Captain Bao Ninh, who was standing just inside the cabin, almost blocking the way in. The captain had confirmed that, whilst a full forensic investigation was being carried out in her cabin, Sue would be questioned in a private part of the ship which had been set up as a makeshift police HQ. In the meantime, Tom caught a glimpse of some officers bagging up what he assumed to be Tony's clothes.

'Is it possible for me to attend Mrs Young's interview?' Tom asked.

'I'm afraid not,' Captain Bao Ninh answered quickly. 'Mrs Young has voluntarily agreed to this. At this stage it is not an interview under caution.' With that he turned around and walked back into the cabin, making it instantly clear that their discussion was over.

Tom could see that Mary was starting to get quite upset, and so he suggested she leave the cabin so that they could head up to the top deck. Although it was now beginning to get dark, he felt a change of scenery might help her escape from the increasingly claustrophobic atmosphere of Sue and Tony's cabin. When they got to the deck, despite a surprising number of guests already being there, they managed to find a place that offered them the privacy they needed.

'I can't believe this is happening,' Mary suddenly said. 'It's like being in a nightmare.'

Tom didn't respond, mainly because he couldn't immediately think of anything to say that might offer her any reassurance. As far as he could see, there was very little, if any, potential good news.

Just then, Huan appeared in front of them. 'Can I please get you something to drink?' he asked in his usual friendly and courteous manner, smartly dressed in his company white polo shirt and black trousers.

'Yes, please,' said Mary. 'I'll have an orange juice.'

'And I'll have a coffee,' added Tom.

A short while later and Huan had returned with their drinks. As he took them off the tray and placed them on the table, Tom looked at him with increased interest, before asking, 'Huan, do you mind if I ask you a question regarding the day Mr Fisher died?'

Mary looked quizzically at Tom. 'I'm sure Huan would rather forget about that.'

Tom, ignoring Mary's comment, went on before she could

say anything else. 'I understand you were working in the bar that evening, when Mr Fisher and the others were there. Can you remember when he left?' In an attempt to help him, he quickly added, 'Was he the first or last to leave, and did he leave with anyone else or by himself?'

'I can't remember, sir. I think he was one of the last to leave, but I'm not certain. One of my jobs is to tidy the bar for the next day. I was busy doing that.'

'Do you remember what time that was?'

'No, sir, I don't. The police have already asked me those questions, and I have been asked not to discuss it with anyone else.'

'Thank you anyway,' said Tom, as Huan picked up the empty tray and headed towards another group of people.

'Did you have to ask him those questions?' asked Mary, clearly annoyed with him.

'Sorry,' said Tom. 'It's just that Huan was working when John, Tony and the others were there. I thought he might be able to help, that's all.'

'And did he?' she asked.

'I'm not sure he was able to tell me anything that I didn't already know.'

Chapter 35

Before either of them could continue with their conversation, they noticed that Jim had appeared and was making his way towards them.

'I was hoping I might find you,' he said. 'Do you mind if I join you?'

'Please do,' answered Mary, making room for him to sit alongside them.

Tom was tempted to ask him if he was here to issue another warning but, given Mary's presence, decided it would not be the cleverest thing to say; it would simply add to her already high anxiety levels.

Jim immediately began to speak. 'I just wanted to ask you something,' he said, before quickly adding, 'It's got nothing to do with John's death.' He continued, with growing excitement, 'Do you remember when I first met your friends Mike and Shelley, and they mentioned that they had originally lived in a place called Totnes? I told you all how Dad had been stationed somewhere around there just before D-Day, and how he had mentioned it many times over the years and had always said he wanted to go back to visit.'

'I do,' Tom answered, 'although I wouldn't describe us as friends. We'd only met a few days previously.'

Jim, shrugging off Tom's comment, and now with even more excitement in his voice, continued. 'I emailed my sister Peggy after our conversation, to ask her if she knew where exactly he had been based. It turns out he had been based in Totnes for about three months before the invasion. I thought it was there but wanted to double-check.'

'That is a real coincidence,' said Mary. 'It just goes to show what a small world it is.'

Tom remained silent, not really knowing where the conversation was heading. He didn't have to wait much longer for the answer.

'What my sister didn't know was that I found some letters, after he died, which hinted he had fathered a child during his time there,' Jim said. 'I never told Peggy about that. She knew he wanted to go back to visit but just thought it was because of the war.' He paused briefly. 'There was also a photo of him with a young woman, who had written the words, To Hank. All my love, Peggy. Hank was Dad's name. I have the photo at home, along with the letters. The woman looked a lot like Shelley to me.'

'Are you saying you think Shelley might be related to you?' Tom asked, his natural scepticism evident.

'Why not?' Jim answered, clearly not put off. 'You hear about these things all the time. Don't you remember Shelley mentioning how her grandmother had a baby when she was very young?'

'That's true, but it's a huge leap to then make the connection you are suggesting. What makes you think you and Shelley might be related? As far as I can see, there's no evidence at all, just a series of coincidences.'

'Strong coincidences, though. That's where I need your help,' he said, his enthusiasm still undiminished.

'My help?' Tom asked. 'I'm not sure I can do anything. As I said, we've only known Mike and Shelley for a few days.'

'But you're a cop. Surely you have contacts who can find things out. I don't want to approach them until I know for sure.'

'Just to remind you, Jim, I'm actually an ex-cop. I retired a few months ago. Why don't you hire someone who is a specialist?'

'I could, but I just wanted to see if you could help first.' He paused briefly, waiting for either of them to answer. When no reply was forthcoming, he tried again. 'Even if it's just having a word with them to see if you could find out anything else about that time. You never know, but they might have some of the letters Dad wrote to Peggy.' He then provided even more encouragement. 'And there's something else. The young woman in the photograph was called Peggy. Later, when he married and Mom and Dad had my sister, she was also named Peggy. Is that just another coincidence?'

Jim's silence suggested how he had now played all his main cards and was waiting for their answer.

Mary looked at Tom before saying, 'I'm sure there's something we could do. What do you think, Tom? You must know someone who could investigate?'

When he answered, it was in a less than enthusiastic tone. 'Obviously we can't promise anything and, anyway, it might not be the answer you are hoping for, but I'll speak with Mike and Shelley if that helps.'

Not for the first time on this holiday, he had found himself in a position where he had been given little choice but to agree to something that he didn't feel comfortable with. Mary's idea of a relaxing post-retirement holiday had now turned into anything but. The very last thing he would have expected, however, was that he had somehow agreed to become part of a historic paternity case.

Chapter 36

'Jim, while you're here, could I ask you something?'

As Jim had begun to walk away, Tom had stood and followed him. It was partly on impulse but also partly about seizing the moment. He suddenly knew this was as good a time as any to ask him something which had been bothering him almost from the first day, when they had all been seated on those small plastic chairs back in Hanoi.

Jim, accepting that he could hardly refuse, given what he had just asked Tom to do, immediately answered, 'Of course. Is here good?'

'Why don't we go and sit over there?' Tom suggested, pointing in the direction of an empty table, away from any of the other guests.

'What is it you want to ask?' Jim asked, after they were both seated. 'I'm guessing it's something to do with John's murder.' His tone became almost accusatory. 'All you seem to have done since then is ask questions. You are starting to get a reputation. Some people don't like what you're doing. They think you're needlessly interfering with the police investigation.'

'I'm just trying to understand what exactly happened that night, that's all,' Tom answered, as even-voiced as possible.

When Jim responded, this time it was in a far more considerate tone. 'Tom, I understand that Tony was your friend, and you are looking out for him, but that's the job of the Vietnamese police. As you told me just a few minutes ago, you are now an ex-cop. Why don't you just leave it to them?'

Tom collected his thoughts before he answered. 'That's all true, but what if I can provide the local police with information which would help speed up their investigation?' He fell silent momentarily before continuing. 'Look, to be honest with you, Jim, I do have my doubts about Tony being the person who murdered John, but that's all they are at the moment: just doubts. I have no hard evidence. Everything is just circumstantial. Actually, a bit like your idea of how you and Shelley are somehow related.'

Tom's candour and analogy appeared to have both reassured and persuaded Jim. 'So, what is it you want to ask?' he asked, albeit without any great enthusiasm.

'What can you tell me about the other two – Bill and Gene – who were in your company back in 1969? It's obvious there has been a lot of animosity between you all. Even when John went back to the bar after you left, apparently there was an argument between them. You yourself have also hinted at it a few times whilst we've all been on this trip. What was it that caused such bad feeling?'

It was clear that Jim had not quite expected this particular question, and it was a while before he answered, in a subdued tone. 'I might have already told you how we spent some time in the mountains, close to the Cambodian border, trying to disrupt the VC's supply lines. A lot of the villages in that region were supportive of the VC and often provided shelter and food, as well as hiding weapons and ammunition for them. Along with other companies, we were given the job of seeking out these sites and destroying their supplies. One day we were asked to carry out an operation at a village called Phong Nha. They named it Operation Resolve.' Almost as an aside, he said, 'I'll never forget the name of that village. It's printed on my brain.' He then continued. 'The intelligence guys had suggested there was a good chance the village was being used by the VC. Actually, it was more a collection of some huts spread over an area of about half a mile. We were all helicoptered into a location about a mile away. 1st Platoon – that's the platoon that included Gene and Bill – got there first. We were still approaching from the other side when we heard continuous, heavy gunfire, and some explosions, coming from their direction. We could tell by the sound of the gunfire it was coming from our guys. When we got there, it was obvious they were still involved in a major firefight. We took up position and started to fire into some of the huts.

After a while the firing stopped, and John, who was our platoon sergeant, approached one of the huts nearest to us. We followed him.'

He hesitated briefly. After a short while, though, he regained his composure and continued. 'Suddenly there were a few shots from a hut we had fired on, and a couple of our guys were hit and went down. John started to return fire, and so we all poured everything we had into the hut. When we were sure there was no more fire coming from it, we carefully entered. We were expecting to find some VC amongst the dead. Instead, we found a few young kids, and what looked like the father and mother and grandparents there, all dead. We carried out a search of the hut, but all we found was a single rifle.'

'So why had they started firing at you?' asked Tom.

'I guess they were scared,' he answered. 'Especially after what they had seen 1st Platoon do to some of the other huts in their village. Talking afterwards to some of the 1st Platoon guys, it seems they had been a bit jumpy, and as they got close to the huts something snapped and they just opened fire. Whether that's true or not, or someone saw something that threatened them, we don't know. What we did know, though, was that one of our guys, Scott James, who had been hit, was lying there, dead. Scott was just nineteen and had only been in 'Nam for a few weeks. John took it really badly and blamed himself for Scott's death.' He paused. 'Of course, after we found out what 1st Platoon had done, we started to blame them for what had happened. In John's opinion, they were poorly led and just too trigger-happy. When we searched the other huts, we found the same scene. In total, we counted twenty-five dead bodies, including two babies and a pregnant woman. A couple of young boys were lying dead at the rear of one of the huts. It looked like they had been shot whilst trying to escape. Many more were just lying there wounded, some with limbs missing and lying amongst other body parts on the floor. A few had survived. I remember seeing a couple of young boys who had survived trying to help the members of their family who were still alive. What made it even worse was that when we searched the houses, we didn't find anything that had been hidden. Not even a sack of rice.'

'So that was the reason for the friction between you,' suggested Tom. 'Gene and Bill had been part of the platoon that had instigated the fight. Was there any sort of official inquiry afterwards into why it happened?'

'Nothing official, no. At the time, there were lots of rumours about similar events that had happened, especially at My Lai, although the story about what had happened there hadn't yet broken. I think the military just wanted to keep it under wraps. It would be bad for morale and just encourage the anti-war groups back in the States. We were all told to forget about it and never mention it again.'

'How did the 1st Platoon guys react when they found out you were on this trip with them? It must have been a shock to them.'

'It was sure a big shock to us. We couldn't believe it, especially after all those years. None of us had mentioned what had happened at Phong Nha until we saw their names on the military trip list. It was like the floodgates opened and all those memories suddenly resurfaced.' By now, it was almost as though Jim were unaware of Tom's presence and just thinking out loud. 'The guys reacted in different ways. I made up my mind to use the trip to try and find some closure, or at least finally to come to terms and accept my part in it. Some of the others, especially John and Bob, were finding it increasingly difficult. You probably saw John's reaction when we met that old guy who had lost his arm in the war. I think it was then when it really started to affect him.'

'Did you discuss it with those from the other platoon?' Tom asked.

'Of course we did. John, especially, wouldn't let it go. He blamed them for what had happened – the massacre and especially Scott's death. He wanted to know why they had opened fire in the first place. The truth, though,' he said, in a more reflective voice, 'is that we would probably have done the same if we had got to the village first. That's what war does to you. It desensitises you and, before you know it, you don't give a second's thought about killing someone. Whether they were the enemy or just innocent people who were in the wrong place at the wrong time. It doesn't matter. All you want to do is get out alive.'

'Did you find out why they had opened fire?' Tom quietly asked.

'Not really, although one of them – I think it was Gene – said they were all smoking weed by then. But that was quite common, even within our own platoon.' He shrugged. 'It just seemed to help them get through the day.'

Tom now realised the time was right to ask a key question. 'Do you think John might have threatened any of them?'

'No. Definitely not,' answered Jim. 'Well, not in the sense you might be suggesting. There were certainly some heated arguments between us, but nothing that might have developed further. We were all just letting off a bit of steam. John did at one point, though, say he might one day give the full story to a newspaper back in the States, but I didn't believe him. I've told you before: he might give the impression of being a tough guy, but deep down he was very sensitive and, as you saw for yourself with that old guy, he could also be very emotional.'

'I understand that, after the argument in the bar that last night, they all started to toast each other. Why would that be, given what had happened? I would have thought that was the very last thing they would want to do.'

Jim looked directly at Tom. 'I'm guessing you have never been in the military. Right? Arguments take place all the time. At the end of the day, though, the camaraderie that develops when your life is at risk every single day overrides everything. Those who have never been in a war can't possibly understand that. The main feeling is that you've survived everything and have all come out the other end, alive.'

Jim turned his gaze towards some indeterminate point in the distance, before continuing. 'I don't know why I've told you all this. I've never spoken to anyone about it since that time here in 'Nam – not even my wife.' He turned and looked at Tom. 'You must have been a very successful cop if you can get strangers to talk to you like I just have.' He paused once more before adding, 'That's all I've got to say. I've probably said more than I intended to, anyway. Please don't ask me any more questions about this. Just leave me alone so that I can finally try and make sense of it all.'

He turned around and walked away from Tom, making it clear that that would be his final word on the subject.

Chapter 37

'You and Jim seemed as though you were having a serious conversation,' said Mary, after Tom had returned to where she was seated. 'What was it about?'

'He was just telling me about his time here in Vietnam. I think the whole experience has thrown up some feelings he hoped didn't exist or, at least, had been forever buried. It must be very difficult for anyone who was there at that time.'

Mary had known Tom long enough now to realise when he wanted to talk and, conversely, when he didn't, and this was one of those latter occasions.

'I think I'll go back to the cabin,' she said. 'I suddenly feel really tired. I might have a lie down before we meet Mike and Shelley for dinner. Why don't you come as well?' she suggested, raising her eyebrows slightly and making it clear that she wasn't that tired.

'Really?' Tom asked, slightly taken aback by her offer. 'You go ahead. I'll be there soon. I'll just finish my drink first.'

After Mary had gone, Tom closed his eyes. Not because he was especially tired, but rather so he could try to make sense of everything that had happened over the past twenty-four hours.

He felt increasingly confident that Tony had not killed John. The only problem was the lack of evidence to back up his confidence.

He was also aware that a theory which had initially been slowly developing at the back of his mind was now steadily, inexorably moving towards the front. This was something he had experienced a few times during his police career. Sometimes it had proved to be a major distraction, and way off the mark, but at other times it had provided him with the route to finally solving the crime. He hoped this was one of those occasions, because right now, if it wasn't, he didn't have a Plan B.

He still had his eyes closed when he heard the unmistakeable voice of Lan very close by.

'Mr Stone,' Lan said. 'I'm sorry to disturb you, but there is a gentleman here who would like to speak with you.'

When Tom opened his eyes, he could see there was a man standing alongside Lan. The man's still-boyish countenance suggested he was no older than twenty-five. He was quite tall with piercing blue eyes, which were complemented by his clean-shaven face and short, well-groomed, dark hair. He was also immaculately dressed in a light-coloured linen suit, button-down blue shirt and matching tie.

'My name is Jordan Griffiths, and I represent the US government here in Vietnam. I work in the consulate at the American embassy in Ho Chi Minh City,' he said with an unmistakeable soft, southern US accent. He didn't bother to offer his hand to Tom, which Tom took as an ominous sign.

'I will leave you two gentlemen together,' Lan said, before turning and walking away.

'How can I help you, Mr Griffiths?' Tom asked. 'Please take a seat.'

As Griffiths sat down, Huan appeared. 'Can I please get you something to drink?' he asked.

'I'm fine, thanks,' replied Tom, whilst Griffiths said, 'I'll just take a soda.'

After Huan had gone, Griffiths began to speak. 'I just wanted to discuss the death of Mr Fisher with you, and the ongoing murder investigation. I have just spent some time with Captain Bao Ninh, who has briefed me on the current status of the investigation.' Without any further preamble, he simply said, 'He has informed me of how you are trying to interfere with his investigation. I just wanted to remind you that Mr Fisher was a US national on Vietnamese soil and, as such, any investigation should be carried out by the appropriate authorities here in Vietnam. I'm sure, if I were to approach them, your own UK authorities would confirm this.'

Tom remained silent as he gathered his thoughts, trying to

compute everything he had just been told. Finally, he said, 'Well, thank you for pointing out to me that it's the responsibility of the Vietnamese police to carry out investigations for any crimes which occur in Vietnam. I would never have known that. Incidentally, what is it specifically I have done which has interfered with the investigation?'

Apparently choosing to discard Tom's sarcasm, and totally ignoring the question he had asked, Griffiths said, 'I'm glad you agree. Can I let Captain Bao Ninh know you will not try to interfere with his investigation again whilst you are on this ship?'

'You can tell him what you want,' Tom answered, now clearly angry with his arrogant approach. 'But, just for total clarification, so that you are not in any doubt: if I come across anything that I feel is material to the investigation, I will certainly bring it to Captain Bao Ninh's attention. I assume the laws here about withholding information are the same as they are in your country and my country. That is, unless you know anything to the contrary?'

An uneasy silence followed, before Griffiths stood up, looked at Tom and said, 'You might find at some point, Mr Stone, that you need our assistance here in Vietnam. Perhaps then you will see there is a reason for the advice I have offered you.'

'It didn't sound too much like advice to me. If I'm being totally honest, it sounded more like a threat.'

Griffiths didn't respond and started to walk away. As he was doing this, Huan arrived with his soda. Tom looked at him and said, 'I think Mr Griffiths has changed his mind.'

After they had gone, Tom took a sip of his drink as he reflected on his conversation with Jordan Griffiths. The more he thought about it, the more difficult he found it to fully understand the reason he was being warned off. It was not as though he had followed Captain Bao Ninh around the ship, checking to see if he was following standard police procedures. Yes, he had made one or two suggestions, and it was clear at the time that Captain Bao Ninh had resented them. It was the fact that the captain had subsequently briefed Jordan

Griffiths about this, and the speed at which he'd done it, which Tom now found troubling. It suddenly crossed his mind that, perhaps, it would all be very convenient if a British national was arrested and subsequently found guilty of the murder, rather than it becoming a long, drawn-out investigation.

Whatever the reason, unless Tom did decide to back off, he now apparently was in danger of causing a potential diplomatic incident. He hoped, however, it was just an inexperienced young man throwing his weight around, trying to scare him off. If that had been his intention, then it had not been successful, as it had simply added to Tom's determination.

Tom suddenly smiled and chuckled to himself. Not only had he been warned by Jim that some of the other guests had not taken too kindly to his seeming involvement in the investigation, but he now was also being threatened by a US consular official for exactly the same thing.

At least he could see the irony in the situation in which he now found himself. In truth, he had not been overly enthusiastic about the holiday when Mary had initially suggested it. She had, however, convinced him that it was an opportunity for them to have an enjoyable, stress-free post-retirement holiday together. After everything that had happened, and especially after the conversation he'd just had, this was probably not the best time, though, to remind her of that.

Chapter 38

Tom took a final sip of his drink and was just about to join Mary in their cabin when Lan reappeared.

'Could I please discuss something with you?' Lan asked quietly.

'Of course,' answered Tom, intrigued. His immediate thought, however, was that Lan was about to reinforce what Jordan Griffiths had just said to him. 'How can I help?'

'It's a bit of a sensitive matter,' Lan said, heightening Tom's sense of expectation. 'Although you are a friend of Mr Young, I understand you are also a British detective inspector. Is that right?'

Tom considered how he would answer this for a moment. 'I wouldn't say I'm a friend of Mr Young. We only met a few days ago, but it's true I like him. As for your other point, I have just retired from the British police force, where I was a detective chief inspector.'

Tom's clarification didn't seem to dampen Lan's apparent respect for his police credentials. Lan was still standing, whilst Tom had remained seated.

'Why don't you sit down?' Tom suggested, in an attempt to remove the awkwardness of the situation.

'I won't, thanks,' Lan said. 'There's something I would like to show you, but not here.'

Tom regarded Lan carefully before responding. 'Where would you suggest?'

'I think the best place would be my cabin. As I share it with Sang and Dung, I will call you on your cell phone when they have started their work. My cabin is on the lower deck, number two.'

There was no opportunity for further clarification, as Lan turned away and headed towards the other side of the ship.

After his conversations with Jim, Jordan Griffiths and now

Lan, Tom wondered who would next want to speak with him. He decided he wouldn't give anyone the opportunity and, instead, started to head back to his cabin. But, not for the first time on this holiday, his plans were interrupted, although this time it was an interruption of his own making.

Just as he was about to walk down the stairs, another man was walking up them. Tom waited until the man was alongside him, at the top of the stairs. 'You're Gene, I believe,' he said.

'That's me,' Gene simply replied, without any great enthusiasm.

'I'm Tom. Tom Stone. I wonder if I might have a quick word with you?'

Gene's suspicion was clearly evident. 'Yes, I know who you are. I think the whole ship knows by now. You're the guy who is trying to make a name for himself.' It was not an auspicious opening.

'And why would I want to do that?' Tom asked, suddenly very aware that this conversation was already not going the way he had intended.

'You're the big buddy of the guy who murdered John. Right? I hear you're a British ex-cop who seems to be speaking to everyone on the ship, trying to get him released.'

'That's not strictly true,' Tom answered, determined now not to respond in kind. 'It's true that I'm trying to help my buddy, but isn't that what all friends would do? I'll continue to do that until he's either found guilty or he's released.'

Gene considered this briefly, before saying, 'What is it you want to talk to me about?' Whilst his earlier outright antagonism had disappeared, there was still little enthusiasm in his tone.

'Why don't we move over there?' suggested Tom, pointing towards the stern of the ship.

As soon as they were there, Tom said, 'I understand you were in the bar the night John died. Well, actually, it was in the early hours of the morning, according to the others I've been able to speak with.'

'That's correct,' Gene replied. 'If you've already spoken to some of the others, why do you want to talk to me?'

'It's usual for every witness to be interviewed in such circumstances. I imagine you've already had that with Captain Bao Ninh. All I'm trying to do is to find out is, if Tony did murder John, what was his motivation? I think I owe at least that to his wife, Sue.'

He waited for a response, and finally Gene, having collected his thoughts, began to speak. 'I've got no idea, although I'd heard they'd had a few disagreements while they were here on the trip. I seem to remember your buddy getting kind of upset when John said something about the Brits not having the guts to take part in the war.'

'Yes, well, I can certainly imagine Tony reacting to something like that,' Tom replied.

'Is that all?' Gene asked. 'Can I go now?'

'There's just one other thing you could help me with, if that's okay.'

'Go ahead,' he replied.

'John had told me earlier that you were all in the same company in 1969. It must have been a real surprise when you found yourselves back together on this trip.'

Gene hesitated before answering, but not before Tom had seen, for the first time, a look of genuine unease on his face. 'You could say that,' he replied. 'Although we were in the same company, we were in different platoons, and so, most of the time, we kept our distance from each other.'

'Was there a reason for that?' Tom asked.

Gene regarded him silently before answering. 'I don't suppose you've been in the military, have you?'

'I haven't, no,' he simply said.

'There's always rivalry. It happens between divisions, companies, and even down at platoon level. We were no different. We always thought we were better than they were. Even now, over fifty years later, it still exists.'

'Really?' asked Tom. 'Even after all of those years?'

'Maybe even more so,' answered Gene. 'Look, I need to go. It's been a pleasure talking to you.' His tone suggested it had been far from it.

*

'You took your time,' said Mary, when Tom arrived back at their cabin. 'I was beginning to think you'd stood me up.'

'No. I just took my time finishing my drink,' he answered, unwilling, at this stage, to elaborate on what had happened. Anyway, it would only spoil the mood.

It was about an hour later, just as they were getting dressed for dinner, when Lan rang.

'Who was that?' asked Mary.

'It was Lan. He wants to discuss the latest update regarding Tony and Sue. He didn't sound too serious, so I expect it's mainly to do with admin arrangements and things like that.' He didn't like lying to Mary, but sometimes it was his judgement that too much information could only make the situation worse. And, anyway, he genuinely didn't know what Lan wanted to discuss. 'I'll be back soon. It shouldn't take too long.' He opened their cabin door and walked towards the main stairs.

It only took a couple of minutes before he was standing outside Lan's cabin. He rang the doorbell and it was almost immediately opened by Lan, who, with some urgency, beckoned him into the cabin and then quickly closed the door behind him.

'Please, sit down,' said Lan, pointing at the solitary chair. His cabin was about the same size as theirs, but, with three single beds in it, somehow it seemed a lot smaller and cramped. As Tom sat down, Lan perched on the edge of one of the beds.

Tom had the impression Lan was finding it difficult to start the conversation, something that he knew was out of character, and so decided to initiate things. 'What is it you want to discuss? Is it related to Mr Fisher's murder? You mentioned that you wanted to show me something.'

'Not really show you something. It was all I could think of at the time.' He immediately continued. 'I wanted to tell you about a conversation between Captain Bao Ninh and Mr Griffiths. It was just before I brought Mr Griffiths to speak with you. He had his own interpreter, and I could hear what they were saying.'

'What was it you heard?' asked Tom, his attention now heightened.

'I heard Mr Griffiths saying how important it was that the investigation should be finished quickly, and how it was in the best interests of both countries if Mr Young was found guilty.' He waited for a response from Tom. When none was forthcoming, he went on. 'It was then that Captain Bao Ninh told him how you had been asking questions, as well as making some suggestions as to how he should conduct the investigation. He made it clear he wasn't happy with what you were doing, and Mr Griffiths said he would handle it. Captain Bao Ninh then asked me to take Mr Griffiths to see you.'

'Do you know if Captain Bao Ninh shared any of the evidence he had with Mr Griffiths?'

'I don't think so, unless they'd had an earlier telephone conversation, which, thinking about it, is possible.'

'Why do you think Mr Griffiths said what he did?'

'I don't know for sure,' Lan answered. 'But, despite the war, there is now a very close relationship between our two countries. The United States is a major investor in our economy, as well as being one of our biggest export markets. There would be a definite incentive to quickly bring an end to an investigation such as this, especially one which might embarrass both countries.'

Tom looked directly at Lan. 'Why are you telling me this? You must realise it wouldn't look good for you if they found out you had told me what they'd talked about. Aren't you, at best, putting your career at risk?'

'I understand that, and I did think about whether I should tell you. But,' he then said, with a sudden burst of authority, 'it just doesn't seem right. To be honest, I don't know if Mr Young did murder Mr Fisher, but it seems they have made up their minds already that he did, just so that there is no bad publicity.' He paused. 'What will you do now?'

'I don't know. I need to think about it first,' Tom answered. 'There is one other favour which you could do for me, though.

I totally understand, however, if you don't want to do it.' This was something that he had been thinking about for some time now and would, back in his old role, have been one of the first things to consider. 'Is there any CCTV footage which covers the bar area on the night when Mr Fisher died?'

'We have cameras all around the ship,' Lan quickly replied.

Tom considered this for a short time before responding. 'Does that mean there would be footage of Mr Fisher being attacked?'

'I've seen the footage showing Mr Fisher and Mr Young having what looked like a fight, but none which showed Mr Fisher actually being stabbed. The CCTV covering a small section of the ship has not been working since the last trip. So that's where they think it might have happened.'

Tom decided not to mention that that was very convenient. Instead, he made do with, 'So there's no actual footage which shows Mr Young stabbing Mr Fisher. Is that right?'

'It is, yes,' he answered, before quickly adding, 'although some of the others in the bar have confirmed Mr Young said he had a knife. Even Sang, who was also there, mentioned it to me.'

'Would you be willing to let me see the footage?' Tom asked, despite knowing that it would place Lan in a very difficult position.

Lan, clearly now considering all the implications of doing so, finally said, 'I don't know if that will be possible. I will let you know if it is.'

The comment about Tony having a knife had taken Tom completely by surprise, as it had never been mentioned previously, or, at least, not to him. Then again, why should it have been? As Captain Bao Ninh, and then Jordan Griffiths, had pointed out to him, he was not involved in the investigation. Notwithstanding this, however, he knew, if correct, it would unfortunately add a new dimension to the body of evidence against Tony. As far as he knew, everything so far had been merely circumstantial.

He suddenly had another worrying thought. What if there was more evidence – this time compelling evidence – which he wasn't aware of?

'Did Sang, or any of the others, say Mr Young had a knife with him when they were all in the bar?' he asked.

'I don't think so. I think he just mentioned he had one. Some sort of chef's knife, I think.' Lan, now sounding a bit flustered, immediately continued. 'But I really don't know.'

'Is there anything else which you think I should know?' asked Tom.

Regaining his normal assurance, Lan said, 'No. I've told you everything. In fact, I've probably told you more than I should have. As I said, though, I really don't know if it was Mr Young who murdered Mr Fisher. That's for others to decide. Or at least I thought it was until I heard Captain Bao Ninh and Mr Griffiths speaking together.'

'Anyway, thank you for sharing this with me,' said Tom. He stood and held out his hand. 'If you do hear anything else, I'd appreciate it if you could let me know.' He paused briefly. 'I'll wait for you to let me know about the CCTV footage. You have my contact number.'

*

'Well?' said Mary, when he was back in their cabin. 'What did Lan have to say? Has he got news on what's happening to Tony?'

Tom had anticipated Mary's question and, like previously, felt it not the right time yet to tell her about what they'd discussed. Rightly or wrongly, he had decided it would only add to both his and her stress and anxiety levels: something which, right now, neither of them needed. 'He just wanted to discuss what they intended to do with Sue and Tony's belongings. He suggested we should pack their things, ready to be sent on to wherever they need them.'

If this was meant to pacify Mary, it had the opposite effect, as she suddenly started to sob quietly. Tom instinctively put his arm around her shoulder and held her hand.

'I can't believe we might never see them again,' she managed, between sobs. 'Poor Sue.'

'Don't give up on them yet,' said Tom, trying to give her

cause for optimism. 'Tony hasn't even been tried yet, let alone found guilty. There's still a long way to go.'

Even as he said this, he remembered what Lan had just told him about the Vietnamese and US officials' intentions to complete this as speedily as possible.

Chapter 39

Later, they were seated in the restaurant at the same table as Shelley and Mike. It was the same one at which Sue and Tony would also, normally, be seated with them. In fact, the table was still set for six people, which, in a way, was an uncomfortable visual reminder of their absence. Not surprisingly, the atmosphere was still quite subdued, although Tom did notice how the level of noise amongst the other guests had increased since the previous day and was now interspersed with the occasional bout of laughter.

Inevitably the first topic of conversation between them had revolved around Sue and Tony, and Tom had, as much as he could or indeed wanted to, filled them in as to the current status. After a while it had become clear that, however difficult, it would perhaps be better if, at least whilst they ate dinner, they discussed other things.

Once they had finished dinner and were drinking their coffees, Tom could see that Mary was becoming quite restless and, occasionally, would subtly nod her head, as if to say, *Go ahead and tell them.* He started to consider whether she was right and now might be a good time to raise the issue with Shelley. Before he could decide, however, the decision was taken for him when Mary, clearly no longer able to contain her own excitement, said, 'We've got something incredible to discuss with you.'

It wasn't quite the way in which Tom would have raised the subject, but now they were committed.

'Why don't you tell them?' Mary suggested, excitement obvious in her voice.

All eyes, not surprisingly, were now focused on Tom.

'Before I do,' he replied, slightly dampening Mary's excitement, although at the same time heightening the overall sense of expectation, 'I have a question to ask you, Shelley.'

'Me?' she asked. 'What is it you want to ask?'

'It might sound a bit strange, but please bear with me.' He hesitated, which again only added to the overall suspense. 'What was the name of your grandmother who lived in Totnes?'

'My grandmother?' she asked. 'Why do you want to know her name?'

'As I said, please bear with me,' he simply answered.

'Her name was Margaret,' she answered, now looking intently at Tom, 'although everyone called her Peggy.'

'Oh my God,' Mary suddenly exclaimed, as she put her hand to her mouth. 'That's incredible.'

Both Shelley and Mike were now even more confused, and it was Mike who asked the obvious follow-up question. 'Why is that so incredible?'

'Before I answer that,' Tom said, 'I'd like to ask just one other question about her. I apologise for having to ask you this, because it relates to the time when your father was born. I'm sure it must have been an extremely difficult time for your grandmother.' He looked directly at Shelley. 'I'm sorry, but I can't think of any other way to ask this. Was she married at the time?'

'Actually, she wasn't,' she answered, in a surprisingly matter-of-fact manner. 'She had become pregnant, but the father had disappeared. Although she did marry a few years later, it must have been very difficult for her, given the circumstances. She was young, unmarried, and there was a war still going on. It was only years later that I found out about all of this when Dad told me.' Looking towards Mike, she carried on. 'She was a wonderful lady who was very good to me. We had some very happy times together, and I still often think about her.'

'I still don't understand why this is incredible,' said Mike, now more than a hint of impatience in his voice.

So Tom told them. He told them about his discussion with Jim, and how Jim had confirmed his father had been stationed in Totnes, immediately before D-Day. He told them about the letters and the photograph of Peggy which Jim's father had kept. and he told them about how he had later named his own daughter Peggy. He finished by telling them about Jim's request, asking if Tom would speak with them and, if possible, try to confirm things, one way or another.

There was a stunned silence amongst the two of them. It was clear, watching the expression on Mary's face, that hers was a far more excited silence.

'I can't believe it,' Shelley said. 'Is he sure?'

'Well, I believe he's sure about his father's story. As to whether it fully matches your grandmother's experience, that's another matter completely. If it doesn't, then it's a hell of a coincidence.' He resisted the temptation to mention how his police career, and all his instincts, had taught him never to believe in coincidences.

'What do you think we should do next?' asked Shelley, as Mike took hold of his wife's hand.

'It's not really a decision I can make for you, but if it was me, then I would want to speak with Jim.'

'I think Tom is right,' said Mike. 'What have we got to lose? If it is a coincidence, then there's nothing really lost. If it isn't, then … ' He didn't need to finish his sentence, as his silence was clear to everyone.

'When do you think we should discuss it with him?' Shelley asked.

'Why not now?' Tom replied. 'Jim is seated in the corner to our right.' He nodded in that direction. 'I've noticed he has been looking at us all the while we've been here. I'm sure he's as anxious – well, probably just as excited as you are. Why don't I go over and speak with him?'

Judging by the expression on Shelley's face, it now seemed as though the reality of what she'd just been told, and the potential consequences, had fully dawned on her. Nonetheless, she managed to say, 'Would you?'

Both Mike and Mary were now holding Shelley's hands as Tom walked over to where Jim was seated. 'I think someone would like to speak with you,' he said to Jim, a smile appearing on his face, after apologising for interrupting their conversation.

'I think you two have a lot to discuss,' Tom said, as he and Jim arrived at Shelley and Mike's table. 'I think we'll leave you to it.'

Mary stood and, once again, gave Shelley's hand a squeeze. 'Good luck,' she said, a huge smile now on her face.

Chapter 40

After they had left the restaurant, Tom and Mary had gone to the upper deck. It was a very still night with hardly any noise, other than the occasional throb coming from the engine of a passing boat or the distinctive, throaty sound of a motorcycle being ridden past where the *Mekong Voyager* was moored. As he took in this peaceful scene, Tom considered how this tranquillity was in stark contrast to the chaos of all the other things he was now having to contend with.

Whilst he had been slightly annoyed when Jim had asked him to speak with Shelley, in retrospect it had proved to be not only something of a distraction from everything else that was going on, but also, in truth, quite enjoyable and satisfying. He hoped they would be able to confirm that they were related, but, somehow, given how the rest of the trip was going, he wouldn't be surprised if it turned out to be a big disappointment for them.

Now, back on the upper deck, the reality of what had happened with John and Tony once again suddenly hit home.

'Why don't we get a drink and have a few moments to ourselves?' suggested Mary.

'Sounds like a good idea,' Tom answered. 'We seem to have spent most of the holiday with other people.' It was clear in his tone that that wouldn't be his ideal holiday.

It wasn't long before Huan appeared to take their order.

'It must be more work for you, having to bring all the drinks from down below,' said Mary. The bar on the upper deck had been closed since John's body had been found.

'It's not a problem, ma'am,' Huan simply replied, before heading off to get their drinks.

'He's such a polite young man,' said Mary.

It wasn't long before Huan returned with their drinks: two generous glasses of red wine, alongside two other drinks on the tray. As he handed theirs over, Tom said, 'Could I ask you, Huan, if you've been interviewed again by the police?' Although he wasn't looking at Mary, he could almost imagine her eyes narrowing as she gave him one of her looks of disapproval.

'No, sir, I haven't,' Huan answered. 'I believe that the police will be ending their investigations tomorrow.'

'Who told you that?' asked Tom, genuinely surprised.

'It was my brother, Sang, sir. He heard the police captain mention it to the American man.'

Tom didn't ask any follow-up questions, realising that they could place Huan in a difficult situation, but continued to watch him as he made his way towards another couple and handed their drinks over to them.

'You're always on duty, aren't you?' said Mary. For once, Tom couldn't make out whether this was intended as a compliment or a criticism. On balance, he suspected the latter.

'If you're referring to my question, I just wanted to know, that's all. Anyway, I did find out that the investigation, at least here on the ship, will be closing down tomorrow, so we should be moving again. That's worth knowing, don't you think?'

'I suppose so,' she replied, albeit without any enthusiasm.

Just then Don and Estelle, together with their son, Brett, appeared at the top of the stairs and, having spotted them, began to head towards Tom and Mary.

'Do you mind if we join you?' asked Don. From the very first time they had spoken to one another, there appeared to be a genuine affinity between Tom and Don, which had been subsequently reinforced by Don's experience in the prison museum, back in Hanoi. 'It's good to see a couple of friendly faces.'

'Please do,' answered Mary, as Brett took a chair from one of the other tables, so that they could all be seated together.

'What a beautiful night,' said Estelle. 'We thought it would be a shame not to take advantage of it. Although, these days, Don likes to stay up late. Don't you, Don?'

'When you haven't got much time left, every hour is

precious,' he answered in his normal, straightforward manner.

'Don,' said Estelle, 'I wish you wouldn't say things like that.'

'Why not? It's true; you know what the doctor said. And anyway, I've always liked to stay up late. I think it's the best part of the day. Your senses are more alive and finely tuned. You see and hear things which you wouldn't during daylight hours.'

'I hope we soon start to sail again,' said Estelle. 'I feel like one of those birds cooped up in a cage.'

Tom thought about mentioning Huan's comment about how he'd heard the ship would be resuming its journey the following day, if only to give her some good news, but then thought better of it. After all, at this stage, it was just a second-hand rumour, and he didn't want to build up her hopes.

'I'm sorry,' Estelle quickly added. 'That was very insensitive of me. I know the man arrested was your friend. It must be very difficult for you both.'

'You don't have to apologise,' replied Mary. 'I can fully understand how frustrating it is for all of the passengers to be stuck here, not knowing when the trip will continue, or even when they will get home.' She paused. 'We were due to fly to Australia in a few days, to visit Tom's son and his family. I'm not sure if that will be possible now.'

This was the first time he'd heard Mary accept there was a possibility that their onward trip might not happen. In a way, it was a relief to him to know she seemed to have come to terms with that possibility, because he hadn't been looking forward to having that discussion.

'If you don't mind me asking, what is the current situation regarding the investigation?' Brett suddenly asked.

'I probably know as much as you do,' Tom answered, not quite with total honesty. 'Actually, in a way, probably less, as you were one of the people in the bar that night and you've been formally interviewed.'

Brett looked at Tom with a hint of suspicion in his eyes but didn't respond to his answer. Instead, he seemed to take a different tack. 'Are you able to tell us what your friend's current situation is? I understand he's still being held in custody in Ho Chi Minh City. Is that correct?'

'As far as I know,' answered Tom, this time with genuine honesty. 'We haven't been able to speak with him, although Sue, his wife, left the ship earlier today to visit him. Their son David is also due to fly in from the UK shortly.'

'You were a senior cop, Tom. Do you think it was him who murdered John?' asked Don, in a way only someone with limited time left could feel unabashed asking.

'I really don't know,' Tom replied, taking Don's question head-on. 'As I keep telling everyone, we'd only known each other for less than a week. What I would say, though, is that during that time, Tony didn't strike me as being the type of person who would stab someone to death.'

'Not even if he was drunk and out of control at the time?' asked Brett.

'Especially if he was drunk at the time. In my experience, you need most of your faculties to be able to do that.'

'But I heard him say … well, we all heard him say he had a knife with him. In fact, I think you'll be able to hear him say it yourself, if you look at the video I sent to you. Surely, if he carried a knife, there was a reason for that? Who would normally carry a knife?' He shook his head. 'Did you take a look at the video?'

'I did, yes,' Tom answered, 'and thanks for sending it. I've watched it a few times now, and Tony is definitely saying something, but, with all of the background noise, I couldn't make out precisely what he was saying.'

There was now a slightly strained silence at the table, which was broken when Don suddenly, and most unexpectedly, said, 'I was awake around the time it happened.'

Everyone had now turned to look at Don. 'You didn't tell me that,' said Brett, as surprised as everyone else, if not more so.

'You didn't ask. No one has asked. I tried to let that police captain know, but he wasn't interested. No one seems to be interested in what a dying old man has to say these days.'

This was the first time Tom had heard Don speak in such an

uncharacteristically self-pitying manner. 'What was it you wanted to tell him?'

'Like I just said, I was awake, sitting on the veranda. If you remember, there had been that big storm earlier in the evening. After it had cleared, I went outside. It was a bit like tonight. Very still, where sound carries much further. As I just said earlier, your senses are more finely tuned at night.'

'So what did you hear?' asked Brett.

'I could definitely hear you all in the bar, including you. You seemed to be enjoying yourselves, and the noise levels got higher as the night went on. Eventually, I managed to funnel out those noises and concentrate on the sounds coming from the river. I even heard you get back to your cabin. You were very noisy, by the way,' he added, clearly intended as an admonishment. 'That was at eight after two.'

He fell quiet for a while, almost as though he had forgotten about Brett's question. Just when Brett seemed about to prompt him, he suddenly started speaking again.

'I was just about to go to bed – by that time the noise in the bar had almost stopped – when I heard loud voices. It was obvious they were drunk. You know, the way drunk people tend to almost shout even though they're standing next to one another. I assumed they must have been in the bar, especially as it was so late.'

Tom was tempted to start asking a few questions but knew that, if he did, it might interrupt Don's flow, making it difficult for him to pick up where he left off. So he simply let Don continue to talk, whilst making a mental note of some of the questions he would later ask.

'Our cabin is next to yours, you know, on level 1, and the noise seemed to be coming from a spot immediately above me. There were two men. I tried to hear what they were saying but could only make out the odd word. What I could hear, though, was that one of the men was your friend. His accent is very distinctive, even though it's difficult to understand.'

'That's true,' said Brett. 'I had a similar problem understanding him when we were in the bar.'

Now that Don's flow had been interrupted, Tom decided to

ask a question. 'What time was that? When you first heard them.'

'It was twelve after two exactly,' he immediately answered.

'How can you be so precise?'

'Because I looked at my watch. I didn't imagine someone would be murdered, but I did think, given the level of noise, there might be a few complaints from some of the other passengers. It doesn't bother me. They are, after all, on vacation, but others might have got upset. Anyway, that's why I checked the time.' Before Tom could ask any follow-up questions, Don once again took them all by surprise. 'It was the same reason I checked my watch the second time it happened.'

'Second time?' repeated Brett. 'You mean after the first one?'

'That's what second time usually means,' he answered, with his own style of sarcasm.

'Are you sure, Don?' asked Estelle, doubt obvious in her voice.

Don didn't respond in any verbally aggressive way. He just said, 'I'm certain. It was at twenty-three after two.'

This time Tom couldn't help himself, and he found himself, a bit unfairly, firing off a couple of questions. 'Was it the same two men, or were they different, and could you make out what they were saying?'

'Which one do you want me to answer first?' he calmly answered.

'I'm sorry,' Tom said. 'Please take your time and just tell it in your own way.'

Don nodded. 'It sounded different and was a bit further away than the first one was. There wasn't any drunken shouting, and it didn't last long. Maybe twenty seconds. No longer. I then heard what I thought was a splash, and then everything went quiet.' He paused. 'To answer your questions, Tom, I don't know if it was the same two men and could only make out the odd word that was said. I think I heard one of them say "'Nam", but, as I said, they were further away.'

'What did you do then, Pops?' Brett asked.

'I went to bed. What else would I do?'

Chapter 41

'Well, that was interesting,' said Mary, when they were back in their cabin. 'How do you think Don is able to remember all of that, particularly the times?'

'His body might be failing him, but his mind is obviously still sharp,' Tom said. 'Also, I suspect his time spent in prison actually helped him to remember things. I read about this somewhere. When you are in prison, especially if it's for a long sentence or, as in Don's case, for an unknown period of time, apparently some people are able to train their minds so they can remember details, especially details relating to their families. I imagine those memories are all you've got to keep you sane.'

'I suppose so,' said Mary. 'He was definitely adamant about the times.'

'He certainly was,' Tom agreed.

'I think I'll get in bed and read my book. It's been a very tiring day,' Mary said, before adding, in a subdued voice, 'I wonder how Sue is?'

Tom decided this was a rhetorical question and so chose not to answer. Instead, he said, 'Do you mind if I look at my emails? I'm keen to know if Milner has sent me one.'

'Go ahead. I know you'll only worry if you don't do it. I've known you long enough to understand that if there's something on your mind, you always want to try and sort it out straight away.' Her voice took on a slightly critical edge. 'You can't just leave things until a more convenient time, can you?'

'More convenient for who?' asked Tom. 'I suppose it's a form of addiction, or at least compulsion. I've never had any tests, but it wouldn't surprise me if I've got some form of OCD.'

This was the first time Mary had heard him admit to this, and she was quite surprised he'd shared it with her. 'I suppose we all have our compulsions. I imagine mine would be crosswords. If I can't finish one – especially if I only need a few more words – then it worries me. Sometimes I even have one of those anxiety dreams where, for example, your hands won't move, or you keep forgetting something important, such as your passport. In my case, though, it's usually related to crosswords. It's amazing, isn't it, how it can play tricks with your mind?'

'Well, I think if this holiday has achieved anything, it's that we've both learnt things about each other that we didn't previously know,' said Tom.

'Yes, and that's a good thing, isn't it?'

'I suppose so, but I suspect only time will tell,' he replied with a little chuckle.

'Why don't you go and see if you've heard anything from David, before I find out anything else about you that I didn't know?'

Tom, suspecting that this was one of Mary's little jokes, didn't respond and instead opened up his iPad and pressed the power button. He looked at his watch, which showed 10.40 pm local time, making it 3.40pm back in the UK.

He quickly scanned his emails but couldn't see anything from Milner. In a strange way he was disappointed, but logic told him it was unlikely there would be a message from him so soon after their conversation. Tom's suggestion to share his information with DCI Shaw would undoubtedly take some time, not least as, knowing Milner, he would need to prepare for the meeting. Milner couldn't simply knock on his door and tell him that he thought DC Shipley had been murdered. He would then have to tell him how he also thought Operation Deliverance had been seriously compromised, and that there was someone on the team who was in the pay of the organised crime network. Such an approach would be unlikely to be successful, at least initially. On top of where and when he would disclose all of this, the more important part would be to put together all the evidence to support his allegations. All of this would inevitably take time and so, logically, it was no surprise that there was no update from Milner. In fact, ironically, it would have been more worrying if there had been a message from him.

He looked again at the headings of the other emails, but instantly decided they were not important – apart from one that caught his attention. It was from his son Paul, so he opened it.

Hi, Dad and Mary,
I hope you are both having a wonderful, relaxing holiday, travelling down the Mekong. I'm sure you are having some great experiences, meeting lots of new people and seeing some wonderful sights, making it a holiday you will never forget. We can't wait to hear all about it.
Anyway, just to say we are all looking forward to seeing you again next week, here in Australia. I'll be in touch again nearer the date.
Take care,
Paul, Kerry, Sam and Holly
PS. Don't forget to send us some photos.

As he read this, he realised just how strange it still felt for Paul to call him 'Dad'. It was wonderful that they had recently reestablished contact, yet, on the other hand, it also highlighted all of those wasted years before that had finally, and only recently, happened.

This contemplative state was interrupted when Mary, looking up from her book, suddenly said, 'Is there anything from David?'

'No,' he answered. 'He's probably too busy to reply anyway.'

'That's good, isn't it?' she asked.

'I hope so,' he answered.

Before Mary could ask any follow-up questions, his phone pinged. He could tell by the number it was a text from Lan, and he opened it.

If you come to the purser's office at 1 am you can take a look.

Tom noted that Lan had constructed the message in a very clever way. It was vague enough to be interpreted in different ways, should anyone, later, start asking questions. His respect for Lan had, as a result, now risen even higher.

Suddenly, though, he realised that this presented him with a problem. How was he going to explain his disappearance to Mary, especially at such a time? He could, of course, just tell her the truth about how he'd asked if Lan could arrange for him to see the CCTV footage. The problem with this approach was that it could backfire spectacularly. It might give Mary hope that Tony was innocent and, therefore, that everything would turn out well. Her concern, especially for Sue, was both touching and genuine. On the other hand, it could just as easily prove conclusively that Tony had in fact murdered John. He really didn't want to – at this stage, at least – do anything which would crush her optimism.

His priority was to finally get to the bottom of what had actually happened in those early hours. But, as he thought about it, he suddenly realised his loyalty towards, and love for, Mary was just as strong, if not more so.

'I think I should tell you something,' he said, now too late to change his mind.

Mary, clearly concerned about what he suddenly had to tell her, put down her book and, with a worried expression on her face, could only bring herself to say, 'What is it, Tom?'

He sat on the edge of the bed and began to tell her. In fact, he told her everything, not just the reason he was meeting Lan at such an unsocial hour. He told her about all his suspicions and why he had those suspicions. He also told her about his brief meeting with Jordan Griffiths and even his threats.

'Oh my God,' Mary said. 'Why didn't you tell me?' This was immediately followed, in quite an angry voice, with, 'I thought those days of you not telling me things were gone.' When he didn't answer, she just said, 'Well?'

'Mary, it's because those days are gone that I've now told you everything. What good would it have done to have given you a running commentary on things? It would only have added to any anxieties you might have had. It was you, remember, who asked me to get involved and see what I could do for Tony.' He quickly continued, 'Although I'd already decided to do so. You know me well enough to know I wasn't going to just sit idly by without at least looking at all the evidence myself.'

Mary seemed to be reassured by what Tom had just said.

'Tom, I'm sorry. It's just that it's come as a massive shock to me.' She momentarily went silent before resuming, this time in a more positive, if not quite cheery, manner. 'So, do you think Tony is innocent?'

'I believe so,' he answered, before offering a caveat. 'Although, until I have definitive proof, I don't want to build up our hopes. That was the main reason why I didn't tell you. What I do know, though, is that the evidence will have to be totally compelling. I get the impression that it would suit the Vietnamese and American authorities if Tony is found guilty.'

'But surely it will be decided on the evidence, won't it?'

'I hope so, but the question is will they allow any evidence to be presented?'

'So, who do you think murdered John?' she asked.

'I really don't know,' he replied. 'That's something I'm hoping to soon find out, though. If I don't, then I've got a feeling it will be too late.'

Chapter 42

After his conversation with Mary, Tom spent the next couple of hours trying to make sense of all the key aspects of this inquiry and what he knew thus far. He had a longstanding and often successful technique of highlighting the salient points, usually on a flip chart: key timelines, potential suspects, links with the victim, possible motives and so on.

He was not one who readily embraced new technology, preferring to stick with his tried and tested techniques. Indeed, this reluctance to fully embrace new technology had been one of the reasons why, when they first professionally came into contact with one another, he and DCI Shaw had, to put it mildly, not seen eye-to-eye. It was during this time that DCI Shaw had publicly accused him of being a police dinosaur. Not surprisingly, especially given the rock-bottom state of his career at the time, this had simply added to Tom's feeling of being no longer being valued and his overall fragile mental state. But that now seemed a long time ago, since which he and DCI Shaw had developed, if not a close friendship, then certainly a growing feeling of mutual respect.

By the time he had finished this, it was almost 12.30am. Mary, unsurprisingly, given how much the day's events had taken out of her, had fallen asleep about an hour previously. As Tom watched, her quiet, rhythmic breathing was somehow reassuring and, not for the first time, he considered himself lucky to have met her when he did.

The last thirty minutes seemed to drag as he waited for his watch to approach one o'clock. Finally, though, it did, and, as he walked towards the door, Mary suddenly sat up. 'Good luck,' she said, a little sleepily. 'I'll wait up for you.'

'You don't have to. I really don't know how long I'll be.'

'I'll still wait up for you,' she repeated, in a way which suggested it wasn't for discussion.

Tom kissed her on the forehead, opened the door and walked towards the purser's office. It was located on the same level as Tom and Mary's cabin, at the end of the corridor and slightly to the right of the stairs which led to the upper deck level.

The door was opened just as Tom arrived, and Lan ushered him inside before quickly closing it.

'If anyone comes, please say you are here to check your account.' Lan was clearly uncharacteristically nervous: not a surprise, given the risk he was taking.

'Wouldn't it be a bit odd, me being here at 1am?' asked Tom.

'Probably,' he simply answered. Without any further discussion, he went on. 'I've already set up the CCTV footage from the time everyone was in the bar. It lasts about ninety minutes from the time they first entered to the time they all left. Do you want to see it all?' His anxious tone made it clear that he hoped Tom wouldn't need to be there that long.

The CCTV equipment was in a small room, although in truth it was little more than a separate, slightly-larger-than-normal cupboard at the rear of the main purser's office, with space for just a single chair. Notwithstanding this, there was still room for nine individual small screens to be mounted on the wall. All of them, except one, were live. Tom assumed the exception was the one which had not been working for the past week.

Tom sat down. 'If you show me how to start and stop it, and then how to fast-forward, I might not have to look at everything.'

Lan spent a couple of minutes showing him the basic controls, and then Tom played with them himself until he felt confident enough that he knew what he was doing.

'I'll be in the office if you need me for anything,' Lan said, before walking into it and closing the door behind him.

Tom had brought a notepad and pen, and he now placed them alongside him. After a few false starts he quickly got the hang of using the machine and was soon working his way through the footage.

He immediately could see that those there were becoming increasingly demonstrative as the amount of alcohol they had consumed increased. At one point it was obvious that some sort of argument had started. John and Bob appeared to be particularly agitated, and there was a lot of finger-pointing between them and the other two from their old company. There didn't appear to be anything physically aggressive, although Tom could well imagine how the noise levels would have increased.

This verbally aggressive part lasted for about five minutes before things appeared to calm down. Tom rewound the tape back to the start of this section and, this time, paid close attention to what Tony was doing whilst the altercation was at its height. In fact, Tony appeared to be enjoying the Americans' argument until John briefly turned towards him, said something and then rejoined the argument. Tony had immediately reacted to whatever John had said to him, and it was only Sang's quick reaction, when he got between them, which prevented it from escalating further. Tony's reaction was then to order another drink from Huan.

Aware that it would be very easy to keep rewinding the tape, and therefore add considerably to the time it would take to view it, Tom slightly sped up the tape until he came to the part where Jim, Bob and John left the bar. This left Gene, Bill, Sang and, of course, Tony still there.

A short while later John suddenly reappeared and was greeted by a sarcastic round of applause. John was followed, a bit later, by Brett, who, like John, appeared to be the target of some ribbing for his late arrival. By this time, though, as Brett had described, they had started the drinking competition, with Huan being asked to keep bringing drinks. Before long, they were all well and truly beyond the point of being able to exercise any self-control as each new drink was consumed in double-quick time.

It was about this point when Brett took the photos and video of them drinking the shots. New drinks were still arriving, but Huan seemed to be struggling to keep up with the demand. Sang eventually took over the task and waved Huan out of the bar.

It looked as though John was claiming victory, as he suddenly turned to face Tony and then raised both arms in the air, as any winner would likely do. If Tom didn't know what was soon about to happen, he would have considered this quite amusing. They might not have been the young men they once were, but there was no doubt that their competitive instincts still burnt fiercely within. By now, though, the earlier hostility had been replaced by tactile, drunken bonhomie, exemplified when John began hugging Gene and Bill, in the over-the-top way in which drunken people often do.

Finally, Tom arrived at the point when the guests began to leave. He reached for his pen and pad, ready to make a note of the times.

Gene was the first to leave. Tom checked the time. It was 2.02am. Bill left next at 2.05am, followed almost immediately by Brett at 2.06am. This perfectly corresponded with the time that Don had given for when Brett had got back to his cabin. John was next, at 2.08am, leaving Tony and Sang in the bar. Finally, Tony was helped to his feet by Sang, who escorted him out of the bar. The time was 2.09am.

Tom ran the footage for another few minutes so he could be sure that none of them had later returned. No one did.

He sat back in his chair and considered what, if anything, he'd learned from watching it.

Well, firstly it confirmed just how much they'd all had to drink. It was excessive by anyone's standard, let alone a group of men in their seventies.

Next, there clearly had been a heated discussion, involving members of the two platoons. The protagonists appeared to be Bill and John, although Gene had also briefly become involved. It also seemed John and Tony had continued their own ongoing disagreement, which had provoked John into saying something to him. Tony's instant response had surprised Tom and, if Sang had not had the presence of mind to intervene, he did wonder where it might have led.

Tom had listened carefully but still couldn't make out if Tony had made a comment about having a knife, although, in truth, Tony's words were all quite slurred anyway. He now knew, however, the exact times when each of them had left the bar, and he was relieved to see that these supported the times that Don had earlier quoted.

He was still considering all of this when the door opened.

'Have you finished yet? I'm worried one of the crew might appear,' said an anxious Lan.

'Nearly,' Tom answered. 'There are just a couple of other things I'd like to see, but I need to switch to the other cameras. Could you show me how to do it? I'll be as quick as possible.'

With some reluctance, and adding to his already high anxiety level, Lan quickly showed Tom how to switch between the screens and then call up the footage. Tom found the part he was interested in and fast-forwarded it to the time when Tony and John were, according to the police, having their fight. Once again, the time – 2.12am – exactly coincided with Don's recollection.

It was immediately obvious that both of them, but especially Tony, were in no state to fight anyone. All coordination between their brains and limbs had deserted them. John had been leaning against the ship's side rail, looking out over the river, when the camera caught Tony walking towards him. 'Walking' was probably an exaggeration, as it was more like a drunken stagger.

As Tony got closer, John turned to face him. There then appeared to be a brief exchange of words between the two of them, before Tony seemed to lose his balance and fell towards John. Not surprisingly, John's first instinct, no doubt taken by surprise, was to push Tony away from him. Tony, in turn, recoiled and threw up his hands, in an apologetic manner. Before Tony disappeared out of shot, the footage captured him walking, still very unsteadily, in the direction of the stairs.

Tom looked away from the screen. If this was evidence that a fight had taken place, let alone something more sinister, then it was not very convincing. In fact, it was the type of event which undoubtedly took place hundreds of times each week in every town in the UK, after the pubs and clubs had closed.

He left the footage running for a few minutes, to make sure

Tony had not returned to carry on their argument. There was no such footage, and John left the screen soon after Tony, holding the rail to keep himself steady. Tom was unable to locate John on any of the other cameras.

Finally, he switched to the screen which covered the stairs leading down to the level where Sue and Tony's cabin was located. He fast-forwarded to 2.15am and waited for Tony to appear. Sure enough, at about that time, Tony could be seen trying to negotiate the stairs. It was painful to watch as, a couple of times, he appeared to misjudge some of the steps and was in danger of falling. It was only due to what presence of mind he still had that he was able to grab the stair rail and prevent it from happening. He then made his way along the corridor until, almost miraculously, he somehow found his way to the door of his cabin. Even this was not without its mishaps, as he'd tried to walk in a straight line but, more than once, ended up bouncing off the wall. On one occasion, as if in slow motion, he fell onto the floor, and it was only on the third attempt that he managed to stand up again. Once again, Tom thought how if the circumstances hadn't been so serious it would have been considered very funny.

By the time Tony arrived at his cabin the video footage showed it was 2.17am. This was exactly the time at which Sue had claimed he had finally got back. As he leaned on the door, it opened and he simply disappeared inside, suggesting, as Sue had described, how he'd fallen into the room.

When Tom looked at his watch, he was surprised to see that he'd been there for over an hour. He quickly went through a mental checklist to make sure he'd seen everything he was interested in. The last thing he wanted to do was to later think of something else and have to repeat this cloak-and-dagger experience. It was very doubtful that Lan's nerves would be able to cope.

Satisfied that he'd seen everything, he was just about to knock on the door to let Lan know he was finished when a sudden thought came into his head.

He quickly went back to the first screen, the one covering

the bar area, where he called up that night's footage again and tried to rewind it. Unfortunately, he accidentally clicked on the fast-forward button and, before he was able to stop it, saw something which stunned him. The screen showed 2.40am.

Chapter 43

Tom rewound the tape just to make sure what he'd seen wasn't some sort of mirage, and it was genuine. It was a while before he could even begin to think straight again, such was his shock. This took the investigation to a completely new level: one which would require not just all his policing skills, but also no little diplomacy.

Eventually, Lan's patience deserted him and he entered the small office, where Tom was still deep in thought.

'We must go now,' he said, in a tone which made it clear it was no longer up for negotiation. 'Please pick up your things. We are leaving.'

Tom did as he was instructed, although, in truth, his mind was elsewhere. They both moved into the purser's office, and Lan poked his head out to make sure there was no one about.

'Won't the CCTV pick us up?' asked Tom, thinking how ironic that would be, given what he'd just been doing.

'I deactivated that particular camera before you arrived,' replied Lan. 'They'll just think the system is playing up again. Now, please leave.'

'Just one last thing, Lan,' he said, much to Lan's annoyance. 'How long are the tapes kept for?'

'Usually, they are kept for each trip. Can we please now go?' he said, almost pleading with Tom.

Tom made his way down the stairs and towards his cabin, as quietly as possible so as not to disturb any of the other guests. Suddenly, a thought occurred to him as he passed Don and Estelle's cabin. What if Don heard him creeping along the corridor, especially at this time of the night? Although that would take some explaining, there wasn't anything he could do about it now.

When he reached their cabin, he made sure he opened the door as quietly as possible. As soon as he entered, Mary said,

'Did you find out anything? Did it show Tony?'

Tom immediately put his right index finger to his mouth and mouthed *shh*. He quietly closed the door and sat down on the end of the bed. He owed it to her to tell her as much as he could. But not everything.

So he told her about the footage in the bar and the apparent argument between Tony and John. He then told her about the drinking contest and just how drunk they all were. He followed this by recounting who had left and when. Finally, he told her about the footage which showed Tony and John's alleged fight and then Tony's subsequent difficult walk back to his cabin.

'So are you saying you don't think Tony killed John?' asked Mary, now replicating Tom's quiet voice.

'I know he didn't,' Tom answered in his most unequivocal tone of voice.

'That's wonderful news,' Mary answered, her face now betraying a combination of utter relief and excitement. 'How can you be so confident he didn't do it?'

'For one thing, he was totally, physically incapable of attacking anyone. If I had presented that footage as evidence, the CPS, quite rightly, would have thrown it out instantly. The other reason is that I think I know who did murder John. All I need to do now is prove it.'

'Who do you think it was, then?' asked Mary, not unreasonably.

He took hold of her hand before answering. 'Mary, it would be best if I didn't tell you. As I said, I need to prove it first. Also, I don't want you to start changing your behaviour. It's important we both act as normally as possible until then. I know it will be difficult, but believe me, it is for the best. Hopefully it will only be for a short time.'

'Okay,' she answered. 'But please be careful. I don't like to think you're doing this all by yourself. Can't you tell someone else?'

'Who do you suggest?' he quickly replied.

Mary didn't answer. Instead, after a short pause, she said, 'I'm sure you're right.'

Although it was now almost 3am, Tom wasn't in the least tired. He knew it was the adrenaline flowing through his veins which was partly responsible. Even if he tried to sleep, he knew, with everything now swirling around in his brain, he would find it almost impossible, and he would simply lie there looking at the ceiling. Like most people, he'd tried that many times previously and found it an almost torturous experience.

By now Mary had closed her eyes again and, as he didn't want to disturb her, he quietly opened the doors and stepped out onto the veranda. Although it was another still, warm night he took the precaution of taking one of the spare blankets with him and settled down, hoping the change of scenery would help him sleep. The last thing he remembered, before drifting off, was the image of what he'd seen in the bar.

Chapter 44

'So that's where you've been,' said Mary, gently kissing Tom on the forehead. 'You don't look very comfortable. Let me make you a cup of coffee.' She stepped back into the cabin.

As Tom stood, a stiff pain in his neck reminded him that he was getting too old to be sleeping on chairs. As he had suspected, he had stayed awake for a while, but eventually the change in location had done its job and he had fallen into a surprisingly deep sleep.

Unfortunately, it wasn't deep enough to prevent him from having an anxiety dream. At the time it had been crystal clear but, like most dreams, now that he had woken, he was struggling to remember the details. The one thing he could remember was that he and Milner had been in a cell in the Hanoi Hilton, both chained to a wall-mounted metal ring. On the other side of the cell he could see Don, also in chains and looking exactly as he did today.

It was incredible how the mind could conflate different concerns, yet somehow seem perfectly logical at the time. Milner's presence in his dream was an indication of just how much, at least subconsciously, Tom was worried about his situation back in the UK. Tom had always thought that one of his strengths was his ability to compartmentalise different problems which were happening concurrently. Clearly, though, this didn't apply to his dreams. He thought it best if he didn't mention any of this to Mary.

It wasn't long before she returned with two cups of coffee and placed them on the small table. 'What do you think you will do?' she asked.

Conscious that they were both outside, and next to Don and Estelle's cabin, Tom raised his finger to his lips and shook his head. It wasn't as if he didn't trust Don and Estelle, but, given the very sensitive nature of the investigation, it would be much better for all concerned if, at least for the time being, he kept it to himself.

Before he had eventually fallen asleep, and whilst his mind was still hyperactive, he'd been able to spend time thinking through all the different scenarios that this new information had suddenly provided him with. Today was likely to be the most decisive one, if not the actual denouement.

Notwithstanding his determination to keep his new suspicions to as few people as possible, he knew that, if his investigation was to be successful, he was rapidly reaching the point when he would need the help of others and so would have to share some of these suspicions with them. So far, just like Captain Bao Ninh's, all his evidence had been largely circumstantial. After his conversation with Jordan Griffiths, combined with what Lan had later told him, he suspected the legal bar to deliver a conviction would be quite a bit lower for the local authorities than the one set for him. He knew, therefore, that any evidence he presented would have to be both provable and unambiguous. There were a few actions, one of which was perhaps *the* most important, as far as evidence was concerned, which needed to be completed today, and he couldn't see how he could do this by himself.

The other major complication was the timetable, which was now, unfortunately, even more limited. If the *Mekong Voyager* was no longer considered to be an active crime scene and the ship was to resume its journey later today, that would definitely make it far more difficult to get the evidence he needed. On the other hand, it would hardly endear him to the other passengers if the ship's sailing was delayed even longer. He already, due to his association with Tony, wasn't exactly the most popular person on board. This would only make matters worse, but, he decided, it was a price worth paying.

Despite all these concerns, the good news was that he had a clear plan in his mind. All he now needed to do was execute it.

It sounded easy, but he knew that every murder investigation had its unexpected twists and turns, and that the greatest danger was when you believed you had thought of everything. It didn't take long for that theory to be proved correct.

Chapter 45

Most of the passengers were once again assembled in the lounge area. Lan had earlier announced that he had some important news to communicate and so had asked everyone to make their way there for his 8am briefing.

Although Tom had been awake for a while, he'd decided he needed a shower to freshen up both his body and mind, and he and Mary had arrived a couple of minutes before the briefing was due to begin. Despite this they had managed to find seats towards the back of the room, not far from Mike and Shelley, who had both waved in acknowledgement.

Lan was positioned at his now-usual place at the front of the room. Given that it had been a very late night for him, as well as, given his other duties, presumably an early start, he was looking remarkably fresh and engaged. Standing alongside him was the ship's captain, although there was no sign of Captain Bao Ninh.

In keeping with his usual punctuality, Lan picked up the microphone and immediately began to speak. 'Ladies and gentlemen, thank you for getting here on time. I thought you would like to hear the good news as soon as possible.' Without any pause, he went straight on. 'The ship will be resuming its journey along the Mekong later today. Unless anything changes, we will recommence sailing at 2pm.'

There was some cheering and applause, although, given the circumstances, it was all fairly muted, reflecting relief rather than celebration.

Lan continued. 'We will, I'm afraid, have to make some changes to the planned schedule, as we have now lost about a day and a half in total. We are still considering how we can make up this lost time, but it's likely we will now arrive in Ho Chi Minh City a day later than the originally planned schedule. At least this will still allow all of you to get your planned flights back home.'

He paused momentarily, allowing this information to sink in. 'I know the shortened stay in Ho Chi Minh City will be a big disappointment for some of you, especially the veterans on board who were looking forward to seeing the city again. On the other hand, I hope you will understand how, given the circumstances, we have had to make some compromises.'

One man had been continuously trying to attract Lan's attention whilst he'd been speaking, although Lan had studiously avoided him until he had finished communicating the main points of his announcement.

'Yes, sir?' Lan eventually said. 'You have a question?'

'I do,' he answered. 'Does this mean that the investigation has ended, and the police are now confident it was the Brit who murdered John?'

'I'm sorry, sir, but even if I knew the answer to your question – which I don't – I would not be allowed to comment. Captain Bao Ninh has made it very clear that this is still an ongoing investigation. Some parts of the ship will still be out of bounds. For example, part of the forward starboard side will remain cordoned off whilst the police continue their forensic investigations. The good news, though, is that the bar area will reopen later today, although it will close at 11pm.'

If this was intended to appease the man, it quickly became apparent that it hadn't worked. 'But what if the Brit wasn't working alone? That would mean the accomplice is still on board.'

It was clear that his comment was aimed at Tom and, with sudden anger rising, Tom was tempted to say something in reply. Fortunately, Lan responded, his own anger now evident, before Tom could say anything. 'Sir, if you have any evidence to confirm what you have just said, then I suggest you take it to Captain Bao Ninh. He is still on board, and I'd be happy to take you to see him right now, if that's what you want.'

When there was no reply, Lan reinforced his point. 'Do you have any evidence, sir? Because I'm sure it would be very important to the investigation if you do have any.'

There was a brief pause before the passenger did eventually answer, and when he did it was with a single word. 'No.'

'Good,' answered Lan, making it very clear that their discussion had now ended. He then carried on as he had before he had been interrupted. 'As soon as we have finalised the revised schedule, I will, of course, let you know. I have also now received confirmation from Mekong Cruises that everyone will be refunded the full cost of this trip. They will also add an extra fifty percent, as a way of compensating you for all the inconvenience.'

This was followed by a faint murmur of approval amongst some of the passengers, although the vast majority, probably out of respect for John, remained silent.

Lan, looking at his watch, said, 'I'm happy to take questions now.'

When none were forthcoming, reflecting Lan's comprehensive briefing, he spoke again. 'I suggest that those of you who haven't already had breakfast make your way to the restaurant.'

Most people took this as their cue to leave the lounge area. As Tom and Mary were making their way out, Mike and Shelley came towards them.

'I just wanted to thank you for everything you did for us,' Shelley said. 'Jim told us how he'd asked you to speak with us.'

'How did it go with Jim?' asked Mary, clearly concerned that it might not have gone as well as they had wished.

Her concerns immediately disappeared, however, when Shelley replied. 'It was wonderful,' she said excitedly. 'We had so much to talk about.'

'What did you agree?' Tom asked, getting to the heart of the issue.

It was Mike who answered. 'Shelley, Jim and Peggy, his sister, will be having a DNA test when we all get home. It's the quickest way to find out.'

'Jim and, hopefully, Peggy will then come over to the UK to stay with us,' Shelley added. 'We'll take them to Totnes, where Jim's dad Hank and my grandmother Peggy first met.'

'Let's not get too far ahead of ourselves,' suggested Mike. 'I think we should just take one step at a time.'

If this was an attempt to dampen Shelley's excitement, then it clearly hadn't worked. 'I can't wait to take them there,' she said, almost as though she hadn't heard what her husband had said.

'Anyway,' said Tom, his mind now back on what he had to do over the next few hours, 'it's great news. I really do think, though, you should take Mike's advice and wait until you have the DNA results.'

'Don't be such a killjoy,' Mary said, looking at Tom, before taking hold of Shelley's hand. 'I'm sure everything will turn out fine.'

'Why did you have to say that?' Mary asked Tom, as they walked towards the lounge exit. 'You could see how excited she was.'

'I was just reinforcing what Mike had said, that's all,' he replied, struggling to understand what he'd done wrong. 'As a matter of interest, and for what it's worth, I'd be very surprised now if they are not related.'

'Really?' answered Mary, now back to her naturally positive self. 'I really hope so. We could all do with some good news.'

As they reached the exit from the lounge, Tom could see that Lan was engaged in conversation with one of the passengers. As they passed by, Tom looked towards Lan but noted that he didn't offer any acknowledgement, not even the slightest change in his facial expression. It didn't surprise him. Lan was probably understandably still very anxious after their time together in the purser's office.

Tom suddenly realised just how hungry he was. He knew how important it was to take in enough food now to get through what would be a long day. At some point, his adrenaline would shut down, and so he would need to eat something substantial. He also knew it might be the last opportunity to eat anything for some considerable time.

When Tom and Mary entered the restaurant, they could immediately see there were people already seated at their usual table. As Tom looked around the restaurant, his attention was drawn to Jim, who was beckoning them over to his table.

'Come and join us,' Jim said, indicating a couple of empty chairs at the table, where he was sitting with Bob and Ruth. It was obvious that they were being invited to sit in the chairs that John and Joany would normally have occupied.

'I'm sorry about that jerk,' said Bob, as soon as they were seated. 'He was talking out of his butt.'

It took Tom a moment to realise he was speaking about the passenger who had interrupted Lan's briefing. 'Don't worry. And anyway, Lan handled it very professionally.'

'He sure did,' Jim said. 'The guy made a fool of himself.'

Mary joined in. 'I don't know why he said that, unless he was just trying to look clever.'

'Anyway,' Jim said, clearly intending to move the conversation on to other things, 'this is the first chance I've had to thank you both for speaking with Mike and Shelley.'

Tom didn't reply, although there was a slightly puzzled expression on his face. Correctly interpreting this, Jim was quick to reassure him. 'Don't worry. I've told Bob and Ruth about it.'

'We're really excited for them,' exclaimed Ruth. 'We could all do with some good news.'

'That's exactly what I said,' Mary replied.

Tom then spoke. 'Without dampening your obvious excitement, I would just say what I said to Shelley. You should wait for the DNA results before you start to make other plans.'

'Too late for that,' said Jim, not in the least bit deterred by Tom's advice. 'I've already spoken with my sister Peggy, and we will be making arrangements to travel to the UK to visit Mike and Shelley. Even if the DNA results don't work out, we'll still go. Mike and Shelley are a fine couple and, anyway, it would be great to see the place where Dad was stationed during the last war.' He then added, almost wistfully, 'He might not have been able to make it back, but we sure can. It's the least we can do for him.' He paused. 'I've also asked Peggy to scan the photo and email it to me. She lives quite close, and I've told her where to find it.'

'I think that's wonderful,' said Mary, clearly moved.

After a short pause, Jim spoke again. 'Perhaps we can all

meet up again. I've looked a map of the UK, and London doesn't look that far away from Devon.'

'That's a great idea. Isn't it, Tom?' Mary said.

'It is,' he answered, suddenly imagining just how fraught the journey to Devon could sometimes be. 'Let's hope we can work something out.'

As they ate their breakfasts, the conversation inevitably turned towards John's murder inquiry. Tom had anticipated this, and, whilst it might be an opportunity to learn some more snippets of information, he was equally aware that he was the person who would be asked the most questions.

It didn't take long for his suspicion to be confirmed. It was Bob who started the conversation with a direct question. 'What's happened to your buddy Tony? Has he been charged yet?'

Tom was beginning to become slightly annoyed with how Tony was increasingly referred to as *his buddy*. He couldn't decide whether this was a form of disapproval or simply the way Americans spoke. He gave Bob the benefit of the doubt. 'I haven't heard anything, although I'm hoping Sue or their son David will call later today to give me an update.'

Bob, clearly not satisfied with Tom's answer, was now even more direct. 'So, what do you think, Tom? As an ex-cop, you must have your own view. Do you think he murdered John?'

'I'm sure Tom doesn't need this right now,' said Jim. 'Let's just leave it to the local police to see though.'

'That's fine,' Tom said. 'Bob's question is a fair one, especially given how close you all were to John. To answer your question, Bob, *no*, I don't think Tony committed the murder. Apart from anything else, from what everyone tells me, he was so drunk he was totally incapable of killing anyone.'

Once again, this did not satisfy Bob. 'So how about the film of them fighting? Then there was the knife. He said himself he had one. Plus, we all know that they didn't exactly see eye-to-eye. It seems pretty straightforward to me.'

Tom decided not to pick apart any of the points that Bob had made. To do so would not only invite further questions but, more importantly, would potentially force him to share the reasons he was refuting Bob's 'evidence'. 'As Jim said, I think it's best to allow the local police to carry out their investigations. I'm sure they are more than capable of doing so,' he said, as plausibly as possible.

Bob clearly didn't intend to let the issue drop that easily. 'Okay,' he replied. 'If you are so sure your buddy didn't do it, that means someone else did – unless you are saying John stabbed himself.' By this stage, he was becoming increasingly worked up. 'If that wasn't what happened, then who do *you* think did it? After all, you are supposed to be the expert.'

Bob's sarcasm wasn't lost on anyone.

'I don't know who did it, despite the fact that you seem to, Bob,' Tom answered, deciding it was time to fight fire with a little bit of his own. Before Bob could respond, and in an effort to draw a line under this, he quickly carried on. 'Look, Bob, why don't we leave it to Captain Bao Ninh? I have a feeling we will all get the answer very soon.'

This seemed to satisfy everyone, although it wasn't difficult to notice that Bob was restraining himself from continuing the conversation.

The rest of their time was spent discussing how, despite the circumstances, they were pleased the cruise would soon be restarting, and what they were particularly looking forward to seeing in Ho Chi Minh City. When it was Tom and Mary's turn to tell everyone what their plans were, Mary mentioned that it now appeared as though they would be able to travel on to Australia immediately after the cruise ended. This inevitably prompted questions about why they were going there.

Tom was glad Mary took over the discussion. It wasn't because he was not looking forward to going, rather that he found it difficult talking about emotional or family-related issues even to people he knew well, let alone those he'd known for less than a week. Fortunately, she didn't mention how Tom hadn't seen his son for over thirty years and had, in actual fact, never seen his two grandchildren until just a few weeks ago.

Even while this conversation was taking place, Tom was

still thinking about what he had to do later that day. If things didn't work out the way he hoped, there was a good chance he would not be invited to join this group for breakfast ever again.

'Why was Bob so aggressive with you?' asked Mary, as they made their way back to their cabin. 'It seemed to me he'd already made up his mind that Tony had murdered John.'

'Sometimes, people who had a close link to the victim need to have someone to blame, so they can have closure. If there is some circumstantial evidence, in the absence of any other potential culprit, then they will latch on to that. I suspect that's what Bob is doing. It always struck me that he and John were probably the two who were closest to each other. He's angry and wants to blame someone.'

'But what about Tony's reference to having a knife? It's not something you would normally talk about, especially when you're on holiday. If he did have one, then where did he get it from? He wouldn't have been able to pack it in his suitcase along with his clothes.'

Tom gave a short laugh. 'You should have had my job,' he said.

'What, and you have mine? Somehow, I can't see you running a florist shop. For a start, you'd have to talk to customers.'

'Now that you put it like that ...' he answered.

Mary's point, about Tony saying he had a knife, was a very good one, and had worried Tom ever since he had first heard of Tony's comment. Irrespective of whether Tony had a knife or not, Tom was still firmly of the opinion, especially now having seen the footage himself, that Tony would have been incapable of using it. On the other hand, he knew his opinion would not stand up in a court of law. Somehow, he had to definitively prove his opinion was the correct one. He was soon to find out if that was to be the case.

Chapter 46

After they arrived back at the cabin, Mary announced that, after the disturbed night, she needed to rest. The last few hours had been very tiring, and, in truth, Tom's lack of sleep was also now starting to catch up with him. He was just about to suggest that he would join her, when he decided he would first check his emails.

As previously, he couldn't quite make up his mind whether or not he wanted there to be an unopened message from Milner. There wasn't anything from him.

What did grab his attention, though, was an email from Peter Andrews. Pete was an ex-colleague, working for the Met, who was based in the specialist Digital Forensics Unit. It was a unit which had proved its value time and time again. Through the use of the very latest software, Pete and his colleagues were able to recover data and messages from almost every device. Messages which criminals thought they had permanently deleted could eventually still be retrieved, providing they had access to the criminal's phone, computer, tablet or laptop. Over the past few years, it had been a major factor in delivering successful convictions. Tom opened Pete's email.

Hi Tom,

Haven't you retired, or was that just a rumour? Looks like you might be doing a bit of moonlighting in your spare time.

I've looked at the video you sent and taken out the background noise (sounded like those guys were really enjoying themselves). I've also enhanced the volume of the conversation, so that you can clearly hear what's being said. As I know you were always a stickler for this type of thing, I've attached a transcript of what was said. If there's anything else you need from me, you know

where I am. Make sure it's something more difficult next time, though!
   Cheers
   Pete

Without any great sense of expectation, Tom had sent the video that Brett had filmed on his phone to Pete, hoping he would be able to work his magic on it.

He quickly opened the video that Pete had reworked, and, with a growing feeling of anticipation, listened carefully to what was being said. After he'd heard it, he replayed the video, before opening the attachment and reading the transcript, just to ensure what he'd heard was correct.

He settled back in his chair and considered what he had just found out. At least he now knew the answer to the knife question. The issue now, however, was what he should do next.

He strongly suspected that it could all hinge on just one point. Now was the time to try to confirm that suspicion, and so he composed a text message and pressed the send button, knowing that his attempt to prove Tony's innocence would depend on the response to it.

Whilst he waited for a reply, he picked up a sheet of Mekong Cruises branded paper and began to write on it. On one side of the paper, he listed all the known evidence against Tony and categorised each point as either factual or circumstantial, whilst alongside each of these points he noted all the counter-evidence. After doing this, he listed all the additional evidence he had gathered. Some of this was factual, and could be readily proven, whilst some of it could be deemed to be simply circumstantial.

As he reviewed what he'd written, it was obvious that, whilst he could now make a strong case as to *who* committed the murder and *how* it had been carried out, there was a glaring omission. As yet, he couldn't offer any explanation as to *why* John had been murdered.

Just as he was contemplating this, his phone suddenly sprang to life. It was a text message, and he could instantly see by the number that it was from Lan.

Ok. I will come to your cabin in 30 minutes. I will only be able to stay for a few minutes though.

Tom realised that Lan's response to what Tom was about to tell him would be crucial. If he agreed, then there was a *possibility* Tom could build a case for Tony to be exonerated. If he disagreed, then Tony would almost certainly be found guilty, and Tom himself would be completely vilified here in Vietnam. Not only that, but, given his profile back in the UK, his reputation would be totally shredded there as well.

Despite the huge risk of sharing his suspicions with Lan, he knew he had no other choice. Time was running against him. If he left it much later then it would be too late. So, yes, it was a risk, but a calculated one, based upon his judgement of Lan's character. His judgement had, in the past, stood him in good stead. He hoped it would not let him down now.

Chapter 47

Tom was gently shaking Mary from her sleep. He felt guilty about doing it, but, with Lan due shortly, it might not fit the serious discussion he was just about to have if she was fast asleep in their bed. Once she had woken, and was sitting up, he explained to her that Lan would soon be arriving and it would be better, given the circumstances, if just the two of them were there.

'If that's what you think, then I'll leave you to talk,' she replied. 'I'll go up to the sun deck. Perhaps Shelley and Mike will be there.'

Tom kissed her gently. 'Hopefully, it won't be long now before it's finished,' he said, deliberately not adding *one way or another*.

'Do you really think so?' she asked, relief clear in her voice.

'Let's hope so,' he answered, as positively as he dared.

After Mary had gone, he went outside to sit on the veranda, hoping it would not only clear his head but perhaps, more importantly, provide him with the confidence and resilience he knew he would need over the next few hours.

Exactly thirty minutes after Lan had sent his text message, there was a soft rap on Tom and Mary's cabin door. Tom took the precaution of closing the door leading onto the veranda. He wanted their conversation to be as private as possible. He opened the cabin door, and Lan, quickly and silently, slipped inside.

'As I said, I only have a few minutes,' Lan said. 'I'm on duty and have a meeting with Captain Bao Ninh and our ship's captain at eleven o'clock. We have to make final preparations for the ship's sailing.' He gave Tom a significant look. 'I believe Mr Griffiths will also be there.'

'Thanks for coming,' Tom answered, as even-voiced as possibly, whilst simultaneously realising that Griffiths' presence could only be bad news. 'I know I keep placing you in a difficult position, and I'm afraid I'm just about to do that again.' He waited for a reaction and, when none was forthcoming, he carried on. 'I'll say to you what I said last time. If you feel you can't do what I'm about to ask, then I will totally understand. I'm just grateful for what you have done so far, because you didn't have to do it.'

Again, there was no response, and so Tom felt he had to keep going. 'Before I get onto what I'm asking you to do, I'd appreciate it if you are able to tell me what Sang saw or heard in the bar, the night Mr Fisher died. I assume, especially as you share a cabin, you have discussed it.'

This time, Lan did answer, although it was evident that he was choosing his words very carefully. 'We heard Sang get back to our cabin, and I could tell he was quite upset. I asked him what the problem was, and he then told us what had happened in the bar. We are all used to guests getting a bit drunk, but usually they just get louder. He said how, at first, they had been drinking beer, but later they started drinking a local Vietnamese spirit. It is very strong and, if you are not used to it, can affect you badly. There was an argument between some of the guests from his group and some from my group – Mr Fisher, mainly.'

'Did he say what it was about?'

'He couldn't understand everything they were saying, but he was sure it was something to do with what happened here, during the war, when they were on a special operation. At one stage, it got very heated, but eventually they calmed down and then they all began to hug each other. It was after that when they started to ask for even more drinks for a drinking competition.'

'Did he say what Mr Young was doing whilst all this was going on?'

'Only that he was also drunk. Mr Fisher apparently said something which upset him. They both got very angry and Sang said he had to separate them, otherwise there might have been a fight.'

'What happened after that?'

'They just carried on drinking, almost as though nothing had happened.'

'What time did Sang leave?' Tom asked.

For the first time, Lan gave him a wary look. 'Why do you want to know? Are you saying Sang might have seen something else?'

'No, I'm not,' Tom replied, in a tone which he hoped would assuage these suspicions. 'I'm just trying to understand when everyone left.'

'He's told all of this to Captain Bao Ninh.'

This time it was Tom's turn to remain silent.

'He said he left after the last guest had gone, just after 2am.' As if to underline the veracity of the time, he added, 'It was about 2.10am when he got back to our cabin.'

'Thank you,' Tom answered. 'That is exactly what I understand, as well.'

It was clear that Lan was beginning to get a bit anxious. He looked at his watch, before saying, 'Is that everything you wanted to ask? I have to go, otherwise I will be missed.'

'Lan,' Tom said, in a way which immediately got his attention. 'I'd like to share my thoughts with you about Mr Fisher's death. I understand it will put you in an even more uncomfortable position, but, if they are correct, then it will prove that Mr Young did not murder Mr Fisher. I can't, however, do this without your help.'

Tom paused briefly, hoping Lan would react to what he'd just said. He quickly realised, however, that Lan wasn't about to respond, so he spoke again. 'Do you want me to carry on? If you do, then I'll also tell you what I need from you.'

Tom could actually feel his own heart rate increasing as he waited for Lan's reply. The silence seemed to be interminable, although, in reality, it was no longer than a few seconds.

Finally, Lan answered. 'Why don't you tell me what you want me to do?'

So Tom told him.

Chapter 48

After his brief meeting with Lan, Tom joined Mary on the sun deck. Shelley and Mike were there with her, along with Jim. As he approached, he could immediately tell just by their body language, let alone the sound of their excited laughter, that they were all in quite an animated state.

'Tom, come and join us,' said Shelley, who was enthusiastically waving in his direction. 'You'll never guess what Jim has just shown us.'

'Is it a photograph of Peggy and Hank?' asked Tom, his tone suggesting that it wasn't just a wild guess.

'How did you know that?' she replied, clearly impressed.

It was Jim who provided the answer. 'I mentioned to Tom this morning how I'd asked my sister to email it to me. I imagine, being an ex-cop, he's trained to remember these things.'

'That, and the fact your iPad is on, and I can see a photo,' Tom said. 'I assume that's Peggy and Hank.'

'Shelley was just saying how the girl in the photo is definitely her grandmother,' Mary said. 'It's such a wonderful story.'

Tom sat down and, sure enough, this was the cue for Huan to suddenly appear. 'Can I please get you something to drink, sir?' he asked in his now customary manner.

'Just an orange juice, please,' Tom answered, knowing he would need a clear head if he was to deal with what was soon about to happen.

After Huan had left, Tom asked, 'So, what are your plans now? Will you still have DNA tests?'

'We were just speaking about that when you arrived,' replied Jim. 'I'm more than happy to go along with just the photo, but, whatever we decide, I think it's important we all agree on the same thing.' He looked at Shelley and Mike as he spoke.

'What do you think, Tom?' asked Shelley.

Tom was taken aback by Shelley's question and needed a short time to compose his thoughts. 'I really don't think I'm qualified to be giving advice on something as important as this. It's such a personal thing and, as Mary will tell you, that is not my strong point.'

'That's true,' Mary quickly replied, before adding, with a slight laugh, 'As I always say to him, sometimes you are so emotionally illiterate.'

'As an ex-policeman, I think I'll take that as a compliment.'

Before this topic of conversation could develop any further, Huan returned with some drinks on a tray and placed Tom's on the table in front of him.

'Have you spoken with your family today?' asked Mary, directing her question at Huan.

'Yes, ma'am. This morning. I told them we would soon be sailing again.'

'They must have been worried about you,' she said.

'A little, but I speak to them almost every day,' he answered. 'My daughter is ill, and my wife wants me to return home. I can't, though, until this trip has ended.' He left to take the drinks to some other guests.

'I hope his daughter isn't seriously ill,' said Mary, clearly concerned. 'I really don't know how his family manage without him. He told us how doing these trips meant he was away for six months at a time.'

Tom resisted the temptation to remind her of what Tony's answer had been when she'd, more or less, said the same thing earlier in the trip. He was just about to take the first sip of his orange juice when his phone buzzed. It was another text message from Lan. It was short and to the point.

Can we meet in 5 minutes in your cabin?

He drank half of his orange juice and then said, 'Please excuse me, but that was an old colleague who needs some information from me. I promised I'd get it to him, but I'd forgotten all about it. I need to go back to our cabin to use my iPad. Hopefully I won't be too long.'

As Tom stood, he caught sight of Mary's expression. It was

the one she always used when she was suspicious about what he had just said. By now he had come to know that look very well. It was her way of making the point that she didn't quite believe what he'd said but was, nonetheless, willing to go along with it. Over the past couple of years, he had surprisingly found this to be one of her most endearing characteristics.

Almost as soon as he'd returned to his cabin there was a light knock on the door. He opened it and Lan quickly stepped inside. He had something in his hand and, whilst remaining standing, got straight to the point. 'I have brought you what you asked for,' he said, without any excitement, as he handed over copies of the passports.

Tom didn't immediately examine them. Instead, he placed them on the desk. 'Thank you. Were you able to find out about the other thing?'

'Yes, I did. They are still there,' he replied. 'I don't know for how long, though.'

Tom was still considering what he'd just been told when Lan said, 'I have to go now. I'm not sure my nerves can take any more of this. Please don't ask me for anything else,' he added, in an almost pleading tone of voice.

Lan opened the cabin door and slipped out as quickly as he'd entered. He had been there for less than a minute.

After he had left, Tom picked up the photocopied passports and carefully examined them. After a short while, he found what he'd been looking for. He took a deep breath and quietly said to himself, 'It's now or never.'

Chapter 49

A few minutes later and he was back on the sun deck.

'That didn't take long. Did you manage to get everything done?' asked Jim. 'You seemed to suddenly be in a bit of a hurry.'

'All done,' replied Tom, as upbeat as possible, choosing not to respond to Jim's astute comment.

Mary, clearly not totally convinced, gave him another of her suspicious looks, this time the one involving a downward movement of her forehead and a slight squinting of her eyes.

'Actually, I've come to take Mary back to our cabin,' Tom said.

'Really?' said Jim, laughing slightly. 'Well, good for you two. You are on vacation, after all.'

'I'm afraid it's something a lot more boring,' replied Tom. Before Jim could respond, he provided some additional explanation. 'I can't find something. I think Mary might know where it is.'

Mary could tell from his body language that he was impatient to leave. 'What was all that about?' she asked, when they were out of earshot of the others.

'Sorry,' he said, turning to face her. 'It was the best I could think of at the time.'

'Well, I don't think it worked because, as far as I could see, no one seemed to be convinced.' Now in a far more serious voice, she said, 'So, what is it?'

'I'll tell you when we are in our cabin.'

*

After the shock and almost disbelief of what she had just been told, Mary remained silent for a brief period, before finally saying, 'Are you absolutely sure?'

'Yes. Well, as sure as I can be,' Tom answered in a controlled and calm manner.

'What are you going to do now, then?' she asked.

'That's another reason why I wanted us to get back here. I intend to now present all the evidence to Captain Bao Ninh. I'm sure he's not going to react well to what I tell him, and there could be consequences for us both.'

'But what can they do? They can hardly lock me up,' she replied, before adding, 'Can they?'

'I doubt they will do that,' he said reassuringly, 'but it's better to be on the safe side. That's why I want you to stay here, in the cabin, until things are a bit clearer.'

'Okay, if that's what you suggest, that's what I'll do,' she answered, now in a supportive tone.

Tom kissed her gently on the forehead. 'Thanks. It will really help knowing you are out of the way.' He paused momentarily, before carrying on. 'There's one other thing.'

Mary looked directly at him, as she wondered what else could he possibly have to say.

'There's a file at the bottom of the suitcase,' he said, gesturing to the suitcase he used. 'It contains a summary of all the evidence relating to the investigation. It's mostly notes, but there are copies of some passports, which I've just added, as well as a reference to where a couple of videos can be found on my phone and iPad. If the worst comes to the worst, could you take it to Jim? I'm sure he'll know what to do with it.'

Suddenly the seriousness of the situation hit Mary hard and she began to quietly cry.

Tom put his arm around her shoulder. 'I'm sorry to make it sound so dramatic, but it's much better for you to now know everything. Remember when I said I'd tell you everything when I considered the time to be right? Well, I think that time has just arrived.'

All Mary could say was, 'Please, Tom, you will take care, won't you?'

'Of course I will. I wouldn't want to miss your scary expressions,' he answered, trying to add a touch of levity to the

proceedings, although Mary's expression suggested it hadn't worked.
'Is that everything?' she asked, quite nervously.
'Not quite,' he replied. 'I need to make a phone call.'

Chapter 50

After his discussion with Mary, Tom had, not for the first time, reviewed everything he knew about the murder. From the successful investigations he had been involved in over the years, he knew the importance of thorough preparation. It was also vital to present any evidence in a logical way which progressively increased the suspense and tension, before delivering the coup de grâce. Now that he had a bit more insight into the personalities of the people involved, he was determined, where possible, to use that knowledge to his advantage.

A few frustrating hours later, the time finally arrived when he would see if all his preparation had been worthwhile. He picked up the summary notes he'd put together and then made his way to the ship's main office, where, thanks to Lan, he knew a meeting was taking place. Along with Captain Bao Ninh, he knew Jordan Griffiths, the ship's captain and Lan would also be there.

He took a deep breath and knocked on the door. It was Lan who opened it and, even to the untrained eye, there was heightened concern and anxiety etched into his face. They both knew everything he'd worked for and achieved during his time with Mekong Cruises was now at risk, with his future being decided in the next few minutes.

Tom gave Lan a reassuring smile and a discreet tap on the shoulder, hoping it would relax him a little. 'I'd like to speak with Captain Bao Ninh. I have some important new information which I believe he will want to hear.'

Lan immediately turned, and Tom could hear him presumably translating what he had just said.

Tom wasn't invited in. Instead, he was surprised to see that it was Jordan Griffiths who came to the door.

'You have some vital information,' Griffiths said. 'Is that correct?'

'It is,' Tom simply answered.

'We're having an important meeting right now, so can you put it in writing? We'll take a look at it when we get some free time.'

'I'm afraid there isn't time for that,' replied Tom, looking him directly in the eye, 'unless you want to be part of a deliberate miscarriage of justice.' When there wasn't an immediate response, Tom carried on. 'Is that what you want? Because, if it is, I'm more than happy to be the main witness for the prosecution.'

He had deliberately said this in a provocative manner, knowing how Griffiths would almost certainly react. When he did, however, it was not in the way that Tom had expected.

'Mr Stone,' Griffiths answered, in a slightly unnervingly calm manner, 'my strong advice to you is to be very careful what you are saying. We have strong libel laws in the US. I will not hesitate to use those laws if you repeat that accusation.'

'Well, let's see if a court of law agrees with you. I'm more than willing to take that chance,' Tom answered, as confidently as he could sound. He knew, of course, that Jordan Griffiths was trying to intimidate him. It was right out of the playbook of most bullies. What he didn't know, however, was how far Griffiths was willing to escalate this beyond straightforward bullying. He was just about to get the answer.

'Why are you doing this?' Griffiths asked. 'I've done a bit of digging on you, and it appears you are a bit of a self-publicist within the British police. You seem to like the limelight and all the attention that comes from being a troublemaker. Is that what all this is about? Do you want to see your name across all the British media again?'

Tom was aware that, so far, he had not been invited into the office to join the others. 'Let me ask *you* a question, Mr Griffiths. What is your role in this investigation? You seem to have now become investigator, prosecutor, judge *and* jury. I thought Captain Bao Ninh was heading up this investigation, but it seems I was wrong.'

'You have five minutes,' Griffiths replied, turning around

and walking back into the office, leaving Tom to follow him.

Whilst the office wasn't overly large, there was still more than enough space for everyone. Tom wasn't invited to sit.

Captain Bao Ninh said something, and Lan translated. 'The captain says he has already warned you about interfering in his investigation. There are laws in Vietnam which punish people for doing that.'

'I'll take my chances,' Tom answered. Lan didn't bother to translate.

'So, Mr Tom Stone. Retired British detective. Please tell us what information you have,' said Griffiths, in an obviously patronising manner.

'Actually, it's retired detective *chief* inspector,' Tom said. 'But I'll forgive your poor research.'

Griffiths had visibly bridled at Tom's comment and seemed as though he was about to reply, but then he apparently resisted the temptation.

Instead, Captain Bao Ninh spoke next, and Lan dutifully translated. 'Why do you think you have evidence that we don't have? It seems you are implying that the Vietnamese police force is incompetent.'

'Not at all,' Tom replied. 'I have never said that. What I do think, though, is that you and Mr Griffiths have, almost certainly for political reasons, decided that it was convenient to arrest Mr Young, based on the flimsiest of evidence.'

Just as Lan began to translate, Griffiths became very angry and, raising his voice for the first time, said, 'I've had enough of this. First you accuse us of being involved in a deliberate miscarriage of justice, and now you accuse us of fabricating evidence. I want you to know that my counterpart in the British embassy, here in Vietnam, is a very good friend of mine. You'll be lucky if you manage not to be arrested for what you have just said.'

'So,' Tom said, 'you're now threatening me with imprisonment. That is what you are saying, isn't it?' When there was no answer, he continued. 'Just for the record, I have at no stage accused anyone of fabricating evidence. What I am accusing you of doing, however, is carrying out a half-hearted investigation. It suits you to have a ready-made suspect. It's very convenient, as it isn't embarrassing and doesn't upset the current US-Vietnamese relationship.'

By now Jordan Griffiths had regained, at least outwardly, his composure and characteristic confidence. 'So, not only are you a famous British policeman, but you're also an expert on geopolitics.' He paused, waiting for a reaction and when none came, he carried on. 'Okay, Mr Ex Great British Detective *Chief* Inspector, why don't you tell us why we are so incompetent and have arrested the wrong man?'

'Before I do that, I would like to invite a couple of others to join us. It will be a bit tight in here, but I'm sure it will be worth it.'

'A couple more?' replied Griffiths, a mixture of concern and puzzlement in his voice. 'Who are they?'

'Well, one you know already, and the other, I suspect, is well known to Captain Bao Ninh.' As Tom finished saying this, he opened the door to reveal the two men standing immediately outside.

Chapter 51

The two men entered the room, and Tom introduced them. 'This is Mr Jason Thomas from the British embassy. I believe you already know Mr Thomas as, according to you, he is a very good friend,' he added, directly addressing Griffiths. 'The other gentleman will be very well known to Captain Bao Ninh. His name is Le Quan Cong, and he is the regional police chief for this region. In other words, Captain Bao Ninh's immediate superior.'

Earlier in the day, after Lan had brought him copies of the passports, Tom had called the British embassy and asked to speak with the person who was involved in Tony's arrest. That person was Jason Thomas. Tom had then explained everything he now knew about John's murder, and all the evidence he had to back up his suspicions. He also told Thomas about Jordan Griffiths' involvement, and how he strongly suspected Griffiths and Captain Bao Ninh were more concerned with getting a quick and convenient conviction rather than the correct one.

After Thomas had carefully listened to what Tom had told him, he had asked a few questions and then, seemingly satisfied with the answers, had asked Tom what he wanted him to do. Tom had told him how the ship was due to resume sailing at 2pm and that the sailing needed to be postponed, so that more extensive forensic tests could be carried out. As Thomas didn't have the authority to do this, he had suggested Le Quan Cong's involvement and said that he would personally immediately contact him.

When 2pm had come and gone, Tom had realised his request had been successful, as the ship was still moored alongside the small jetty, showing no signs of resuming its sailing. It was then simply a case of waiting until Jason Thomas and the regional police officer could both get to the ship. It had been just before 3pm when Tom had received a text message from Thomas to confirm they had arrived and were just about to board.

'Do you know what this is all about?' Griffiths asked, directing his question at Jason Thomas.

'I do, Jordan,' Thomas answered. 'In fact, I probably know a good deal more then you, but I'll let Mr Stone explain.'

Tom took a deep breath and began to speak. 'I think we can all agree that Mr Fisher and Mr Young didn't always see eye-to-eye about things, and there are plenty of witnesses who could confirm that. On the other hand, they did have something in common. They were both ex-military who had been involved in dangerous situations during their careers, and so, at least in my opinion, shared an almost grudging mutual respect.'

'Your opinion?' repeated Griffiths, sneeringly. 'You are obviously an expert now on human behaviour.'

Tom ignored this and carried on. 'It's also clear that, during the night Mr Fisher was murdered, they'd both had a lot to drink and, by the time they had stopped drinking, were considerably the worse for wear. There is even a video, taken by Brett Simpson, which graphically shows this. It's my strong belief that, even if Mr Young had wanted to murder Mr Fisher, he was physically incapable. One look at the ship's CCTV footage, showing the two of them together, would confirm this.'

Lan was having difficulty keeping up with the translation but interjected after Captain Bao Ninh said something. 'He asks about their fight by the side of the ship. It was around this time that Mr Fisher disappeared. He also says Mr Young had boasted about having a knife. One of the people at the bar said he mentioned something about having a chef's knife.'

'Again, look carefully at the CCTV footage,' Tom said. 'There was a bit of pushing, but that's all. As far as him having a knife is concerned, he certainly didn't have one then.'

'Just because you couldn't see it then doesn't mean he didn't have one. He might have been putting on a drunken act, and hiding the knife, because he knew there was CCTV. He could easily have stabbed him and thrown the knife into the river,' Lan said, once again translating for Captain Bao Ninh.

'Except that according to the post-mortem Mr Fisher's body showed multiple stab wounds, not just a single one,' Tom replied. He paused briefly before continuing. 'You've mentioned that the witnesses were sure he'd said he had a knife. What exactly do you think he said?'

Once Lan had finished translating, Captain Bao Ninh took out a small notebook from his pocket and said, 'This is the witness statement from Brett Simpson.' He began to read it. '*As they were drinking, Mr Young suddenly said he had a sharp chef's knife.* As you said earlier, Mr Simpson took a video of him actually saying this. I've seen the video. I don't think even you can dispute what he said.'

'That wasn't my question. My question was what *you* thought he'd said on the video, not what Mr Simpson thought he'd said.'

There was a silence in the room as everyone turned to look at Captain Bao Ninh, waiting for him to respond.

When no response was forthcoming, Tom continued. 'Have you ever been to Yorkshire in the UK?' he asked, directing his question now at both Jordan Griffiths and Captain Bao Ninh.

It was Griffiths who answered. 'What the hell has a place called Yorksheer got to do with this?'

'Well, it's got everything to do with it,' Tom replied, further increasing the suspense in the room. 'Mr Young lives in a place named Sheffield, which is a city in Yorkshire. People from Yorkshire have a very distinctive accent. Sometimes it's even difficult for people from outside Yorkshire to fully understand what is being said.'

'Hang on,' said Griffiths, once again displaying a rising anger. 'Are you now saying, because he had an accent, we didn't hear properly?'

'That's exactly what I'm saying,' answered Tom.

'Well, good luck with that in court,' he replied, this time with an undisguised contemptuous laugh. 'Jeez, I've heard everything now.' He faced Jason Thomas. 'Are you going to let this guy carry on like this, or are you going to stop him?'

243

'Actually, I'm rather enjoying it,' Thomas answered, with a slight laugh.

'Well, I'm not willing to listen to any more of this crap, even if you are,' Griffiths said, as he made to walk towards the door.

It was then Le Quan Cong spoke for the first time since he'd entered the room. 'I think you should stay and listen to what Mr Stone has to say,' he simply said, although in a very authoritative tone.

Tom took this as his cue to continue. 'I sent Mr Simpson's video to an ex-colleague of mine. He's an expert in digital forensics who was able to remove all the background noise, so as to hear precisely what Mr Young said.' It was his turn now to refer to his notebook. 'What he actually said was the following: *This is sharper than a Sheffield knife.*' He immediately continued. 'Just so you know, Sheffield built its reputation on the production of steel and, especially, cutlery. That's knives, forks and spoons. What I just read out to you is a common saying in that part of Yorkshire. He was referring to the sharpness of his drink and relating it to the sharpness of a knife made in Sheffield.' He waited for a reply, and, when it was obvious that none was about to come, he continued. 'I will send you the enhanced video, together with a transcript of what he actually said.'

It was now clear to everyone in the room that Tom had their full attention and any further attempts to discredit, belittle or denigrate him would probably simply work to his advantage. In retrospect, it was probably his mention of digital forensics that had begun the change from an atmosphere of contempt to some degree of respect.

After a while, and having regained some composure, it was Jordan Griffiths who next spoke. When he did, it was in a tone devoid of any of his previous aggression or attempts to ridicule. 'Okay, so he didn't say he had a knife, but that doesn't mean he couldn't have got hold of one from somewhere.'

'Good point,' answered Tom, in a similarly reasonable manner. 'Except that he was back in his cabin, having passed out, when Mr Fisher was murdered.'

Chapter 52

'How could you possibly know that?' asked Jordan Griffiths.
'I know because there's a witness who is willing to testify to that effect.' Tom once again turned his attention towards Captain Bao Ninh. 'Mr Don Simpson – that's Brett Simpson's father – tried to tell you this, but, for whatever reason, you didn't take him seriously and wouldn't even listen to what he had to say. Maybe it was because he's an elderly, frail gentleman – which he is. But he's still got a very sharp and retentive mind. He was awake, sitting on the veranda, at the time when Mr Fisher was murdered, and made notes of all the times he heard different things. His cabin is more or less immediately below where it almost certainly took place. It was a very still night, and he was able to make out what generally was going on above him.'

Tom once again referred to his notes. 'This is the chronology of what happened that night. At 2.02am, Gene left the bar and then Bill left a little later at 2.05. Mr Simpson's son, Brett, left at 2.06 and got back to his cabin at 2.08. Mr Fisher then left at 2.08, and Mr Young was the last to leave at 2.09. Then at 2.12 Mr Simpson heard Mr Fisher and Mr Young raising their voices at each other. At 2.17 Mr Young returned to his cabin, which, incidentally, the ship's CCTV footage can verify. Finally, at 2.23am, Mr Simpson heard two other voices – one of which I believe was Mr Fisher's – after which he then heard a splash, as if something or somebody had fallen overboard.'

'How do you know all of this?' asked Griffiths, as Lan tried his best to keep up with the translation. 'You keep referring to CCTV footage. How do you know what the footage shows?'

Even though Tom had anticipated this question, it was the one he had least been looking forward to answering. In the event, his nervousness was short-lived, as Lan, setting aside his translation duties, suddenly began to speak. 'It was because I showed Mr Stone the CCTV footage.'

There was a sudden silence in the room before Tom broke it. 'I had asked Lan to let me see the footage.'

Before he could say anything else, Griffiths interrupted. 'You do know what you've done, don't you?' He turned to the ship's captain, who, so far, hadn't said anything, although he did speak enough English to follow what Lan had just revealed. 'I'm sure, captain, that is against your company's rules and is probably a disciplinary issue.'

It was phrased and delivered in such a way that it was clear he wasn't expecting an answer. Despite his assumption, however, the captain did answer. 'I don't know. That will be for others to decide.'

This seemed to disappoint Griffiths. 'Well, if any company property had been misused in the US, it would be an instant sackable offence.' As if to further strengthen his point, he added, 'At the very least.'

'If Lan had not decided to do this,' Tom said, 'then the information I have just taken you through would not have been available and an innocent man would, most probably, have been falsely imprisoned. Incidentally, imprisoned based upon ...' He paused before saying, 'Well, let's be charitable here and say an incompetent and half-hearted police investigation.' He carried on when there was no response. 'There's one other thing we haven't got to yet, but it's important to point out. If Lan hadn't bravely decided to share the footage with me, then a murderer would still be walking free. If anything, in my opinion, Lan should be promoted.'

'Are you saying someone else has been arrested?' asked Griffiths. 'Who?'

'That's exactly what has happened, but I'll get on to that shortly,' Tom replied. 'You may remember how I asked if you could forensically examine the area where Mr Fisher and Mr Young were seen fighting. If that was where the murder took place, then there was a strong chance you would find blood samples, especially given how Mr Fisher was killed.' After Lan had translated, Tom continued. 'My understanding is that nothing was found. Is that correct?' he asked, directing his question at Captain Bao Ninh.

Clearly understanding what he had been asked, Captain Bao Ninh just said, 'Yes.'

As it was obvious the captain wasn't about to add anything to his answer, Tom continued. 'I also asked if you could carry out a forensic analysis of Mr Young's cabin, as there were samples of blood on the furniture, including the bed. I'd explained to you that it was all Mr Young's blood and how it had got there. There was no evidence of Mr Fisher's blood anywhere in the cabin. Again, is that correct?'

Again, no translation was required. 'Yes.'

'So, just for the record, let me summarise why I'm certain Mr Young could not have murdered Mr Fisher. Firstly, despite what some witnesses thought they'd heard him say, he didn't have a knife. Secondly, the so-called fight was no more than a bit of drunken pushing and shoving. Next, as Captain Bao Ninh has just confirmed, despite the violent nature of Mr Fisher's murder, absolutely no blood samples or even specks of blood were found where he and Mr Young supposedly fought. The blood found in Mr Young's cabin was his own blood, the result of hitting his face on the wardrobe when he got back to his cabin. CCTV showed that was at 2.17am precisely. There was no further footage of him reappearing. There is also a witness, Mr Don Simpson, who later – at 2.23 am, to be exact – heard two men arguing, one of whom I propose was Mr Fisher. This brief argument was followed by a sudden splash, as you might expect to hear if someone had fallen overboard.'

'Okay, so, if Mr Young didn't commit the murder, who did?' asked Griffiths. 'You said you'd arrested someone already.'

'Actually, I haven't. As you quite rightly have said on numerous occasions, I have no jurisdiction in this country. It was Le Quan Cong who made the arrest. That's why, even as we speak, a new team are carrying out a more detailed forensic examination on part of the ship. They are also seizing certain items for DNA analysis.'

Captain Bao Ninh's understanding of English suddenly miraculously improved and, without any translation, he said in a clearly angry manner, 'You have no authority to do that. I am in charge of what happens on this ship.'

'Not any longer,' interjected Le Quan Cong. 'As of right now, you have been relieved of your duties.' He then repeated this in Vietnamese, so that Captain Bao Ninh could be in no doubt about what he'd said.

Not surprisingly, Captain Bao Ninh looked crestfallen, and even Griffiths abandoned his usual confrontational style and, with uncharacteristic contrition, said, 'He was only doing what I suggested. If anyone is to blame, then it's me.'

'I think we'll leave that to your people, if you don't mind,' said Jason Thomas.

There then followed an awkward silence, whilst both Jordan Griffiths and Captain Bao Ninh tried to come to terms with the full implications of their involvement in this investigation.

Surprisingly, it was Griffiths himself who broke the silence. 'So, if I am for the chop, at least tell me who did actually murder John Fisher.'

Tom looked in the direction of Le Quan Cong for approval. When he nodded in consent, Tom simply said, 'It was Huan.'

Chapter 53

'Huan?' Griffiths repeated. 'Who the hell is he?'

'He's one of the ship's crew,' answered Lan. 'He works mainly as a waiter and barman and has been with Mekong Cruises for a few years.'

'How do you know it's him?' Griffiths asked, still clearly puzzled as to why his name had never been mentioned previously. 'Are you sure?'

'I hope so,' Tom replied, 'as he's just been arrested.'

Everyone in the room was now waiting for Tom to provide the evidence for this unexpected arrest. So he began. 'Huan was working in the bar the night Mr Fisher was killed. It's his job, not only to serve drinks, but also to tidy up the bar after everyone has left. This means he's often there into the early hours, and well after the last guest has left.'

'So,' said Griffiths, 'are you saying there is actual CCTV showing him committing the murder?'

'No, I'm not,' Tom answered. 'That's because there isn't any. Mr Fisher was murdered at the side of the ship where there was no CCTV coverage. The camera for that particular section had been faulty for about a week and hadn't yet been repaired.'

Captain Bao Ninh suddenly said something to Lan, who then duly translated. 'He wants to know, therefore, what evidence do you have?'

'I'll get to that in a short while. In the meantime, it might help if I run through how my suspicions gradually built up.' After the briefest of pauses, he continued. 'The first time I came across Huan was when he served drinks to a few of us on the sun deck. He was wearing a white, open-neck polo shirt and black trousers. He had a very distinctive wooden emblem, showing a carving of a bamboo plant, hanging from his neck, which was held by a length of strong cord. We asked him what it represented, and he was very happy to talk about it. He said how it had a spiritual significance for all the people who lived in the part of Vietnam where he came from. All the while he was telling us this, he kept stroking it, either out of superstition or reverence, or maybe simply because it provided him with some sort of reassurance.' He paused as if he had suddenly remembered something. 'Actually, it made quite an impact on some of our group, and so it wasn't something I could easily forget. Anyway, each time after that, when he served us, he was wearing the same uniform: white open-neck polo shirt and black trousers, with the bamboo symbol very visibly hanging from his neck. The day after Mr Fisher's death, Huan wore the same colour shirt and trousers. What was different, though, was that his polo shirt was now buttoned up, so that neither the symbol nor even the cord were visible. At the time I did think it was a bit strange and definitely out of character for someone who clearly took great pride in not just wearing it but also displaying it.'

Whilst Tom had been giving his explanation, Jordan Griffiths had shown uncharacteristic self-restraint by not interrupting him. Even though he now appeared to be reconciled to the fact Tony was not the murderer, his natural belligerence couldn't be constrained any longer. 'Are you going anywhere with this dress code story?' he suddenly demanded. 'It's all very interesting, I'm sure, but do we really need to know what a young waiter wore?'

'I'm nearly there,' Tom replied, not rising to Jordan's sarcasm. 'After I'd looked at the footage of the guests in the bar and seen them all leave, I started to rewind to take another look. Unfortunately – well, at least for Huan – I accidently hit the fast-forward button and, before I could stop it, Huan reappeared in the bar. It was 2.40am.'

'Surely that wouldn't be surprising,' Griffiths said. 'After all, as you said yourself, part of his job was to clean up after everyone had left the bar, and the last one didn't leave until almost ten after two.'

'That's true, and it wouldn't normally have got my attention, except that, for some reason, he'd changed his shirt. Earlier he had been wearing his white polo shirt. Now he'd suddenly changed into a red one. So the question I asked myself was: why would he do that, especially as it was so late? Normally, if you'd got something on your shirt, and you were the only one there, and just about to finish your work shift anyway, you wouldn't bother changing it.' Tom looked at Jordan Griffiths, who, as usual, was immaculately attired. 'Well, I wouldn't, anyway,' he added.

Just then there was a knock on the door and Le Quan Cong opened it. It was one of his officers. Le Quan Cong stepped outside and had a brief conversation with him, before returning and saying, 'Excuse me, I am needed elsewhere.'

After he'd left, Tom resumed. 'Apart from carrying out a thorough forensic analysis on that part of the ship where there was no CCTV coverage, the team are currently retrieving the clothes which Huan had originally worn that night. They will be sent for DNA analysis. I'm pretty certain they will find evidence of Mr Fisher's DNA on them.'

'How do you know the clothes will be there? If that was me, they – along with the weapon – would be the first things I'd get rid of,' suggested Griffiths.

'That's a good point and, in fact, I'm sure that's exactly what he did with the knife. As far as his clothes are concerned, they are still on board – or at least were a few hours ago when Lan found them – and that was the first question I asked him when he told me they were still there. Perhaps Lan could answer that one?'

Everyone turned to face Lan, who, if he was surprised by Tom's invitation, certainly didn't show it when he answered. 'That's an easy one. All staff are issued with two sets of the clothes they will need for each trip. Shirts, trousers, outdoor clothes, and even a suit if you work in the restaurant. After each trip they are then dry cleaned and later returned. If they are lost or somehow damaged as a result of their own carelessness, then the cost is deducted from their salaries. Staff will go to great lengths to make sure that doesn't happen to them. I think Huan thought he could last out until the end of this trip. I found his trousers and shirt at the bottom of his cleaning basket.'

It was just as Lan was finishing his explanation that Le Quan Cong returned. 'I can confirm we have found clothes belonging to Huan in his cabin. There are many spots of blood on one shirt and a few on the trousers. They will be immediately sent away to see if they match Mr Fisher's blood.'

'So, is there still a chance they won't match?' asked Griffiths, in a way which suggested that was still the outcome he hoped for.

'Not now,' he answered, 'because Huan has just confessed to the murder of Mr John Fisher.'

Chapter 54

The guests were, once again, assembled in the ship's entertainment room.

'I'm sure you have noticed how the ship hasn't, as yet, resumed sailing when we had planned.' Lan had the microphone in his hand, with the ship's captain standing alongside him.

There had already been a general murmur of disquiet in the room, but when Lan had made his opening remark, it increased notably.

'Just the three hours, so far,' someone shouted.

'Yes, I'm sorry about that, and there will, unfortunately, now be a further delay.' Before anyone could ask any questions, he immediately continued. 'I apologise, but new evidence has come to light regarding the death of Mr Fisher, and so the police have to carry out additional forensic searches before they are willing to let the ship sail.'

Immediately the room became a shouting match as guests competed with each other to have their questions heard. Lan was having trouble trying to regain even a slight semblance of control. Eventually, though, when it was obvious he wasn't going to answer anything until people had stopped shouting, the noise gradually reduced until, once again, the room became totally silent.

'Thank you,' Lan said. 'I will try and answer your questions, but, please, I can only do this one at a time.'

Immediately, a man raised his hand, and Lan pointed towards him.

'What new evidence have the police got?' the man asked.

'I'm sorry, but, as this is an ongoing police inquiry, I am not allowed to comment. What I can say, however, is that the new evidence is very significant. I won't, though, be able to answer anything related to Mr Fisher's death.'

'But did the Brit still carry out the murder?' asked another guest.

'Or are they looking for his accomplice?' asked the same

man who had alluded to this possibility at an earlier meeting. Without waiting for a reply, he followed this up with, 'I told you, didn't I?'

'I'm sorry, but I can't answer that. I'm here to answer questions regarding the ship's arrangements.'

The man was not about to let this go, especially now that he evidently felt, at least in his own mind, he had been vindicated. 'Funny, though, isn't it? That other Brit, the ex-cop, is not here. I guess he's already been arrested.' Whilst Tom had not been named, everyone knew who he was referring to.

It was Jim who came to Tom's defence. 'That's complete BS. You're just making it up now, especially as you have absolutely no evidence to support it. You know there are laws to protect people from what you just said. I, for one, would happily sign any legal document to witness how you, in public, have just slandered an innocent man.'

'Let's all try and calm down,' said Lan, acting as peacemaker. 'I'm sure everything will soon be resolved, and we can start sailing again.'

'When is that likely to be?' someone asked.

'Hopefully, by this time tomorrow, we should be on our way. The police officer in charge is determined to finish his investigation as quickly as possible. That's one of the reasons why there are more police on board right now. As soon as I know, I will communicate the new itinerary to everyone.'

There were a few other questions, but, basically, there wasn't anything else of importance which Lan could add to what had already been said.

As they began to leave, suddenly, raised voices could be heard towards the front of the room. Lan and the ship's captain quickly made their way there to find out what was happening. The man who had suggested Tom was a murder accomplice was partly lying down, attempting to pull himself up. One side of his face was already showing signs of swelling.

'Are you okay?' asked Lan, offering him a hand to help him stand. 'What happened?'

'I think he tripped,' Jim answered, before heading towards the exit door.

Chapter 55

It was a few days later, and most of the guests, having earlier checked into their hotel in Ho Chi Minh City, the Regal, were now having dinner in the main restaurant.

After Huan's arrest, the ship had been given permission to resume its journey at midday the following day. The consequence of this was that they had lost over two days from the published holiday schedule, and this meant, unfortunately, they would only be staying in the city for about twenty-four hours before they had to get their flights home. Unsurprisingly, news of Huan's arrest had quickly spread throughout the ship and, equally unsurprisingly, had become the main topic of conversation amongst the guests, with much wild speculation as to why he did it.

'Here's to Tony and Sue,' said Mary, raising her wine glass in celebration of their return. Sue and Tony, along with their son David, who had earlier that day arrived in Hon Chi Minh City, were seated next to Tom and Mary. Lan, recognising that they would benefit from a certain amount of privacy, had arranged for one large, circular table to be set up in one of the more exclusive private rooms in the hotel, and it was here that Mary was giving her toast.

Even while Le Quan Cong was finalising the forensic examination on board the ship, he had notified the authorities in Ho Chi Minh City, where Tony was being held, to immediately release him. Jason Thomas, the representative from the British consulate, had returned to Ho Chi Minh City to help effect his release and to provide any consular assistance which might be required. Not surprisingly, it had been a very emotional occasion when Sue and Tony had rejoined the others, earlier that day.

'I'll drink to that,' replied Tony.

'Oh, no, you won't,' Sue quickly responded. 'Not after

what happened the last time you had a drink. You'll just be having soft drinks, at least until we are back, safe and sound, in the UK.'

Jim rose to his feet. 'I think we should also raise our glasses to my old buddy John.' There was a slight but unmistakeable tremor in his voice as he mentioned his name. 'It's ironic, really, when you think about it. He managed to survive the time we all spent here in 1969, but not a vacation, fifty-plus years later. I will never forget you. So, John, this is from your brothers in arms. To John.'

Everyone then repeated the toast, and Jim sat down.

This time it was Tony who stood up. 'This might only be orange juice,' he said, indicating the drink in his hand, 'but it's the best orange juice I've ever tasted, and I owe that to one man.' He looked directly at Tom. 'I'll bet you would never have thought you'd hear me say this, but Sue and I are so grateful to have met you. Who would have thought, if we hadn't sat next to you at Heathrow airport, we wouldn't all be here tonight, and I would still be in that cell?'

It was obvious that even Tony, a man who liked to present himself as someone who didn't rate personal emotion, had suddenly become quite moved. Probably in an attempt to disguise his feelings, he added, 'I just wish he hadn't been a bloody southerner.' Although this was lost on the Americans who were there, they politely joined in with the laughter that followed Tony's comment, allowing him some time to regain his normal composure. 'Mr Tom Stone,' he then said, whilst raising his glass.

After everyone had repeated Tony's toast, Tom, himself now slightly embarrassed, simply raised his own glass in acknowledgement.

'Come on, Tom, why don't you say something?' said Sue.

It wasn't the type of thing he was comfortable with, at least not in such a social situation as this. Nonetheless, especially as Mary was almost pushing him to his feet, he felt as though he had little choice.

'Thank you, Tony, but I'm sure you would have done the same. Unless, of course, it had been a southerner.' This settled

Tom down a little, and he was then able to say a few things he had wanted to say.

'You should be aware, though, that it wasn't due to just my and Mary's efforts. Quite a few other people here, in different ways, also helped. Don, for example,' he said, pointing towards where Don was seated with Estelle and Brett. 'If it hadn't been for his extraordinary ability to recall specific times then I would not have had the confidence to carry on. So, Don, I hope your time back here in Vietnam was worthwhile and better than the last time you were here. You certainly made a difference to Tony and Sue's lives.'

One or two people immediately began to applaud and, in a matter of moments, everyone took to their feet to join in. It looked as though Don had become overcome with emotion, and Estelle placed a comforting arm around him.

'I also really have to acknowledge the role that our tour director, Lan, played in all this,' Tom said. 'If I said he was unbelievably brave, putting his career and livelihood on the line on more than one occasion, then I would still be massively understating his contribution. As per usual, Lan is on duty, in the main restaurant, making sure his guests are having the best possible time. Hopefully, we'll get the chance to tell him this before we all leave Vietnam.'

He took a sip of his wine before he carried on. 'We should also acknowledge Jim's part in this. Despite some major reservations, he was still able to provide me with key information relating to their time here in 1969. Most of you here have not heard the full story yet, but suffice it to say, like the others, it was crucial to Tony's release.' Tom looked at Tony. 'Incidentally, Tony, what you missed whilst you were otherwise engaged was how Jim was able to demonstrate that he can still look after himself. I think the man with the swollen face and black eye will vouch for that.'

Jim raised his right arm and made a fist, clearly proud that his exploits were now common knowledge.

'Not only that,' Tom went on, 'but it looks as though he has found some long-lost relatives in Shelley and Mike. That alone would have been incredible, but, with everything else which has happened, I think we can all agree that all the memories we now have of this trip will never be forgotten.'

'Last but not least, as they say, I just need to thank Mary for the support she has given me over the past week. There were times when I couldn't tell her everything, but, despite her undoubtedly knowing this, she still trusted and supported me, even during those times when I doubted myself.'

Mary, recognising that this was probably the closest Tom had ever got to showing real emotion in such a setting, took hold of his hand and gave it a slight squeeze.

Chapter 56

After they had finished eating, a less formal atmosphere had quickly developed and, as usually happens on these occasions, individuals had changed seats in order to speak with different people. Lan had now been able to join them and was seated next to Tom.

Of course, what everyone wanted to know was *why* Huan had murdered John. Whilst some people could guess as to his reason, most in the room only had a patchy understanding. Rather than speak to individuals, or to small groups, Tom decided to tell everyone at the same time and answer any questions as he went along.

'When was it you first started to suspect Huan?' asked Tony.

'It's fair to say my suspicions about Huan had grown ever since I'd seen him with his polo shirt buttoned right to the top. Don't you remember how he'd shown real pleasure and pride in showing off the carving of a bamboo plant that hung around his neck? In fact, he was specifically asked what it represented, and he seemed more than happy to tell us. So I was puzzled as to why, suddenly, he didn't want anyone to see it. It might seem fairly innocuous, but it just stuck in my mind. There was either a genuine, innocent answer to that question or he had something to hide. Being an ex-policeman, I naturally, automatically suspected the latter. Anyway, that certainly raised my suspicions.' He paused. 'It turns out he didn't want to show it because it wasn't there. When he was being interviewed, he admitted that John had pulled it off, presumably during the attack, leaving a nasty-looking welt on his neck.'

'So what happened to it?' asked Jim.

'I don't know for sure, but I suspect it's now lying at the bottom of the Mekong.' Tom then carried on with his explanation. 'Then, on the CCTV footage, after everyone had left the bar, by pure chance ... well, actually due to my technical incompetence ... I'd seen him return to the bar, wearing a different-coloured shirt to the one he had been wearing less than an hour earlier.' He turned to face Tony and Sue. 'When he served us drinks, he always wore a white polo shirt and black trousers. That's what he was wearing for most of the evening in the bar, but when he returned, he had changed his shirt to a red one. It was really at that point my suspicions increased to a much higher level. So I asked Lan if he could obtain some additional information for me.' Tom looked in Lan's direction. 'If he had refused, which he would have been more than entitled to do, then none of us would be sitting here tonight, so thank you, Lan.'

This prompted a spontaneous round of applause, although all Lan could bring himself to do in response, clearly embarrassed by the sudden attention, was to give a perfunctory nod of his head.

Tom continued. 'Fortunately, Lan agreed. I'd asked him to find out if Huan's original polo shirt was in his room. It was, and it was this which the police later took away for forensic examination. It proved to be the most incriminating evidence, as John's blood was on the shirt, providing unequivocal proof that Huan was, at least, at the scene when John was stabbed. Later, when the police presented him with this evidence, he admitted to having stabbed John.'

'We'd heard Tony's blood had been found at the side of the ship,' said Bob. 'Sorry,' he added, looking in Tony's direction, 'but we thought John must have put up a fight and, at that point, you'd also been cut.'

Tony, clearly in no mood now to hold any grudges, just said, 'I'm certain he did. He wasn't the type of man to go down without a fight.'

Tom resumed. 'Actually, the only place where any of Tony's blood was found was in his own cabin. But this was because he'd fallen into the wardrobe when he returned and cut himself. Do you remember that?' he asked directly of Tony.

'Of course he doesn't,' answered Sue. 'He doesn't remember anything, because he was completely blathered.'

'Just for the benefit of our American friends here,' said Tom, '*blathered* means worse for wear, usually as a result of having drunk too much.'

'In which case I think there have been a few times on this trip when many of us have been, what's the word? Blathered?' said Bob, to much merriment, at least amongst the men there.

When the room had quietened, Tom continued. 'The other thing I'd asked Lan to do was to try and get a copy of Huan's passport. He'd already confirmed that all passports – that's staff as well as guests' passports – are held on the ship. He managed to do this and, when I saw the copy of his passport, it was immediately clear what the connection was. Unless it was a coincidence almost equalling Jim and Shelley's, I now had a possible motive as to why he might have killed John.' He turned to look at Jim and Bob. 'Huan was born in Phong Nha.'

Whilst this didn't mean anything to the majority of those in the room, the significance was not lost on the two of them. 'Are you saying what I think you are?' Jim asked, visibly shaken.

'I'm afraid I am,' Tom simply replied. 'I know this must be difficult for you to hear, and I can imagine you might prefer not to relive the events that happened there, so I'm happy to leave it at that.'

Bob and Jim, both clearly shocked by Tom's revelation, didn't immediately reply, no doubt realising that what they might hear next would bring back very difficult memories for them. Jim looked towards Bob, as if seeking his approval. Bob simply shrugged his shoulders, and, after another brief pause, Jim just said, 'Go ahead.'

'John, Bob and Jim were part of 3rd Platoon during their time here, back in 1969. In fact, John was platoon sergeant. They had been tasked with destroying any supplies that were going to the Viet Cong, and had been told by their intelligence section that supplies were being hidden in a village named Phong Nha. But that intelligence was incorrect and, as a result, twenty-five innocent people living there were killed and many more wounded.'

The room had suddenly taken on a more sombre atmosphere, far removed from the celebratory joviality of earlier. Tom once again looked at Bob and Jim, as if seeking their approval to continue. Bob nodded his head in agreement, whilst Jim was looking down, concentrating on the wine glass in his hand.

'A few of Huan's relatives were amongst those who died,' Tom said. 'Specifically, his grandparents, one of his great-grandparents, and his father's younger sister and baby brother.'

'Oh my God,' said Ruth, turning to look at her husband. 'You never told me that.'

'It's not the sort of thing you go round mentioning,' Bob answered, his normal, slightly aggressive tone now totally absent. 'I wish I had, but the truth is I just wanted to try and forget all about it. I think we all thought that.'

'So why come on this trip,' she asked, 'if you wanted to forget?'

'I don't know. I was hoping to somehow get the answer to that whilst we were here.'

It was Tony, with a palpable tension now in the room, who next spoke. 'How do you know all of this?'

'It was Sang, Huan's brother, who later told myself and Lan,' Tom said. 'Their father, who was just a small boy at the time in 1969, was one of the survivors. He later married, and Sang was born in 1988, and Huan followed later in 1992. I don't suppose it's the type of thing a family would ever forget. I guess some people are affected more than others, and it looks as though Huan was one of those people.'

'But how did he know about 3rd Platoon's involvement?' asked Brett.

'I don't know for sure, but I suspect he'd heard snippets whilst serving in the bar.' Looking again at Bob and Jim, he went on. 'You've mentioned how you'd had a few heated discussions with some of the men who were in 1st Platoon. Huan's understanding of English was very good and, as he was constantly bringing drinks, it wouldn't have been that difficult to put two and two together. Especially if he'd heard Phong Na being mentioned.'

When there were no more follow-up questions, Tom continued. 'Sang did confirm that Huan had become increasingly morose as the trip progressed. Apparently, Huan now says he couldn't reconcile all the drinking and laughter with what happened to his relatives. It seems that watching the celebrations in the bar was when he finally snapped.' Tom turned his attention towards Don. 'Incidentally, you mentioned how you thought you'd heard someone say *'Nam* just before you heard the splash. I suspect, although I don't know for certain, that what you really heard was Huan saying *Phong Nha*.'

'But why select John?' Brett asked.

'Perhaps it was because he was in the wrong place at the wrong time. Sometimes things are that simple.'

'You mean it could have been one of us? Me, for example?' asked Bob.

Tom decided no answer was required.

Chapter 57

The dinner started to break up when people began to head to bed, leaving just a few of them seated at the table.

'We can't thank you enough,' said Sue. 'If it hadn't been for you, Tony would still be in prison.'

'Well, as I said,' Tom replied, 'it wasn't just me.' He paused briefly before turning to face Tony. 'How were you treated in prison? At one point, Mary was concerned you might be tortured,' he said, with a slight laugh.

When Tony didn't immediately answer, Tom spoke again, although this time the laughter had been replaced by concern. 'You weren't, were you?'

'I'd have liked to see them try,' Tony answered, in a voice which suggested he wouldn't have entirely minded. 'But no. There was nothing like that. They just kept asking me the same questions. Why did I do it? What did I do with my knife? They'd placed a piece of paper and a pen in front of me and kept saying how, if I signed it, and admitted to killing John, then it would be taken into account during the sentencing. It was there even when they left the cell.'

'Weren't you frightened?' asked Mary.

'Not for myself. I knew from my special forces training what they were trying to do.' When he spoke again, it was if he were just talking for his own benefit. 'It was strange because, even though it was a long time ago, I suddenly could still clearly remember those training sessions. Funny, that, isn't it?'

'When did you find out you were going to be released?' asked Mary.

'I suspected something was up last night. Someone came in, brought me some better food and took away the pen and paper. Later, a Mr Thomas from the British consulate arrived and told me I was free to leave. I couldn't believe it at first. I thought it was a wind-up and they were playing games with my head, and I might have said something to him to that effect. Anyway, he said he had a message for me, from Sue, and it was then I was convinced.'

'What was the message?' asked Mary.

'She said that I would now be able to watch the Owls again.'

Before anyone could ask the obvious question, Sue provided it. 'The Owls are Tony's favourite football team, Sheffield Wednesday.'

Tony took up the story again. 'No one other than Sue would know to say that. Anyway, twenty minutes later I was in the British consulate, having a celebratory beer.'

'He's forgotten to say how David and I were also there to meet him,' said Sue, slightly annoyed he'd mentioned beer but not them.

Tony put his arm around her and kissed her tenderly on the cheek. 'You two were the best sight any man would want to see.'

Mary looked towards Lan. 'How about you, Lan? What will you do next?'

'I'm not sure,' he answered, his intonation betraying his sense of uncertainty. 'The entire crew have been given time off by the company. I'll use that free time to think about what I want to do next. I've been with Mekong Cruises for a few years now, and so maybe this is a good time to look for something different. Perhaps I'll move to another country and have a clean break.'

'That would be a shame,' Tom answered. 'Your country needs people like you.'

When Lan didn't reply, Mary said, 'Well, whatever you decide, I'm sure you'll make a great success of it.'

Now it was Lan's turn to ask a question. 'What do you think will now happen to Captain Bao Ninh?'

'Difficult to say,' replied Tom. 'But I suspect his career with the police is now at an end.' After reflecting further, he carried on. 'I hope, though, that's the only thing that happens to him. There's no doubt in my mind he was pressured by Jordan

Griffiths to conclude the investigation as quickly as possible. Whether someone above him had told him to do that, I suppose we'll never know. Anyway, as far as Griffiths is concerned, it wouldn't surprise me if he is quietly reassigned to another US embassy, somewhere in the world.'

Tom now asked Lan a question in return. 'Do you think there will be any repercussions from what's happened here? For example, the fact it was a Vietnamese national who killed an American Vietnam veteran. Might it negatively affect the tourist trade?'

'I don't know,' Lan simply answered. 'Hopefully just the opposite, and people will see how my country is not afraid to arrest, and convict, one of its own citizens if it's proved they committed a crime.'

Chapter 58

It was early afternoon the following day, and all the guests had already left for the airport to catch their respective flights home. Tom and Mary, however, were still at the hotel, as their flight to Melbourne wasn't due to take off until much later that day. Lan had arranged for them to keep their room for as long as they needed it, as well as for them to have an early dinner in the main restaurant. A taxi had been arranged to take them to the airport at 8pm.

It had, unsurprisingly, been quite emotional when the others had left the hotel.

They had, of course, exchanged contact details and promised to keep in touch with each other. Lots of photos were taken and, as Sue filmed it, Tony had insisted on saying a few heartfelt words of gratitude towards Tom and Lan for effecting his release. Jim had repeated his promise to travel to the UK and that he wanted them all to meet up again. Mary and Sue, in particular, had both found it difficult to control their emotions, whilst Tom and Tony had made do with a manly hug and handshake. As was the case with Jim, promises were made to get together again in the near future.

Tom had surprised himself by realising just how difficult it was when he had to say farewell to Don and his family, especially knowing how ill Don was. But it was when he and Lan had said their farewells that he had felt the most emotional, as he knew just how much Lan had risked, and this had been reflected in their long, final embrace. For Tom, a simple handshake would normally suffice, but this somehow felt different. Ever since he had first met Lan in Hanoi airport, he had been hugely impressed, first of all by his professionalism but, latterly, by his physical and moral courage, and Tom had told him just how privileged he felt to have met him. Lan had promised to keep in touch with him and let him know whatever he finally decided to do in the future.

'Tom, I've invited Sue and Tony to come and stay with us,' Mary had announced, just before everyone boarded their coach. 'It would be really wonderful to keep in touch, especially after everything we've been through together.'

'That's a good idea. We should definitely do that,' Tom answered, wondering just how they were going to fit in all of the other different trips they had now committed to.

After everyone had departed, and Tom and Mary had finished their packing, there were still a few hours to kill, and so they decided to walk to the same small bar where they had first met John and his friends. As before, as they quietly sipped at their beers, they quickly became mesmerised by the apparent traffic chaos which was happening just a few feet away from them.

'Despite everything that has happened, aren't you glad we came?' asked Mary.

Tom considered her question carefully before answering. 'I suppose I am now, but I'm sure I would have felt differently if Tony was still being held in prison.'

'But he's not,' replied Mary, taking hold of his hand. 'I'm so proud of you.' She kissed him on the cheek. 'We've met some wonderful people who I'm sure we'll keep in touch with.' She then carried on, as if she'd suddenly remembered something. 'Who would have thought that Jim and Shelley were related?'

In truth, Tom had found it fascinating to see how a relatively brief holiday trip could change group dynamics so much and create new friendship groups. Jim, for example, had now become almost physically connected to Shelley and Mike, whilst Bob and Ruth had found the company of Don, Estelle and Brett to be enjoyable. Inevitably, Sue and Tony had never strayed too far from Tom and Mary, whilst Sue and Mary, although so different in many ways, had clearly formed a particularly strong relationship. And then there was the relationship between himself and Lan.

'Well, it's a holiday I don't think we'll ever forget, that's for sure,' he replied.

'Exactly,' Mary said. 'We would never have experienced all

this if you had still been with the police. It's definitely given me a taste to do more. What about you, Tom?'

But he didn't get the chance to answer Mary's question because, at that moment, his mobile phone rang. He could see, from the name that came up, that the caller was one he would least expect, and immediately he could feel his heart rate increase. It was unlikely to be good news.

'Let me just take this call,' he said. 'It's a bit noisy here.'

He walked away from the street until he found a less noisy location, and then pressed the accept button. 'Hello,' he simply said.

'Is that Tom?' the voice asked. It was Sir Peter Woodward, the Metropolitan Police commissioner.

Tom had come into direct contact with Sir Peter a few times over the past couple of years and had always found him to be a decent and very fair person. Even though it had been Sir Peter who had effectively had the final say in ending Tom's career, Tom still had the utmost respect for him. Notwithstanding this, it wasn't every day you received a call from someone in his exalted position.

'It is. I wasn't expecting to take a call from you,' Tom said, with genuine understatement.

'No, I suppose not. Anyway, I hope I haven't caught you at an inconvenient moment. I understand you are currently out of the country. On holiday, according to DC Milner.'

At the mention of Milner's name, Tom's anxiety level increased even further.

Before he could answer, Sir Peter carried straight on. 'I'm here with DCI Shaw and DC Milner. Commander Fernley is also here. They have just informed us about an extremely serious matter. I understand from DC Milner you might know a little about Operation Deliverance already.'

This was a difficult one to answer, as Tom obviously didn't know how much Milner had told Sir Peter. He also knew that Milner's decision to confide in him was potentially a breach of confidentiality and therefore, theoretically at least, a disciplinary matter. Given how Milner had only recently been subjected to one of those disciplinary hearings, and had subsequently been demoted, Tom was struggling to find the correct thing to say. He settled on, 'Well, he told me about the recent surge in OCN crimes and how he was now part of the team set up to try and bring them down.'

Sir Peter was astute enough to know that Tom was giving him the vaguest reply possible. 'I suspect you know a bit more than you are admitting to, but that's not why I called you. In fact, it's just the opposite.'

Tom, for the first time, suddenly had an inkling of where this discussion might be heading, although he remained silent.

'I believe it was you who suggested to DC Milner that he should take any concerns he had to DCI Shaw,' Sir Peter said. 'Is that correct?'

'Yes, that's correct,' Tom answered.

'Hmm,' said Sir Peter. 'Well, I think that was a very astute piece of advice. DC Milner and DCI Shaw have just taken myself and Commander Fernley through all of the evidence they have to support their conviction that Operation Deliverance has been compromised. I don't need to tell you just how serious this is.'

Despite this, he then went on to say just how serious it was. 'Not only has a serving police officer been murdered, but, if this were to carry on for much longer, then it's not too much of an exaggeration to say that the whole credibility of the Met would be impacted. As you know, it has been a difficult time recently for the Met, and we are only now starting to regain some degree of trust with the public. If it was shown that serious gangland crime is currently being committed with the active assistance of a police officer, or, God forbid, officers, then at best it would set us back considerably. At worst, however, it could conceivably result in yet another root-and-branch investigation and reorganisation, with everything that entails. Wouldn't you agree?'

Tom realised how Sir Peter had very cleverly led him to this point. 'Yes, it's possible, I suppose,' he answered.

'Good. I was hoping you would say that, because we would like you to help us prevent exactly that from happening.'

Although Tom had increasingly suspected the conversation

was heading this way, it was nonetheless still a shock to him and, therefore, something he couldn't just agree to, or reject, straight away. 'You might remember how I retired not that long ago. I don't really know what I can do to help.'

'You are being too modest,' Sir Peter immediately replied. 'In fact, you are *just* the right person to help. You are officially retired, and so no one would be expecting you to be involved. That means you can do things without raising any suspicions.'

'But what exactly can I do?' Tom asked.

'I'd like you to set up and run a covert operation with the objective of exposing the informer or informers – if they exist – in our current special investigation team, as well as providing information that will help to bring down the OCN, who, I think, call themselves the Westie Crew. The best way for us to restore the public's trust is to put away their gang members.'

'Put like that, it seems so simple,' Tom answered with a laugh. 'Is DCI Shaw happy with this?'

'You are on loudspeaker, so let's allow DCI Shaw to answer for himself,' said Sir Peter.

DCI Shaw then spoke. 'Hi, Tom. To answer your question, not only am I happy with it, but it was me who suggested it to the commander and commissioner. It would be your operation, although you would report to me.' His voice took on a far more informal tone. 'Look, Tom, we know each other well enough now – our faults as well as our strengths – to make this work. I need you. *We* need you, to put an end to the Westie Crew and all the vicious criminal activities they are involved in.' More sombrely, he went on, 'I don't need to remind you what it's like to lose an officer,' a clear reference to the death of DC Bennett. 'DC Shipley was a young officer, recently married, who was a valued member of my team. He's now dead – murdered by the Westie Crew. Not only that, but his death was set up to look like the suicide of someone who'd been in their pocket. At the very least we owe it to him, and his family, to correct that injustice.'

Tom could sense that this was said with genuine feeling, and he couldn't help but feel moved by DCI Shaw's words. He didn't immediately answer, however, as he tried to think through all the possible implications of agreeing to the request.

'How much time do I have to think about it?' he asked.

'You need to decide now,' answered Sir Peter. 'The entire operation is currently on hold, although we obviously haven't said this to the members of the team. We just can't afford any more mistakes or setbacks. The future of the Met could depend on what we do next.'

An anxious, extended silence followed. 'Are you still there?' asked Sir Peter.

'I am,' Tom answered. Almost before he could give it any more thought, and as if he were having some sort of out-of-body experience, he heard himself saying, 'Okay. I'll do it, subject to one or two operational conditions.'

'That's great,' Sir Peter quickly replied. 'Liaise with DCI Shaw on those. When can you get here? We need to start the planning and develop a new strategy straight away.'

'I'm actually preparing to fly out of Vietnam at the moment.'

'Even better,' Sir Peter said. 'That means you will be able to start soon. Contact DCI Shaw when you are back in the UK, and thanks again for agreeing to this.'

With that, the conversation ended, leaving Tom, mobile in his hand, simply staring straight ahead, still unable to believe what he had just agreed to. His almost hypnotic state was interrupted by Mary.

'Tom? Do you want another drink, or do you want to head back to the hotel?'

Tom took a deep breath and said, 'Mary, I think I need another beer.' He paused very briefly before adding, 'I need to tell you something.'